Boomtown

Boomtown

a novel

Greg Williams

SEWANEE WRITERS' SERIES / THE OVERLOOK PRESS

This is a work of fiction. Situations and characers are the author's invention. Any resemblance to specific persons living or dead is concidental.

First published in the United States in 2004 by
The Overlook Press, Peter Mayer Publishers, Inc.
Woodstock & New York

WOODSTOCK:
One Overlook Drive
Woodstock, NY 12498
www.overlookpress.com
[for individual orders, bulk and special sales, contact our Woodstock office]

NEW YORK:
141 Wooster Street
New York, NY 10012

∞ The paper used in this book meets the requirements for paper permanence as described in the ANSI Z39.48-1992 standard.

Library of Congress Cataloging-in-Publication Data

Williams, Greg.
Boomtown : a novel / Greg Williams.
p. cm.
1. Electronic commerce—Fiction. 2. Young adults—Fiction. 3. Businessmen—Fiction. 4. Internet—Fiction. 5. Manhattan (New York, N.Y.)—Fiction. I. Title.
PS3573.I449257 B66 2004   813.54'22   2003063978

Book design and type formatting by Bernard Schleifer
Manufactured in the United States of America
FIRST EDITION
ISBN 1-58567-450-8
10 9 8 7 6 5 4 3 2 1

For Elizabeth

ACKNOWLEDGMENTS

For their role in publishing *Boomtown*, I am grateful to Wyatt Prunty and Philip Stephens of the Sewanee Writers' Series, Tracy Carns and David Mulrooney of The Overlook Press, and my agent, Scott Miller of Trident Media Group. This book has benefited from the skillful copy editing of Robert E. Jones, managing editor of the *Sewanee Review*. I am especially indebted to my fellow novelist Margot Livesey for her invaluable editorial guidance through several revisions of the manuscript.

Part I

1. Bright Future

ON THE MORNING OF JANUARY 1, 2000, JONATHAN SCARVER awoke to find his body still whole and healthy, his home intact, and his wife sleeping soundly beside him. He pushed back the comforter and got up to check on the kids. They too were asleep, still perfect, and perfectly safe. Downstairs he started the coffee. Gently, to avoid waking his family with the harsh clink of glass on glass, he placed the empty bottle of Cristal into the recycling bin. Somehow a case of that premium champagne, intended for the AllMinder.com launch party, had wound up stashed in his office. Funny how that happens. He had managed to smuggle it home one bottle at a time in his computer bag, and seven hours ago, at midnight, he and Olivia had popped this one to ring in the new millennium. Technically it wasn't that, he had heard—the old millennium still had one more year to go—but people who liked to explain that were about as much fun as those who'd begun appearing on CNBC to carp that Internet stocks were overvalued. Aww, did somebody miss the boom? Is somebody a little risk averse? This was no time for numerical technicalities. Our meter had turned, and that was that.

In the television room Jonathan checked New York 1. To keep the account of last night's inevitable mayhem from reaching the ears of his sleeping family, he turned the volume so low that the hiss and gurgle of the coffeemaker in the kitchen nearly drowned out the voices of the anchor and the shivering on-scene reporters, and he had to sit on a footstool directly in front of the screen, his ears just inches from the speakers. Lay it on me, what happened last night, what got blown up, what biological weapons were unleashed in Times Square, and how long before they will spread to my home, a mere forty-minute train ride from Grand Central Station?

What a surprise. Not just his home but also the city—and apparently the whole entire world—had survived the New Year's Eve that many had prophesied would be a night of a thousand calamities: chemical, biological, and nuclear terrorism; computer bugs leading to massive power outages, plane crashes, and the inadvertent launch of intercontinental ballistic missiles. A new age of apocalypse. Jonathan knew of one man who, back in June, had quit his job at a downtown Manhattan PR firm, moved to some remote spot in one of those rectangular midwestern states, built a bomb shelter, and stocked it with guns, ammunition, water, and freeze-dried food. How did that guy feel right now on such a wonderful New Year's morning, this Noah with a boat but no flood? Was he glad to have been wrong? Or disappointed that the heavens had not punished the foolishly ill-prepared, who had scoffed at his sensible precautions and were even now remembering him smugly as they stepped out of their unfortified Westchester County homes, wearing nothing more protective than a bathrobe and slippers, to fetch from the curb the *New York Times*?

Back inside with the paper, Jonathan heard the coffeemaker gasp up the last of its brew. He poured himself a steaming cup and sat down at the kitchen table. At that moment—the hot coffee, crisp *Times*, warm house, perfect family—perhaps overcome by irrational exuberance, he might have been tempted to make the outlandish prediction that the NASDAQ market—recent charts of which looked like a stairway to financial heaven—would grow yet another twenty percent before April Fool's Day. And he would have been right.

2. Small Town NYC

"THERE IS NO DOUBT THAT SOONER OR LATER YOU'LL PLAY scenes in which lust is the main motivator and sex the ultimate goal. Sometimes you are the prize and sometimes you are the pursuer. It happens all the time in real life, so why do those moments so often seem fake on stage and screen? The idea of this exercise is to get in touch with the reality of lustful conflict that you experience in your own lives, so that when the time comes for you to fake it you won't be faking it. It will be"—here Willa Bernhard paused for effect, lowering her voice to a whisper that was still, because of her stage training, somehow loud and exclamatory—"*true!*"

She took a moment to meet the eyes of each student with an intensity promising that you, yes you, are the talented one, unique among your classmates, soon to be awash in lights and money. It was at least in part what they were paying for—the faith of their coach, the personal, special connection to this red-haired woman with the craft-fair copper bracelets and the mesh gym bag, this onetime soap star. The draw could not have been the hard folding chairs or the privilege of honing their craft in this so-called "studio," the second floor of a former

Garment District sweatshop where the clanging of radiators only underscored the lack of actual heat. The cold air of January 4th gusted unopposed through a broken windowpane, bringing with it the aroma of Chinese food and the diesel grumble of delivery trucks. Here Willa's students congregated faithfully every week, believers for whom stardom was just one lucky break away.

Twelve students, fifty bucks a head, and Willa taught four classes per week. There were times when Nicole Garrison, one of the Tuesday night twelve, envied Willa for having failed her way into what seemed like such a pleasant lifestyle, but more often she envied Willa for ever having been a working actor, once upon a time able to pay the rent and buy groceries and maybe even take a trip or two with money earned from acting, instead of living on tips, as Nicole did.

Willa had been a regular on the top-rated soap opera of the midnineties, *Love and Loss,* a stint that ended three years ago when the producers resolved her contract dispute by poisoning her character into a coma. Ever certain that the conniving Meredith McCallister would suddenly recover and she herself be written back into a job, Willa accepted payment from her students with about as much enthusiasm as she might have collected food stamps from the government. This was not her proper station in life. Teaching was a temporary gig made necessary by the slings and arrows of outrageous fortune. Soon her star would rise again, and she would no longer have time for these wanna-bes, not all of them without talent, to be sure, but all lacking that elusive *je ne sais quoi* that made her own talent so "uncategorizable," as one of her college acting teachers had remarked, the poor guy, still up there in New Haven, apparently content to teach rather than *do.*

Nicole Garrison wasn't bad, Willa had to admit—but if your beauty was so delicate that most people missed it, as Nicole's was, were you still beautiful? The camera wouldn't miss it. In the mock screen tests, which the class watched on a thirty-six-inch television, Nicole was the star and her fellow students swallowed their envy. Theater, no. She lacked a certain bigness required of live performers. The distance between stage and audience would render undetectable her delicate jaw and the subtle slope of her cheekbones. Willa took some consolation in that.

"But as I explained last week," she continued, pushing back her hair, clinking her bracelets, "there's a twist to this exercise. I want us to mix it up a bit, broaden our perspective, see how the other side feels. I want you to play the part of the last person who tried to pick you up. Or, if you are the pick-up-er, I want you to play the part of the pick-up-ee. Not only that, but I want both actors to be of the same sex, and if that seems weird to you, if that seems unreasonably impulsive, not to say *kinky*, then get used to it. During the course of your career you will be asked to do all kinds of weird things by producers and directors, and for all intents and purposes right now I am your director." She pivoted on one heel, again doling out her one-on-one stare. "So, who's going first?"

At the inevitable volunteer moment, Nicole always felt a motivating twinge of guilt. Back in elementary school and high school in Colorado Springs, when the teacher asked *Who knows?* she had always been the first to reach for the ceiling. She might have done so now if this assignment had not been, for her, such a stretch. Although men were always trying to strike up conversations with her—the gym was the worst; so much to talk about: the temperature, her technique, do you need help adjusting that seat?—the encounters never lasted

long enough to be dramatically satisfying, for Nicole had per-
fected the deft preemptive mention of her live-in boyfriend.
There were guys all over the city who had never met Dale
Caulfield, creative director at NYCDigitalArts.com, didn't even
know his name, but knew that he was fortunate to have a girlfriend so apparently untemptable, this long graceful beauty
whom a few of the more perceptive men correctly guessed—
her posture? the tilt of her head?—had spent years studying
ballet.

She was still trying to come up with possible material
when to her relief Gina Sullins volunteered. Just a year or two
out of college, still young enough to have proclaimed too loudly right before this very class that she would never be one of
those actresses who lies about her age, young enough that in
her closet she kept a stack of Kappa Kappa Gamma sweat-
shirts, still in good condition, which she wore to acting class
without embarrassment or irony, she would probably deliver a
scene straight out of those blocks of the Upper East Side that
had been colonized by fraternities and sororities. "Naturally,"
she said in front of the class, "I'm the one someone's trying to
pick up." She cocked her head and batted her eyelashes, calling attention to her vanity in a way that was supposed to make
it endearing.

A little too curvy for the current national taste, she did
what she could to play her figure to advantage. Any change
in emotion spurred a generous repositioning of that ample
ass, always a scene stealer. Nicole considered it a phony
move, akin to a melodramatic rolling of the eyes or the
swoonish placement of a wrist against the forehead, and
wished that Willa would call her on it. "Okay, I work at
Tonik," Gina continued. "We have a lot of events for the cool-
er companies. Advertising firms, dot coms, that sort of thing.

And I'm a waitress there, and this is a scene from an office holiday party we had a couple of weeks ago."

"Pick someone to be you," Willa said.

Gina tried to hide her pity as she considered which of her fellow students to choose. Some were already twenty-*eight*. How sad. She settled on one of the older ones. "Nicole, you want to be me?"

At first Nicole didn't think it was a good casting call—she possessed neither the ass nor the clueless confidence. But in front of the class she was already finding the character: twenty-three-year-old barely former sorority girl, confused to find that, contrary to what the lying commencement speaker had said, the world *wasn't* at her feet, confused to find herself filling drink orders at Tonik instead of slapping legal briefs onto Sam Waterston's desk on *Law and Order*, not even dating a celebrity yet. For Nicole, assuming that point of view—nascent disappointment—was disconcertingly easy. Not so long ago it had been her own. Now she wished she could have the nascent part back.

"Am I interested in this guy?" she asked.

"He's not quite up to my standards, and he's like thirty-something, so a bit old for me." Gina threw a hip-sized curve into her voice. "Maybe if I were in my late twenties already. Not that I mind responding to his constant e-mails." Some of her classmates laughed at that. "You'll see when we get there."

When the scene began, Nicole pretended that her left hand was the order pad on which she scribbled with an imaginary pen. Silently she took orders from imaginary patrons, working her way toward Gina, who, leaning against the wall, had struck a cocksure pose: half-drunk pussy hound with hungry eyes and parted lips. It was overdone, but to humorous effect, and drew titters from the rest of the class.

NICOLE

Hi, can I get you anything from the bar?

GINA

(*pitching her voice low*)

You know, you look so familiar to me. Are you an actress?

NICOLE

Isn't everyone?

GINA

(*even as a guy, unable to keep from cocking her hip*)

I really have the utmost respect for anyone who gives it a shot. I think that is so cool. (*beat*) Am I crazy or is there something chemical going on here. Don't answer that. How about we get together for some drinks after the holidays? Get to know each other a little bit.

NICOLE

(*flirting as if she is Gina*)

As long as you're single. I don't date attached men unless they're producers or casting agents.

GINA

Well, to be perfectly honest, because I'm an honest guy, I do have a girlfriend. But it's not serious. To tell the truth, the relationship has just about run its course. I mean, she's a special girl, very special, but we've drifted apart. Forget drinks, how about dinner? (*handing a business card to* NICOLE) Here's my info.

Nicole stared down at the small rectangular card in her hand.

DALE CAULFIELD

CREATIVE DIRECTOR

NYCDIGITALARTS.COM

Her first thought was that this was some kind of prank. Perhaps she had dropped Dale's card from her own wallet here in the classroom, and perhaps Gina had picked up the card, and was playing *gotcha*. Then the more plausible explanation settled in. "This is the card he gave you, the guy at the party?"

"That's the actual card."

Willa gently admonished the actors to stay in character. But Nicole couldn't. She had just learned in front of twelve other people that her relationship with Dale had "run its course." Pending only the confrontation and the tears, she was single.

She walked slowly up Eighth Avenue without bothering to cinch her coat against the cold. It was after eleven p.m., and around Port Authority the ratio of menacing to normal people had shifted in favor of the former. "Yo, wassup wassup!" "What, you too good to smile for a brother?" She trudged past them. Dale had always made her promise to take a cab home for safety, but right now she was amenable to oblivion.

Sometimes New York was too small.

Shopping to furnish their apartment two years earlier, having taken the big step of cohabitation, a first for both of them, Nicole and Dale had run into one particular couple at three different stores: Bed Bath & Beyond (hefting the linens), Home Depot (inspecting fixtures), and Circuit City (picking up a DVD player to enhance all those future quiet evenings alone together). The smiles of recognition went from weak to weaker. It was irritating to face your own socioeconomic reflection and not necessarily like what you saw. That's me? It was worse to behold the curves and youth of your prospective sexual replacement—or, actually, hadn't Gina said she was only mildly interested? That somehow made it worse. Nicole found herself maddeningly offended on Dale's behalf, embarrassed for him, and also by him: my boyfriend tried to pick up Gina? And *failed*? Aiming low was all the more pathetic if you missed anyway.

Turning the acting class incident over in her mind, she never once thought, *I can't believe this happened in a place as big as New York City.* That Dale had been handing out his business card at all was unbelievable. That he had handed it to Gina from Nicole's acting class somehow made perfect New York sense.

3. Reckoning

NICOLE DID NOT CONFRONT DALE RIGHT AWAY. FIRST SHE wanted to find and commit to an apartment so that she would be unable to weaken in the unlikely event that he pressed her to stay. With a sense of optimism that surprised her, she scanned the *Village Voice* for any share that was immediately available and met two other criteria: cool location (genteel Gramercy Park, finally?) and under $700. But prices were a shock. In the end the best neighborhood she could afford was the East Village. Last January her parents, who lived in Colorado Springs, had traveled to Denver to see the touring version of *Rent*. That's what they would think about the East Village: lots of drug taking and ill-advised sex in an environ-ment of monetary privation and raucous music. Not the place for their daughter. Out of concern for her safety they might even prefer that she continue to live in sin in Hell's Kitchen with graphic designer Dale Caulfield, who, though spineless and engaged in a ridiculous profession, might at least manage to raise his voice enough to scare off an intruder. What was she going to do now? Get help from one of those *Rent* drug addicts who are always low on cash and bursting into song?

A coworker and confidante at the Film Center Cafe suggested Brooklyn or Queens, some very colorful neighborhoods,
she said, but Nicole was unable to reconcile that with her idea
of living in New York. To most of the nation, and to anyone
who had grown up in Colorado Springs, New York was only
and always the island of Manhattan. Leaving Manhattan
would amount to leaving New York, and that's how it would
play back home, too: she's failed, she had to move out of the
big city, we'll get her back soon.

During the rest of the week that she spent looking, there
were moments with Dale when she found herself wanting to
take the more convenient and financially secure course and
stay with him. Home early enough on Wednesday to watch the
evening news with her, he made a few insightful comments
about the American political landscape, and then, during a
commercial, asked, "Is everything all right? You seem a little
distant." She pleaded exhaustion from her waitressing shift
and from preparation for an audition tomorrow. "Acting class
has been tough too," she said. To help her snap out of her
funk, he insisted that he would prepare dinner the following
evening. When the time came, he ordered from his favorite
Indian restaurant but still made a big show of serving her.
During the meal he listened to the story of the audition, his
supportive remarks helping her laugh off the degradation
inherent in waiting for two hours just to find that not only was
this merely a student short film rather than a SAG independent feature, as advertised in *Backstage*, but also that the young
director, still in his acne years, planned to shoot, in his apartment, a scene of "tasteful" lesbian erotica during which he
would make a nude cameo appearance. Dale was suitably
indignant on her behalf.

The meal and the conversation were pleasant enough.

Dale was not without his redeeming qualities. So maybe she shouldn't go through with leaving him. After all, he hadn't cheated on her, as far as she knew, had only given out his business card while drunk. And—the real problem—declared that their relationship had "run its course." Maybe that had been just a momentary lapse.

Her confidante at the Film Center Cafe seemed to take Dale's side. Folding the napkins, she said to Nicole, "Think about it. Do you really want a man who, physically, wants only you for the rest of his life?"

The question dented her resolve. Her first reaction was *Yes, I want to be the only one he wants forever.* But wouldn't that guy, if he even existed—and what were the odds?—be a clinging loser? Wasn't it strange to value reckless lust in a man at the beginning of a relationship, when all was exciting, and then be shocked later to find that it is not entirely specific to you? Maybe even if he had gone home with Gina she could deal with that. But she kept coming back to "run its course." The comment had risen in importance to become the core offense of the incident because it cast her as boring and validated her parents' negative assessment of her living arrangement. Religion aside (though of course with them it was always front and center) they'd warned her Dale wasn't committed. He didn't put a ring on her finger, did he? Why buy the cow, her mother had asked, when you can get the milk for free? Nicole didn't look at it that way, but now she considered that she herself might not be destined to enjoy the stability of a long-term commitment. She was good at city-girl poverty and getting by and keeping her ambitions alive on a thin dime, but choosing the right guy to love? Apparently not one of her talents.

Difficult at first, reimagining her future without Dale soon became alarmingly easy, and then it wasn't so alarming anymore. Saturday night she watched with odd detachment, flat on her back, while Dale got the milk for free (thanks, Mom), working himself up into a grimace, which he directed at the wall, and then lying beside her to catch his breath as if at the end of some kind of solo exertion. He might as well have just lifted the air conditioner out of the window. She might as well have been someone else. It was a liberating epiphany. If he was staying with her out of obligation and convenience, wasn't it better to find out now?

His sweat dried on her chest, and soon it was gone. In the same way the rest of him would soon disappear.

A few hours earlier, only four days after the Gina incident, Nicole had committed to her new place, one bedroom in a three-bedroom fifth-story walk-up in the East Village. At a coffee shop nearby she had written a check to her new roommates for the rest of January's rent. Her room was available beginning Sunday afternoon, tomorrow. Nicole had already culled from her closet the clothes she no longer wore and delivered them to the Salvation Army, Dale commending her social conscience. The remaining clothes she packed into two suitcases Sunday morning while Dale was still sleeping. Enough space was left for her acting books and the bud vase she would place on the windowsill of her new room.

Wearing only boxer shorts, and rubbing his eyes, Dale came out of the bedroom and regarded the suitcases. "Couldn't find the laundry bag?"

"I agree with you," she told him. "Our relationship has run its course."

"What?" He kissed her on the cheek and headed for the coffeemaker.

"Our relationship. That's what you said to Gina from my

acting class when you tried to pick her up. You remember, the voluptuous little waitress at Tonik?"

"Gina Gina Gina"—as if trying to place the name. "Tonik." Guilty. She could tell by the way he busied himself with the coffeemaker while trying to formulate an exculpatory response. "I'm not sure I know," he finally said, "what you're talking about."

As Nicole recounted to his back what had happened in her acting class, he seemed to grow smaller. Finally he turned to face her. He was immediately apologetic for having given out his business card with questionable social intentions—a "drunken mistake"—and assured her that he'd never touched Gina.

"That's the least of it," Nicole said. "Run its course?"

"I never said that. If I did I was drunk. You know I'd never leave you or toss you out on the street."

"I'm not some charity case. I'm not some *responsibility* or *obligation*. I can get along fine on my own."

"Come on now, I don't even want to think of you trying to make it in the city by yourself. I love you too much."

"I guess I realize, no you don't."

Perhaps if he had not launched into a speech about how irrational she was being, how hysterical, perhaps if he had not, with a bit too much satisfaction, pointed out that she did not make enough money to pay the rent even on a studio apartment, she would not have stomped the floor, clenched her fists, and yelled that she did too make enough, enough at least for a share, and she had one lined up already. But he did and she did.

He held her by the shoulders. "Okay. You want me to beg. Fine. Please don't go. I love you."

She shook her head. "Don't you ever think that maybe you're just afraid of change?"

Even now, all full of love, he had no decent explanation for why he had not at least informed Nicole about—if not invited her to—the NYCDigitalArts holiday party. "I think you had an audition that night or something, I don't remember exactly." Other people had brought their girlfriends and boyfriends, according to Gina, who had no idea why Nicole was interested enough to stop her after class and ask a bunch of questions about a so-so party two weeks in the past.

"Let me pay back your deposit." He put his hands on her shoulders, his face so full of optimistic entreaty that he might have been proposing marriage. "You'll continue to stay here with me, we'll be together. If you want me to sleep on the couch for a while, until we patch things up, that's fine. We could even go see a counselor."

"I paid rent through the end of the month. I move in today. You can't buy me out of the deal."

He let go of her shoulders and broke eye contact. Arms folded he began to pace. "Look, do you even know these people? How do you even know the other girls can pay?"

"Two girls and a guy."

"Whatever. You're not an East Village type." He was recovering some of his defensiveness. "All this just because I gave my business card to Gina Sullins?"

"Great. Do you happen to know her middle name too?" She had been determined to get through this without crying, but now it was an effort to keep the corners of her mouth level and her chin steady.

"It's not like I'm in touch with her."

She unloaded her final round of ammunition. "According to what Gina told my *whole* acting class, she really enjoys your e-mails."

He didn't miss a beat. "It would've been rude to just not

respond! I suppose you think I should've ignored her." He ran his fingers through his thinning hair, a gesture that had been fetching in the days when his locks would spring back over his forehead but now—now that he was balder—made him look older and slightly demented. "This city sorely lacks for civility, and whatever I can do to make it a little more hospitable . . ." Getting nowhere, he stopped. "Well, you aren't going to be able to get your couch out of here today. So maybe you can come back when you're calmer and we can continue this discussion without all the emotion."

The only way to keep from crying was to raise her voice. "You don't seem to think very highly of me. You probably think no one else will want me—"

"No, no, you're beautiful, you—"

"—but I can tell you I *walk away* from other men all the time. All the time. It's not too much to ask you to show similar restraint, or at least a little discretion. Someone from my acting class?"

"How was I supposed to know that?"

"You can keep the sofa. I'm sure you'll *use* it more than I would."

He waited for the meltdown. She had loved that damn couch. She had gone into debt to buy it and have it delivered to their apartment. Over the past few months she had sat on it for hours as she worked on her lines and ran through her voice exercises. She took a step closer to him— yes, this was going to work, he thought—and she extended her hand. He reached out to pull her in for an embrace that would be the beginning of the reconciliation and rebuilding. She opened his hand, placed something there, and stepped back. He looked down. In his palm lay her set of keys to the apartment.

And she was already struggling to get her suitcases out the door.

"Don't expect me to help you," he said.

In not pursuing her, he took a gamble that she would be unable to go through with this. But as he poured his coffee in the alcove kitchen he felt his face slacken with the truth that Nicole was not coming back. He would never again hear the familiar weight of her footsteps descending to street level. He wasn't hearing it this time either; the suitcases were throwing her off, their ominous knocks and thumps underscoring the drama of her departure. He would never again hear her key in the lock and the turn of the deadbolt when she came home, for he held her keys now in his palm. Never again her light steps on the hardwood floor, the smell of her papaya shampoo in the bathroom, the sight of her reading Uta Hagen on the prized sofa that, vacant, would always remind him of what he had lost for having been too much himself.

The planning that must have gone into this! He checked the closet and saw that her half—her three-quarters, actually —was empty. He remembered the massive donation to the Salvation Army on Friday morning: she had known even then. This realization had him rethinking every recent conversation, searching for the signs he should have recognized. He sat down on her couch, his couch now, closed his eyes and took a deep breath.

He imagined her regal posture as she surveyed the city, hers alone now, from the back of the cab carrying her downtown toward her new life. He imagined a gaggle of female friends assuring her over coffee and cake that she had done the right thing. He would be the villain in a story that she would refine over time for maximum gasp factor. *He did what?* How happy, sturdy, and sensible she would be from now on.

He would have been surprised to know that by the time her cab crossed Twenty-third Street she was in the middle of a full-blown face-scrunching cry, just as he was surprised at his own suddenly easy composure, and the pleasure he took from leaning back on the couch. From now on he would be able to raise his shoes to the off-white armrest without Nicole snapping at him. I can be the villain, he thought, I don't care. I can be single, fine.

Had he so misjudged Nicole and himself? If his greatest love and future wife had just walked out the door, why did he feel so free?

4. Drinking and Dialing

ON HIS WAY TO THE BATHROOM, SHUFFLING, HUNGOVER, his stomach queasy, something like thumbs pressing against the backs of his eyeballs, Brad Smith noticed his cell phone on top of the television. At the sight of it he immediately felt a sense of dread, which, judging by his call log, was well founded, for at an inappropriate hour—to be precise, at 12:32 a.m.— probably as soon as he had walked in the door after having a quick drink for six hours at Zarela, killer margs, he had phoned and for forty-two minutes, apparently, conversed with one or both of his parents, after midnight most likely his father.

What had he said?

Yes, he recalled now his father's groggy "Hello?" He vaguely remembered trying to sound sober, reasonable: "Oh, no reason, just haven't talked to you in a while." He was heartened to recall no yelling. Probably, he tried to tell himself, the conversation had gone just fine. Probably the sound of Dad's voice had scared up Brad's debate team elocution, left over from high school, fifteen years ago, back when he was still living up to his potential.

He winced at himself in the bathroom mirror. He was

used to being handsome—according to one girlfriend, "chiseled"—and would be so again in a few hours, but until then the look was classic hangover bloat. One of these days his face was going to get stuck like this. He took a long piss, so exactly the color of margarita that it almost felt cold. Then he went back to bed for a few minutes. He was going to get up and go to the gym before work. Because everything was perfectly fine. He had not had too much to drink last night, a Sunday. The conversation with his father had been cordial and informative, even at 12:32 a.m. After a good sweat at the gym, a productive morning at work, and a nice, big, curative lunch, he would call Dad again and have another normal conversation to prove to himself that everything was all right. In a few minutes he would rise and get his life moving.

He awoke two hours later, at 9:00 a.m., to the ringing of his phone, the land line. He had to be at work for a meeting at ten. The caller ID screen listed Anonymous. Should he? Shouldn't he? He took the chance.

"Bradley, Bradley, good, I'm glad I caught you, it's your Uncle George."

"George!" Oh, why had he answered the phone? This was going to be about the oil thing again. "I'm running a little late."

"It's a rare person who can hear opportunity knocking and have the courage to open the door, and I've always thought you were that kind of person—you're just like me, Brad. So we really need to talk about this investment opportunity. You haven't told your Dad about this yet, have you?"

"No." That was the last thing Brad was going to do, not least because his father had asked him to please let him know if George ever came around looking for money, because that would mean he was using again and should be back in rehab or jail. Brad was afraid his father would be enough of a hardass to call the cops and enough of a softy to feel guilty about it forever. He didn't want his father's conscience on his conscience. "I'm not going to tell him."

"Good, we'll cut him in when the time comes, and then he'll be proud of his little brother, won't he? Because if you come up with a way to bypass the Panama Canal, the Panama Canal, man! This is huge! Instead of sending the ship through, you pump the oil from one side through our pipeline to another ship waiting on the other side. How great is that, man? The best ideas are always so simple. See, it was all connected to Noriega and shit, that's why no one wanted to touch it. Understandably. But now he's in jail in Miami, so the pipeline makes perfect sense."

"George, I have to get ready for work."

"But you know people on Wall Street, right? You could broker the deal that gets the whole thing going." Brad closed his eyes and let him talk. George had been his favorite uncle, the wild one, the one most likely to take him to an R-rated movie and let him drink a beer out of the fridge and stay up as late as he wished. Handsome, too, always with good-looking trashy women around and guys talking about "going drinking" and being shushed by George whenever they mentioned any activity related to something called "blow" or "snow." Brad had been too young to recognize the indications of drug use. Only bad people did drugs. George wasn't a bad person. *Ergo* . . . But then George started getting arrested. "Threw his life away," Brad's father often said. The squandering of potential topped his list of grave and stupid sins. "Got into Vanderbilt, perfect grades for the first three years, on his way to becoming an engineer, and then he just dropped out!"

Ever aware of this judgment, George was prone to launching into unprovoked arguments against it. "Maybe working at a golf course isn't exactly living up to all I could have been, but everything happens for a reason, Brad. See, caddying, you get to network with all the bigwigs. That's how I got my friends in high places. That's how I met the Panama Canal guy."

There was a sniffle in there. George was crying. "Have you been drinking again?" Brad said. Still hungover himself, maybe even still a bit drunk, he felt ridiculous for asking, a hypocrite taking the high road. "Never mind. Look, let's talk later." Brad cut short the conversation with a promise that, yes, he would indeed talk with George later, extensively. Just after he hung up the phone, it started to ring again. George again no doubt. *And another thing* . . .

This time he ignored it. When he stepped out of the shower, the ringing had stopped, George probably having drifted off into a drunken, dreamless sleep like the one from which Brad had just awakened. He wiped a circle of steam from the mirror and checked his face. Some of the familiar angles had returned. The call log on his cell phone, however, had not improved.

In his wallet he found a woman's business card, and now he remembered talking to her, some account executive at an ad agency. Pretty, if he remembered correctly, and went one-for-one with him on the tequila shots. He had not kissed her, he remembered that much. There had been brief, clumsy barroom groping, plenty of unsubtle innuendo, and the suggestion—no, the promise—that he would e-mail her today. It had seemed like a good idea at the time. But now, no way. If he did run into her again in some bar or other after work sometime, there would be an awkward hour or two when they would still be sober, and taking care of that as fast as they could while each wondered, *What was I thinking?* No, he wasn't going to contact her. What happens at happy hour *stays* at happy hour.

Walking to AllMinder's Twenty-third Street office in the cold morning sunlight, the sidewalks of Park Avenue South dense with prosperous workers of the new economy, Brad began to feel a little better. We were only ten days into the new millennium, and he lived and worked in the world's ultimate city, for which the rest of the planet—in those rare moments when he thought about the rest of the planet—was but a vast support mechanism, as even the most remote root of the tree indirectly serves the biggest apple.

5. Wildly Successful and Profitless

At the Monday Morning Meeting, Jonathan Scarver, general manager of AllMinder.com, announced that with the hiring of another director of business development and an online ad sales coordinator the company had just surpassed the hundred-employee mark. Before the sentence was out of his mouth he was leading the assembly in a round of applause.

"This is a milestone for us," Jonathan said. "When I think back to how small we were when we first started, and it was just me and Barbara and Brad over in our offices in the Garment District." He shook his head. The *Garment District!* "I'm really so proud of you all and grateful to you for taking us as far as we've come in not even twelve months. I think we all deserve a big hand, not just for what we've already done, but for what we're going to do going forward."

Another round of applause. Jonathan read the names of the new employees and pointed them out across the room. He was aware that his enthusiasm might sound, to a cynical person, suspiciously like bullshit. As a young man it had never occurred to him that someday he would be the one passing out the corporate Kool-Aid, but what the hell, he believed every word he was saying. AllMinder's Initial Public Offering in June was going to go through the roof, giving him a nine-figure fortune, and most of these clapping employees would find themselves with more money than they could ever have hoped for if they had lived anywhere other than Silicon Alley in New York or Silicon Valley in California. Not for the first time since that cold New Year's morning when he arose ahead of his family to find that all was surprisingly right with the world, Jonathan thought about that ridiculous guy who had moved out to the Midwest to hunker down and await the collapse of the social order. Loser. Coward. Looking over the applauding crowd Jonathan saw the faces of the brave, these new-economy soldiers who were helping to change the world for the better, and he, he was their wise commander in chief.

Hungover Brad Smith was among the listeners, miming applause as he assessed the new hires. The online ad sales coordinator was a cute thing not even a year out of college. He rode the elevator with her earlier this morning. Stepping off she turned the wrong way, toward the stairwell rather than toward the lobby. She blushed and explained that today was her first day. It sounded so fresh: *Today is my first day.* Brad found himself wondering if she was one of those twenty-two-year-olds for whom thirty-three-year-olds did not register. Or the reverse: she looked straight through the untested, immature guys her own age. Perhaps she used to have crushes on her college TAs. If so, maybe there was hope for Brad.

"Isn't that right, Brad?" Jonathan was talking to him.

"I'm sorry, what?"

The assembled employees laughed at that, the PR guy not paying attention. Jonathan said, "The new floor? The renovation?"

"Oh, yeah." In anticipation of rapid post–IPO headcount growth, AllMinder was taking over another floor of the building and had commissioned an architect to redo it. The initial concept drawings that Jonathan liked best showed a work environment that, in Brad's unstated opinion, not so vaguely resembled the interior of the starship *Enterprise*. Construction was scheduled to begin the second week of April. AllMinder would occupy the finished space in July, shortly after the IPO. "It's going to be great," Brad said. "The feeling is that we shouldn't look like any old cubeland. We should look like a dot com. We're going to get a pinball machine and maybe a couple of vintage arcade games. Jonathan here has approved the in-office use of those annoying scooters that you're always having to dodge on the streets these days, and so we're getting some of those in." Brad's turn to lead the applause.

Jonathan said, "You can all consider this new floor a reward from Farouk," as in Farouk Kharrazi, who, through his Kharrazi Enterprises, was AllMinder's lead investor and most active board member, a volatile man of never specified Middle Eastern origin. "As you know, Farouk has given me free reign to run the company as I see fit and to make the hard spending decisions that we have to make in order to attract and retain employees and site visitors in this highly competitive environment. I consider the new floor integral to meeting that challenge."

Looking around the room, Brad wondered if he was the only one who had gone out last night. He was approaching an age—or was he years past it?—where a night of indulgence was no longer something to be bragged about, the hangovers no longer a sign of life being lived to the fullest but perhaps exactly the opposite. At thirty-three, if you repeat stories of drunkenness outside the secret society of your fellow partiers, it is only to your own potential embarrassment and career peril. For a thirty-three-year-old the line was *had a couple of drinks*, not even a few and certainly not a lost count of margaritas followed by two or three "one last" shots of tequila. No, that would be frowned upon. And your couple of drinks had no effect on work. That was part of the game at thirty-three. The new Biz Dev guy, he played the game. Brad could tell, and not just by the job title. The real indicator was the face: a little puffy and the eyes still dim with recovery. Looking at him Brad detected the possibility of one of those beautiful friendships, the greater portion of which transpires with elbows on an oaken bar, and eye contact made mostly in a mirror above rows of bottles in their gemstone gleam.

As the meeting broke up, Brad went to the kitchen to pour a cup of coffee. Jonathan appeared beside him. "I'm telling this to everyone," he said. "Do me a favor and don't put anything about the new floor renovation in your report." Every week Jonathan compiled progress reports from key staff members and e-mailed them to the board members. "There's no need to distract Farouk with that kind of non-business information."

"You haven't told him?" The renovation was going to cost four million dollars, most of that Farouk's.

As more employees wandered into the kitchen Jonathan lowered his voice. "Don't be myopic. By the time the bill comes in we'll already be traded on the NASDAQ, and it won't be a big deal that we spent the money. Anyone who comes into the office is going to be impressed with us, more likely to do business with us, more likely to write favorable articles about us if AllMinder exists in a cool working environment. I'm just worried that Farouk wouldn't understand that right now. In not telling him, I'm protecting him from his own shortsightedness." He checked his watch. "I've got to meet with Barbara about an HR issue."

Back at his workstation, Brad opened his weekly report and deleted the paragraph he had written about the new floor renovation. Four million dollars was a lot of spending to keep from Farouk, but Jonathan was right: with the stock market soaring and the IPO imminent, there was no need to worry.

6. The Snooping Tech Guy

AMONG THE ATTENDEES OF THE MANDATORY MONDAY Morning Meeting was Steven Bluestein, a systems administrator with a penchant for literary science fiction. He never listened closely to the people on the business side, the Jonathan Scarvers, the Brad Smiths, guys who didn't understand the nonmonetary significance of the Internet, its transformative evolutionary properties, countless giant steps for mankind. Even as he clapped on cue and feigned interest in the new floor that he already knew would be reserved for the Scarvers and Smiths of the organization, he was thinking of something he had read online recently: that the Internet had become a sort of collective consciousness, the best ever uncensored macro expression of the human mind, with space for everything from pure hate to a longing for universal respect and love. It mirrored the paradoxes of human thought and behavior, which even within a single individual could run the gamut. Most of the time, OJ wasn't going around stabbing people, and it wasn't hard to imagine Jeffrey Dahmer helping a little old lady cross the street—*what a nice young man*—while at the same time wondering which of the tasty meats in his freezer he was going to thaw for dinner.

Now back at his cube, sipping his coffee, Steven considered that in the kitchen a few minutes earlier neither Brad Smith nor Jonathan Scarver had noticed him. Even as he reached around Brad to grab a couple of packets of sugar, he remained invisible to those two professional backslappers. Different types of jobs attracted different personality types; negotiators, PR people, and figurehead general managers were, in Steven's view, necessary evils. Stick them on the fancy floor, make them feel important, give them a wink as you sign off on their padded expense reports. Meanwhile Steven paid for his own deli sandwiches.

Well, at least he did manage to glean from his job some free entertainment: he read everyone's e-mail. That was how he knew, among other things he wasn't supposed to know, that the newly renovated floor would be reserved for Biz Dev, Marketing, and Strategy. The technologists—only the most important people in the whole company—would be left behind in the windowless space they currently occupied. Every now and then Jonathan would walk through with some business prospect or job candidate, like a factory owner giving a tour.

It was easy to justify browsing through anyone's and everyone's e-mail accounts. He had to keep everything up and running, for on his network resided all company documents, and on his machines, hosted at Exodus, resided the company's Web site, without which there was no company. The enemies were hardware failure, software misconfiguration, and, most fearsome of all, computer viruses. A brick-and-mortar company didn't have to worry about its place of business suddenly vanishing because a brainy fifteen-year-old, from the comfort of his own bedroom, creates an e-mail-borne virus that some clueless nontechnical employee like Maria Massimo opens, infecting the entire company and possibly—given the right, or rather *wrong,* series of coincidences, errors, and security lapses—bringing down the whole site. For AllMinder that was a constant threat, and Steven the only sentry. What better way to make sure the e-mail accounts kept working properly than sometimes to read the messages as they went through?

He might have to admit someday, if he were ever questioned about it, that there were plenty of better ways. The volume of mail coming into AllMinder was so great that no one person could possibly eyeball all of the attachments; and you couldn't detect a virus just by looking anyway. Short of total abstinence, the systemwide antivirus software that Steven had already installed was the best prophylactic. There was no legitimate reason for him to read other people's e-mail. If there was a problem he would hear about it right away. He had only to put his feet up, open whatever science fiction book he was into at the time, and wait for his pager to beep or his phone to ring. You simply could not conduct business without e-mail in the year 2000 any more than you could have done without the United States Postal Service in 1950. A tool that had once been viewed with suspicion, as a novel luxury, a potential distraction, perhaps best reserved for the executive levels, like the better dining room or corporate jet privileges, had become the preferred—nay, the essential—method of communication for almost any sit-down job. People who worked within comfortable talking range of one another, their desks perhaps even side by side, often communicated company matters only in e-mail, the better to create a record that might help resolve any subsequent disputes.

Reading AllMinder e-mail, Steven found the usual pettiness that suffuses any human organization. Several of the product managers predictably referred to Vlad Morovsky, the mental runt of their group, as Moronsky or sometimes simply

Moron. At one time or another nearly everyone turned "Kharrazi" into "Crazy." The guys in Biz Dev regularly circulated inappropriate sexual material, including humor and photographs, and made plans to go to "the place," which Steven inferred from context was some local strip joint, probably Tens, just a couple of blocks away on Twenty-first Street. He had never been to such a place, not because he didn't like the idea of seeing half-naked women—he liked that idea very much—but rather because he feared that despite the bills in his fist they would ignore him and move on to better looking prospects. Rejection under such circumstances—the inability to buy attention even at a place where it was sold—would be too heavy a blow for the ego to bear.

Alcoholic PR guy Brad Smith received e-mails from women he met in bars and to whom he had given his business card. "Hey, enjoyed meeting you last night, I was SO drunk though. We should get together and have a non-slurring convo, don't you think? I'm free this Friday." If Brad ever replied, it wasn't on the company e-mail. He either phoned or used a Web-based service, probably Hotmail. Most likely though he did nothing. Sometimes the woman would send a follow-up: "Hey. There was something wrong with our e-mail yesterday and maybe you didn't get the one I sent you . . ."

And Jonathan Scarver, married Jonathan Scarver, was receiving—and, as fast as he could, forwarding to Human Resources Vice President Barbara Lubotsky—e-mails from AllMinder's director of customer service, an attractive woman based in Florida, whom apparently he had not called after that "great dinner" (her words) to which he had treated her last time she was in New York for meetings. "I know there was a connection," she wrote. "There was definitely a spark, Jonathan, you can deny that all you want, but it's true. And it *wasn't* on work time, so I don't think either of us has anything to be ashamed of. I feel really close to you, and I just have to ask, didn't you want to come back to my hotel that night? Are you really happy in your marriage? You seem so concerned about whether or not you're behaving 'appropriately,' but this kind of love is never 'appropriate' (what a boring word!) and I'm just asking you Jonathan to grow up and listen to your soul." In his brief replies Jonathan revealed that he had informed HR of this "harassment." Barbara Lubotsky's verdict: "We need to document everything and terminate her immediately." And that was the end of that. Except now something seemed to be developing between Jonathan and Barbara.

And Barbara herself was the subject of spiteful exchanges between some of the entry-level coordinator girls, who daily picked apart her tasteful corporate attire. Steven found that odd. Wouldn't the coordinator girls be better off emulating the VP's attire the way he, fresh out of college, had taken note of his boss's backpack and had bought one just like it? Instead they dressed not for work but for going out afterward, so that they wouldn't have to go home to Jersey to change. At the copier, at the coffee machine, coming out of the restroom, they looked as if they were about to hit the dance floor. When they walked by, Steven could almost hear the soundtrack of their anticipated evening.

One of them, Maria Massimo, a soft, curvy Italian girl, had a boyfriend whom she called, respectfully, Mr. Green. Apparently he was well endowed and a fantastic lover. She was quite explicit about this. She wrote to her girlfriends of "multiple big screaming Os." Often she canceled plans with them because "Mr. Green is calling."

"Steven," she would sometimes ask, "can you help me with my computer? I can't get my browser to stay open."

He wasn't really a desktop support guy—the lowest rung on the Information Technology ladder—but Maria had a tendency to touch his arm when asking for a favor, as if his muscles (what muscles?) were her only hope for getting out of some movie-worthy predicament. Hero Steven Bluestein would find himself closing his science fiction book, lowering his feet to the floor, and following her back to her cubicle.

He almost laughed when, once, before allowing him to touch her keyboard, she closed down Microsoft Outlook and said, "Can't have you reading my e-mail."

Although he was glad to be of service to Maria, Steven generally liked to keep a low profile. So it was a validation of sorts that even Jonathan Scarver, who prided himself on being a man-of-the-people CEO and who seemed to have at least some notion of the nature and importance of the contribution of Systems to the daily operation of his company, always referred to him as Steven Brownstein. Once he did it in front of three VPs, none of whom corrected the miscoloring of Steven's last name, perhaps because they suddenly weren't sure of it themselves.

Brad Smith, being a gregarious corporate communications type, could be counted on to put the Blue in there, but his attempts to seem like he really gave a shit always failed. "So, reading another science fiction book, I see," he said to Steven in the elevator. "What's the general theme?"

"It's too complicated to explain. I wouldn't be doing the book justice."

"C'mon, give me the"—looking around at the walls of the descending box—"elevator pitch."

Steven shrugged him off. "You'll have to read it. It's a good one."

Without touching the book, Brad made a show of craning his neck to see the title.

"I'll put it on my list," he said in a tone that baldly, yet somehow inoffensively, declared he would do no such thing, not least because there was no list.

"Why don't you ever write back to these women you meet in bars?" Steven wanted to ask. Instead he zipped his book up in his backpack and waited for the elevator doors to chime open.

7. Goals Versus Lifestyle

BRAD STEPPED OFF AND WALKED BESIDE STEVEN BLUESTEIN almost as if they were heading out for a drink together. That'd be a laugh. The guy never went out, hence all the reading time. At least once a day it occurred to Brad that he should do more reading—stay in on a Friday night, kick his feet up, and really get into a novel, perhaps one about New York. Or *write* one about New York. The city foisted that dream upon its inhabitants and then booked them solid with life. Like many who woke up, worked, and played there, Brad felt he was living the novel that he wanted to read, if only it existed, or the one he would write, if he could ever find the time. After his windfall, after the stock options, then he would isolate himself somewhere, maybe in a little cabin on the coast of Maine, though he'd never been there (were there cabins on the coast?), and really get to work putting his own novel on the page. But he suspected writing about New York while living somewhere else was a little like trying to record in sobriety what it feels like to be drunk. You get the mechanics right—you know how to make a martini and that it is cold; you know which way the avenues run and that they are spaced farther apart than the cross streets—but you can't describe the anxious high that keeps your feet on so many sidewalks, your ass in so many cabs, and your belly at so many bars.

The new online ad sales coordinator was walking toward him from the entrance to the lobby, and he found himself parting company with Bluestein and stepping in her way, smiling. He introduced himself, got her name again (Rebecca), and asked how her first day was going.

"Great!"

"Good, I'm glad, it's a fun place. So how'd you wind up in online ad sales anyway? A field that didn't even exist when you entered college."

She rolled her blue eyes. "It's not my first choice, to tell you the truth. I wanted to be in communications or marketing or PR, but I needed the job. I was an English major at Bates."

"Interesting. Maybe I'll try to rope you in for a PR activity or two."

"Oh, I'd love that."

"I'll have to clear it with your boss, of course, but I think I can do that."

"That would be so cool."

Brad had three unfilled spots already approved for his department, which right now consisted only of himself. On the one hand, he didn't really need the help, and if the time ever came, he would have a hard time justifying the hires to Farouk Kharrazi. On the other hand, that wasn't stopping anyone else. His counterparts were hiring like mad, and he worried that if he did not do the same he would lose influence to their bloated departments. More than a decade his junior, Rebecca would have been a perfect entry-level addition. He would have to speak to Barbara Lubotsky about why he wasn't seeing any good résumés. Was PR last on her list?

Over a Caesar salad, which he ate alone at a restaurant on Park Avenue South, Brad tried to imagine how a secret fling would play out. It always begins with an ostensibly innocent conversation like that one back in the lobby. The conversations continue. On the surface they're harmless enough. The savvy pair of potential lovers, feeling each other out, are careful to flirt only when there are no witnesses, and to keep things verbal, deniable, subject to two interpretations, one of them casting the nascent relationship in a perfectly appropriate professional light, the other hinting at sexual possibilities. Then there is a night out for drinks. Perhaps two or three colleagues are supposed to join, but they cancel. Or perhaps these unwitting chaperones depart after a drink or two, leaving you and your preferred workmate unsupervised at the bar. That's when things really get rolling. The city, your silent partner, looms up large and romantic and dangerous through the movie screens that are the windows on all four sides of a cab zipping downtown. And then at a little spot you wander into because of its conspiratorial lighting you offer up a boozy observation that makes sense at the time, something like, "New York seems so big, and it is, but then maybe in a neighborhood you don't know very well you find this perfect little corner table, and you're with someone interesting, please forgive my Manhattanite understatement, it would violate my sense of irony to express just how enthusiastic I am about sitting here in present company. Help me remember this, I'll put it in a book: New York is such an intimate place, really, as small right now as the space between us." She would buy into that. For a moment, at least, it would be true. And the rest of the night and the next few weeks would be easy, everything existing in the paradoxical realm of casual passion that was the unsustainable ideal for Brad and his kind. You could fuck like porn stars at night and then not talk during the day. Perfect for the guy, but generally, in Brad's experience, increasingly objectionable to the woman. She starts to make things a little more obvious at work, maybe even tells some of her friends. Maria Massimo gives you a knowing look, and you wonder, *How did she find out?* Pretty soon Rebecca remarks that it sure would be convenient if she could leave a toothbrush and a change of clothes at your place; and, by the way, her parents are coming in for the weekend and they would so much like to meet you.

Brad found himself chewing his croutons with angry gusto, promising himself that he would do whatever he could to keep Rebecca the online ad sales coordinator, the probable clinging psycho, at a distance romantically, though he did intend to follow through on his commitment to throw her some PR work. It was the only decent thing to do. But there would be no affair. He really needed to stay in and read more.

After lunch he sat on a bench in Union Square, the cold air on his cheeks helping his hangover recovery and bracing him to dial area code 404. Atlanta. His parents. Time to supplant the drunken late night call with a perfectly normal one.

"Hey, Dad, how's it going?"

"Me, I'm fine. The real question is how're you?"

Brad winced. So it had been that obvious. "What do you mean?"

"Well . . ."

And they spent the next ten minutes sparring about his condition. Brad apologized for being so oblivious of the time. "I was perfectly fine until someone gave a toast near the end of the night and insisted, absolutely insisted, that everyone do a shot of tequila. It would've been rude not to participate." He was anxious to know what he had said but didn't want to ask.

Several times he pointed out that he'd been "fine at work this morning."

"You seemed unduly concerned that we think you should be married by now and living in the suburbs. We just want you to be happy." Brad had no response. Had he really gotten into all that? "You were talking about the shingle women and the shingle ads in New York. I honestly thought you were talking about some kind of construction until you said shingles *bar*."

"Heh-heh. That tequila, that's bad stuff." Brad made too obvious an attempt to change the subject. "You should see the Saint Bernard I'm looking at right now. I don't know how people keep these big dogs in the city. They must have huge apartments."

Dad's voice softened. "You've got to give yourself time to think, Brad. Contemplation is a necessity. If it all passes by in a blur, what have you got? You know what the Greeks used to say about the uncontemplated life. Besides, you don't want to end up like George, not that you ever could, I shouldn't even joke about it."

Had the old man found out about his brother's crazy Panama Canal scheme? Probably not. He'd already be out in Arizona, sticking George back into rehab. "Yeah. Look," Brad said, "I won't be calling you so late anymore. I'm really going to cut back on these social outings, but I am in PR, after all, and my colleagues don't tend to do their socializing at Starbucks. I'm cutting back though."

His father ignored Brad's unkeepable promises and asked about work.

"Great guns, Dad. Great guns. Still planning for the IPO, and if we do anywhere near as well as other companies in this space have done, I'll be able to afford some of that free time you're talking about. Maybe I'll go somewhere and contemplate my life and write."

"It's a bubble. It's a bubble. If you look at long-term stock trends, it's just so obvious that these past two or three years are a complete anomaly, so you better hurry with your IPO. I mean, do you realize how crazy this is? How much have you guys spent, about twenty million?"

"More like fifty."

"Fifty million! To hang out and make a Web site that brings in no money? It's a sign that people are off their rockers."

Brad sighed. Dad just didn't get the new economy. The old rules didn't apply. Even respected analysts at major investment banking firms were saying so. His father had worked patiently for thirty years at the same insurance company, exercised good judgment all along the way, and in fact had enjoyed a remarkable career, rising from entry-level risk analyst almost all the way to the top, bailing out with a golden parachute when it became clear that he was in danger of being offered the CEO spot, which he could not have turned down and which probably would have eaten at least five years into his retirement. "Think of all the golf I would have missed," he sometimes remarked.

Now he continued. "I just hope you can cash out before the crash, or that you won't be disappointed if you can't, because if you get used to thinking of yourself as rich, you'll drive yourself crazy when it doesn't pan out."

"After the IPO, I should be fine." Brad had calculated that he would be worth anywhere from three to ten million dollars. It was one of the reasons he couldn't get too worried about running up his credit card debt. "The bubble needs to last for another year, that's all. Come on, you don't think we can make it to January of 2001 with the economy still running like this?"

"To give you an idea of what I think the odds are on that,

I don't have any tech stocks. About the drinking, son. I know some people manage to be both drunk and successful, but I'm not sure that's the goal you want to aspire to."

Brad found himself nodding. He loved his father but ignored his advice, and found it frustrating that the advice was always so unassailably sensible. If only his father could have been one of those unreasonable, heavy-handed fellows, rebellion would have been so much easier on the conscience. Alas, the old guy was always right. Stop drinking so much. Stop counting your chickens before they hatch. The stock market cannot sustain itself at its current level. Who could argue?

8. First Grocery Trip

FOR THE FIRST FEW DAYS, NICOLE SUBSISTED ON FRUIT AND her staff meal at the Film Center Cafe, the cost of the move having depleted her bank account into the low double digits. But by Thursday she had worked some good shifts, and the roommates had cleared a quadrant of the refrigerator for her. Plenty of room for skim milk, yogurt, and fruit. Her two shelves of the pantry would hold graham-flavored breakfast cereal, soup, pasta, and several cans of tuna. In the freezer, a box of low-fat ice cream sandwiches.

Walking back to her new apartment from the grocery store she carried her bounty in plastic bags that pinched her gloved fingers together, pulled her shoulders down within her puffy coat, and declared to all who saw her, *Hey, I live around here now.* She felt so great about it that she stopped at a corner convenience store and exchanged one dollar for a rose, which the clerk carefully positioned in one of her bags so that it might survive the rest of the trip home. She made small talk with him while she adjusted her scarf before stepping back outside. Dale had often remarked disdainfully that cheap flowers sold by delis, rather than by qualified florists, would shed their petals before the end of the day, and she had bought this one as much in rebellion against his admonition as to fill the bud vase on her windowsill.

Her new neighborhood was so different in character from Hell's Kitchen that at times she felt as though she had moved to a different city altogether, but no, she could look north and see the Empire State Building and the Chrysler Building, and southwest to the World Trade Center towers. This was every bit as much New York as the Theater District, which had been her home until Sunday and where she still worked at the Film Center Cafe, serving neighborhood residents and tourists who wandered in off the street with playbills rolled in their fists.

It was only the more intrepid tourists who wound up down in the East Village and the Lower East Side, and as Nicole explored her new neighborhood, having been "booted" from Dale's apartment (she was working on her revisionist story about the breakup), she discovered a sort of refugee sensibility that suited her state of mind.

Of course she had been down here several times before. All New Yorkers visit the area sooner or later. She had performed a series of showcases at KGB on East Fourth Street, Dale comprising five percent of the audience. Together they had eaten Mexican at Mary Ann's, strategizing about how best to get her seen by agents and casting directors, and then they had walked off the meal on the East Village streets, gazing into other restaurants and novelty shops. As they passed a tattoo parlor, Dale shook his head.

"I don't see why anyone would do that."

"Oh, come on, I'm practically the only one in my acting class who doesn't have a tattoo."

"Body modification, they're calling it now. People are getting little devil's horns stuck under the skin of their foreheads.

I'm a graphic artist, trust me, styles will change, and someday all these people will wish they hadn't done this, because—and this is something I think will really grate on them—it will be *out of fashion.*"

Several times since moving out, it had occurred to her that she should get a tattoo, a small one, discreetly placed so that it wouldn't become a caricaturable feature in the heat of the spotlights she hoped were about to swing her way. One of her female roommates had a little half-moon on her ankle. Something like that maybe. Then she caught herself. One thing to buy a deli rose, quite another to get a tattoo she didn't really want simply to scandalize Dale in the event that she saw him again. That he was still such an influence irritated her. She was going to have to guard against the habit of imagining her daily choices through his eyes. She felt that only when he no longer crossed her mind would he truly be out of her life.

She lived with three people: a painter (with the half-moon tattoo), a drummer, and a writer. They were also a bartender, a waiter, and a proofreader—that's where the rent came from—but their jobs did not define them. From the first day, when she did not see any of them until after midnight, it had been clear that they would keep to themselves. She could tell there would be the usual share-type problems, brief arguments over who used all the hot water or who left that bowl in the sink, but on the whole it was a respectful, civil arrangement. Though they did one another small favors, they would never be lasting friends; though they did one another small crimes, they would never be lasting enemies.

Four days into her new living arrangement, she still did not miss Dale—perhaps, she realized, because during their cohabitation they had seen very little of each other during the week.

Even if she had not moved out on Sunday, by today she would have seen him for only about three waking hours in total. He was out the door by eight-thirty or nine while she was still sleeping off her late night Film Center shift; if he went out for dinner and drinks after work, as he often did, he wouldn't be home until nine or ten, when she was still at Film Center taking orders, or in acting class, or, too rarely, spending a precious night off at home, enjoying time alone. *How was your day? Fine but exhausting. How was yours? Fine.* A little CNN and then off to bed. Sex usually waited until rare occasions of simultaneous sobriety and alertness on Saturday or Sunday afternoons. In her new East Village apartment she noticed his absence most at night. It was hard to sleep without him; rather it was hard to sleep without a warm body next to her. But she would get used to that. She was not yet remotely interested in finding someone else to share her bed. In fact it occurred to her to impose upon herself a period of celibacy, to abstain even from dating and to resist the well-intentioned efforts of restaurant coworkers and actor acquaintances who wanted to set her up with so-and-so. You could tell a lot about people by whom they tried to fix you up with, and a lot about yourself. Back when she was new to Manhattan, the sell would have been about the potential boyfriend's good looks and what a great career he was about to have in some arts-related profession. Now it was about how, after the inevitable disappointments that had accumulated in his thirty-three to thirty-nine (and once forty-five!) years of life, he was still in pretty good shape, with a nice practical job in, say, health insurance, and was back in the city because of his recent divorce. She went on none of these proposed blind dates. This was a time for being alone, for getting to know herself directly rather than through the eyes of some man she was trying to impress.

In the cab coming down to East Fourth Street after storming out on Dale—in the trunk her two suitcases full of clothes, books, toiletries, and that bud vase—she had been crying not so much for Dale as for the passage of time, its inexorable destructiveness, the impossibility of preserving the good of the past without forgoing the good of the future, the cruel requirement of progress that we must leave people, things, and parts of ourselves behind. There was loss in that—on the morning of her departure she had felt it acutely—but there was freedom too, and hope, and she was beginning to feel that now.

She unpacked her groceries. In her room she cut the stem of the rose and placed it in the bud vase. Dale was wrong about the fragility of deli-bought flowers; this one would remain fresh and perfect for more than a week.

9. Browsing at the Bookstore

Nicole had no idea how close she came on Wednesday evening, week two of her escape from Hell's Kitchen, to meeting Brad Smith. Having decided against going out that night, having determined instead to broaden his world by staying home and reading, after work Brad went not to a bar but righteously and with difficulty to the Union Square Barnes & Noble, where he browsed the fiction section, overwhelmed. The store stocked three or four copies of each book—about the width of a bottle, a comparison that nearly drove Brad straight to nearby Cibar.

Nicole was in the store at the same time, at a table stacked with books about acting. After some deliberation, for she could afford to buy only one book, she settled on *True and False* by David Mamet and took the escalator back downstairs.

Brad glimpsed only a flash of profile that too quickly became the back of her head as she descended to the next floor. Her unconventional beauty wouldn't have registered with Rinehart and some of his other happy-hour buddies, but Brad was more than susceptible. In the space of a few seconds he constructed the rest of her face, imagined her life, and felt an attraction so unreasonable and unfounded that he knew he could never confide it to anyone. He had to go talk to her right now or risk losing her forever to the current of the city. He returned the novel in his hand to its place on the shelf and took a step toward the escalator.

"Brad!"

Directly in front of him, as if just to block his path, AllMinder geek Steven Bluestein, wearing his backpack and holding two new science fiction books. "Hi, Steven." Brad took a step sideways, casually, as if this chance meeting were pleasant enough and see you at work tomorrow. But Steven stepped sideways too. "You come here a lot?" "Not really." Anyone else would have detected Brad's distraction and let him go, but not Steven.

Most of Steven's colleagues in Systems lived in New Jersey, where the wife took care of three or four kids in a house that smelled of curry. They tended to go straight home from work and stay there. They did not break away on a Wednesday evening to roam the aisles at one of Manhattan's larger bookstores and then maybe grab a brew a few doors down. For Steven, this sort of chance meeting in Manhattan was like the beginning of some sci-fi story, a couple of space warriors hailing each other in the market square and then cementing the budding alliance with a few pints of space-age mead. "Hey, after you pick out your book, want to grab a brew over at Heartland?"

Brad couldn't bring himself to be rude. Perhaps he could dispense with Steven in a few sentences and then race downstairs in time to catch the woman at the register or just happen to be leaving with her. Hold the door for her. Depending on the wait at the register, he guessed he might have as long as three minutes. He glanced at his watch. "Oh, I'm never one to turn down a beer, but unfortunately today I can't."

"Really?" Steven was standing there grinning, oblivious. "Why not?"

"I've already made plans, I just can't."

"Oh. Are you going to go see a movie or something? I wouldn't mind seeing a movie."

"No, no movie." He glanced toward the escalator again. "Look, Steven, if you must know, I have plans concerning a girl, and I'm sort of late, so if you'll excuse me—"

"Oh, sure, sure. Believe me, I understand that. Maybe another time?"

Already on the escalator, Brad called back, "Sure." He took the steps two at a time, but downstairs he found no sign of the girl whose face he had seen only partially and yet somehow perfectly. In front of the store he looked both ways, finally deciding to take a last ditch stroll through the small park across the street, where perhaps she had stopped at the dog run to watch the pets enjoy their brief respite from the leash. No such luck, she wasn't there.

Even as they shared the city, saw the same newscasts, walked the same streets and passed through the same doors sometimes mere minutes apart, Nicole and Brad had no idea how close they came, several times, to meeting each other and having so many of life's questions answered. Someday it will occur to Brad that it was a good thing Nicole did not meet him at that time in his life, when he was boozing too much, womanizing methodically, and grossly overspending in anticipation of his post–IPO wealth. He will remember with chagrin the way he almost chased down that girl on the escalator in Barnes & Noble, having seen only the back of her head. And Nicole too will be glad not to have met Brad then, for she was in defensive mode, having been "dumped," to hear her tell it, and having little success to show for years of struggle in New York.

She was so unimpressed with herself that she would have been insurmountably suspicious of anyone who expressed interest in her; guy just wants to have sex with a struggling actress, thinks my failure makes for desperation.

After finding no sign of the woman whose face he hadn't quite seen (Nicole was already well on her way home to the East Village), Brad went back upstairs at Barnes & Noble. He chose a novel about Paraguay, intending to read well into the night.

"Plans fall through?"

"Hi, Steven. Yeah." He weighed the book in his hands. "You still want to get that beer?"

And so he had two with Steven at Heartland Brewery; then a few more by himself at Cibar on his way home. For months thereafter, the book he bought would remain on his dresser, still in its Barnes & Noble bag.

10. The Happy Hour Demographic

AT FOUR P.M. BRAD GOT THE HAPPY-HOUR E-MAIL FROM HIS friend the devil, who worked at GSR Investments and made a heartbreaking multiple of Brad's salary. "El Teddy's at 6:30," it read in its entirety. It was addressed to twenty-four people. That David Rinehart could come out at all on a Thursday was itself something of an occasion. His sixteen-hour days tended to make him a rare sight until Friday night, when he suddenly became the ubiquitous center of all after-work activities for the twenty or thirty friends who regularly partook of his largesse at various bars. Actually, Rinehart had missed the last two Fridays, and Brad had been meaning to send him an e-mail to find out what was up.

Brad's first inclination was to say no; he was going to stay home and read the novel he had bought yesterday. But after drinking last night he felt as if the weekend had already begun. No point in staying in, especially not on a Thursday. "I'm in," he wrote. Send. After all there was a chance, tiny but not non-existent, that he'd run into the Barnes & Noble girl again, which would certainly never happen if he stayed home.

Brad had spent most of that morning in a meeting with

Jonathan and the investment bankers who were going to take AllMinder public in June, making him richer, he hoped, even than Rinehart. Farouk Kharrazi had phoned in from L.A. Confined to the speaker phone, unable to bolster his proclamations by waving his arms or pounding the desk, Farouk tended to yell in compensation. His strong accent and idiomatic confusion sometimes resulted in comedy. "We are eating a dead horse," he said, interrupting a circular discussion about market capitalization.

Jonathan hit the mute button. "See what I have to deal with?" he said to the bankers. "The other day he told me we needed to do something by the sweat of our bras."

Brad had two action items coming out of the meeting: first, write a press release touting the impressive increase in traffic to AllMinder.com since the start of the national prime time advertising campaign (commercials that featured a talking orangutan driving a delivery truck); second, brainstorm with the marketing department to come up with a company mission statement.

"Something like All Things to All People?" Brad joked.

"Exactly," said the lead banker, "but say it in a way that expresses our clarity of purpose."

Don't mention profit, the bankers advised him, use *revenue*. Don't mention site visitors, use *eyeballs*. No need to mention that AllMinder was spending six million dollars per month more than it was taking in, and that this discrepancy would increase as AllMinder hired additional staff and upped the marketing spend to get more eyeballs and *brand recognition*, another term Brad now tossed around more frequently, it seemed, than he said *hello*. Obviously, leave out the traffic analysis, which showed that visitors to the site rarely if ever returned. They were not loyal users but merely the curious and the easily influenced who had seen one of those orangutan commercials. Didn't matter. As long as the eyeballs kept coming, the likely market capitalization was in the low billions, some sliver of which had Brad's name on it.

The IPO market was so hot right now that the investors didn't seem to care that AllMinder was still "adapting to changing market conditions," as Brad wrote in one press release, "by repositioning the company for a seamless alignment with the demands of the marketplace." In other words we don't know exactly what we're doing yet—all things to all people indeed. "The company continues to accrue talent at a rate of about five new hires per week," Brad also wrote. In a job market so hot that a developer could drop his business card on the subway after work and have two offers by morning, the mere fact that you could attract and retain workers was a validation of your business plan.

Done with draft one of this press release and ready to hit happy hour, Brad approached Jonathan Scarver's office shortly after five. Through the glass walls he could see the general manager looking perfectly busy and decisive, the Visionary, ever aware that he was on display to passing subordinates. He had recently taken to spiking his hair with gel.

"First draft of that press release is in your e-mail," Brad said. "Want to get a quick drink? Some friends of mine are going to El Teddy's."

"Is Steven Brownstein coming? Your new drinking buddy?"

Brad shook his head. "No, and it's Bluestein."

"Apparently you guys are quite the buddies now, according to him."

"I ran into him at Barnes—"

"Oh, I know, he's telling everybody the whole story. Two wild and crazy guys."

"Anyway, you want to go to El Teddy's or not?"

Jonathan tapped his wristwatch. "Commute," he said. "I've gotta catch an early train tonight, but thanks." He was thirty-eight, had been married for ten years. Behind him were photographs of his good-looking wife and children, his anchors up in Westchester County. "It's not bad. I get a lot of work done on the train," he often said. It was the party line for commuters. It must have been in the welcome packet for new residents up in Westchester. "Tell your colleagues who reside in the city that you get a lot of work done on the train. Be careful to imply that they would be more productive if only they too had the advantage of valuable train time immediately before and after work." Brad, who liked to report how pleasant his own commute was—that walk up Park Avenue South —always muzzled his skepticism. The one time he had taken Metro North—to attend an oddly scheduled Thursday night engagement party in Westchester—the regular commuters had begun their ride with the best of intentions, reading and working, looking alert; but within ten minutes they were falling asleep, mouths hanging open, heads bobbing, as if succumbing to an invisible gas being pumped in by the diabolical Mass Transit Authority. The illusion was so compelling that Brad had lowered his window a couple of inches to get some air.

"I'll read over your press release on the train," Jonathan said.

Watch out for the sleeping gas, buddy.

In the cab on the way to El Teddy's, Brad checked his home voicemail. Three, all from Uncle George. "Listen man, I really should get your work or cell numbers in case I have to report any important developments in the pipeline plan, which I do, by the way. Not surprisingly." Slurring. Delusions of grandeur. "There's two sides to every story. I *had* to get to Phoenix that same night, and I didn't have a car, that's what the judge just wouldn't understand. Even your dad started preaching about how I should've taken the bus instead of some random dude's Trans Am. The bus? You know how long that takes? I'm trying to put together a major international oil deal and *you* are not helping one bit. You need to see the opportunity here, man. You know how long it takes a ship to go through the Panama Canal? A shitload of a long time, man. Plus they have to pay a toll. If you could set up a pipeline that ran right alongside of it, you'd be rich! If you call home and check your messages, you got to call me back. Keep in mind, there is no difference between me and you. If I'd had your opportunities, I'd be riding this dot com boom too."

Click. Next message, this one even more disjointed. Apparently the president of the golf club was unhappy with something George had said to his daughter, and had berated him about it in front of several other members. "The whole time I was thinking 'Panama Panama Panama, Oil Oil Oil.' I'm going to come in and buy out that golf course and that guy's going to be sticking his own damn hand in the toilets, which I told him I did not sign up for. So listen. Give me a call."

Click. Last message: "You know I've always been proud of you, I've always seen a lot of myself in you. I think we have a lot of the same weaknesses, and it is those weaknesses—our ability to take a chance, Brad!—that are going to make us way richer than the steady people like my brother, your dad. Don't you get that, man? I *had* to get to Phoenix, so don't be holding that whole grand theft auto thing against me. And as for the drugs, well, I'm for legalization anyway. Call me, please!"

Brad shuddered. Geez, was that just the booze? Is that what *I* sound like? Or what I'm going to sound like someday? The very thought made him crave a drink. El Teddy's was coming up on the left side. Through the bulletproof partition he said to the cab driver, "This is perfect, thanks."

Brad told Rinehart about Sunday night. "I actually went into work on Sunday, toned up a press release. On my way out I stop at Zarela figuring I'll eat at the bar, some good Mexican food and a beer or two, nothing major. While I'm there I start talking to a couple of girls, and one of them isn't bad. They both want to get into the Internet business, and I'm their personal expert. They're drinking margs, I switch to margs."

Rinehart was nodding along. "That's what I respect about you, you're always working. Solo dinner on a Sunday night? Brad Smith sees that as an opportunity to play the lonely card, the obviously single card, the Internet expert card, the soon-to-be-IPO-rich card." Rinehart was not quite handsome, but his bearing conveyed a level of success and potential that plenty of women evidently found attractive. His dates so invariably evoked a clothing catalog that Brad was not surprised, a few weeks earlier, to recognize one of Rinehart's exes in a lingerie ad in the *New York Times.*

"So far so good, right?" Brad said. "I didn't wake up with her, and I already tossed her business card. The problem is the call I made to my parents." He told Rinehart about the forty-two minutes that were logged in his cell phone but not in his memory. He had told no one else. Rinehart would be supportive, would tell him to suck it up, not to worry about it. Rinehart worked so hard that his own drinking binges were few and far between; thus deprived, he would support no attempt at moderation in his friends.

"I honestly think I have to quit drinking."

Rinehart put a hand on Brad's shoulder. "If you do that, if you join AA or whatever, I'm going to get all your friends together and we're going to have a reverse intervention. 'You used to be fun,' we'll say. 'You used to hang out with us.' 'Where be your flashes of wit?'"

"I know, I know. But don't you sometimes think it might be fun to sit at home with a book or something? I bought a book last night."

"If I'm not at work I can't stay in," Rinehart said. "Because I'm always wondering where the party is. Look, have you talked to your dad since then?"

"He told me to slow down and contemplate my life."

"That sounds like a good idea." Rinehart pointed at Brad's empty glass. "Ready for another?"

Their conversation took place at a volume that would have made it audible across an empty gymnasium, but at packed El Teddy's the words barely cleared the eighteen inches that separated their faces. A crowd of people three deep waved twenties in a vain effort to get the attention of the bartender, but Rinehart had built up so much tip equity that he had only to glance toward the bar to order another round for his party, which grew as the recipients of his e-mail continued to arrive. Excusing himself from Brad to go play host, he shouldered his way toward some new arrivals. With a fresh margarita, Brad found himself stepping up to Julia Dorsey and one of her girlfriends, who, interestingly enough, moved away, leaving Brad and Julia to each other.

"Hi, Brad!" Julia pecked his cheek. A skilled partier, she held her cigarette without burning any of her fellow sardines, and her drink without spilling it on the toes of her sleek black boots. "I was just telling this story . . ." about a friend of a friend of a friend, some guy whose girlfriend had just broken up with him because she found out that he had given his business card to one of the girls in her acting class. "And get this, here's how she found out . . ." She told a version of the story she had heard from a guy in her office who had been flirting with a temp whose roommate was in the acting class and had seen the action firsthand. "And so apparently she gets her boyfriend's business card and she's like, 'You whore, this is my boyfriend,' and the whole class was like, 'Uh-oh.' Apparently it was like an episode of Springer."

"That sounds like urban legend to me," Brad said.

"I'm serious."

"Well, the guy is a lucky bastard. Probably saved himself from getting married and moving to Westchester."

"I hope you're not expecting an argument from me on that point."

"Not at all, that's why I like you."

The tide of the crowd shifted, separating him from Julia for a period of three and a half drinks. Then he found himself pushed by the crowd and, he would have to admit, by his own drunken volition, back into proximity with her. Again they enjoyed the relative privacy sometimes afforded by an oblivious crowd. Her coarse good looks, which she had spent freely in places like this over the past ten years, attracted him into making eye contact too intensely during a conversation about relationships in New York City. "Dating a woman here is like musical chairs," he was saying. "You gotta date them when they're young and don't want to get married. If you're stuck with a woman when she turns thirty? Suddenly, magically, you're the one. How did you get to be that way? No one ever

thought you were 'the one' before. And that's why the divorce
rate is so high and married couples are so irritating. They don't
belong together, but they don't want to admit it. They just got
caught when the music stopped."

Julia said, "It's better than living in some small town where
you marry the first person you ever have sex with. I'd be the
wife of a mattress salesman in San Diego, my only consolation
being that his father owns the store and someday this whole
empire of mattresses would be mine and Billy Ballentine's
alone, and Billy, being a man, would die first, heart attack
probably, and then it would all be mine. I'd be the Mattress
Queen!" She thought for a moment. "No smartass comments,
please." She turned her glass up. The rim, pressing between
her eyes, deposited a grain of margarita salt there.

Brad touched it away. "But I mean, that's why I'm always
attracted to women you say are far too young for me."

"Because they don't love you?"

"Absolutely. It's bachelorhood preservation. They're not
thirty, so I'm not 'the one.'"

"Well, I may be thirty, but I'm not looking for 'the one.'"

"You say that now, but if we sleep together pretty soon
you'd want to see a movie or get brunch, and I'd agree, and
before you know it we'd be trapped in a meaningless dating
relationship. Next thing you know, I'm on the train to
Westchester."

"Brad Smith." Shaking her head she flashed a set of professionally whitened, absolutely straight teeth. "Rest assured,
I'd never marry you."

"That kind of turns me on."

"Really." Julia rotated her glass and sipped from where the
rim was still salty. "I like you a lot, Brad, but I don't love you."

"We might have a short but happy future together."

She shrugged. "Sure. Sometimes I *am* the mattress queen." She laughed hard enough to justify squeezing his upper arm. Playing along, he touched the small of her back. "I just thought of that time," she said, "when you brought that kid, practically, to Rinehart's party."

It took Brad a moment to remember the episode. "Hey, she was drinking age."

He had known Julia for three years and had never seen her without a glass in her hand, could not imagine her shutting out the distractions of her life long enough to lose herself in a novel or even in one of those lengthy *New Yorker* profile pieces that left Brad at once humbled and inspired. She paged through fashion magazines, read some of the blurbs, but she abandoned the crossword puzzle or the sex quotient self-assessment survey—indeed, the whole issue entirely and for-ever—at the first chirp of her cell phone. She was one hundred percent party girl, all the time. Work was a party. She was brilliant at it. A successful salesperson for an enterprise sys-tems software company, she supposedly made several hundred thousand per year. She dressed expensively, if not well, her taste subtly revealing a mall rat upbringing. It was easy to imagine her as the wife of a San Diego mattress magnate, with enough money to buy a big house in La Jolla, in front of which she would hang a woodcraft sign, THE BALLENTINES, much to the consternation of her MBA neighbors. In college her lack of interior life would have repelled Brad, but he had long gotten over his attraction to the psychologically damaged, the glori-ously self-tortured. For now, give me a girl who likes to drink, fuck, and travel. Julia *seemed* to fit the bill, but that was just an act, Brad suspected. She would have sex with him, sure, and pretend at first that it was no big deal. Then she would begin to require nonsexual time and attention. A friend's engagement would prompt a period of self-pity and hostile sulking. Still, thought Brad, she was looking pretty good tonight. He hadn't had sex in more than four weeks; an old girlfriend, in town on business from L.A., had done him a favor. That was perfect. If she became too demanding, he could say, "C'mon, we're three time zones apart!" Not that he had heard from her.

Over Julia's shoulder he saw Rinehart walking toward him, using both hands to carry three full margaritas in a precarious triangle. He was wondering if he should accept the fresh drink or leave with Julia right now. Get the sex out of the way, see if she could live up to her talk. "You know," he said to her, "I'm kind of surprised we've never hooked up before."

"Me too."

Brad set his empty glass on the bar and relieved Rinehart of two of the full margaritas. He passed one to Julia. Rinehart took her empty glass and set it on the bar.

"You have got to be the richest waiter in New York," Julia said.

Rinehart's shoulders rose. "What do you mean by that?"

"Nothing, it was nothing, I was just kidding, Rinehart. Relax."

"I'm not your waiter. I'm *buying* your drinks."

Brad said, "She was just kidding, man."

"David," she pleaded. It sounded odd. No one called Rinehart by his first name. "Forget it, I'm sorry. Here, I'll pay for my drink."

"That really *would* make me the waiter, wouldn't it?"

Brad noticed the runny nose, the agitation. He pulled him aside. "You've been doing a little something?"

"You got a problem with that?" Rinehart said. Then, suddenly beaming, "You want some?"

Brad answered no and no. He had tried the drug only once, swearing never again because it was too expensive and too . . . too perfect. At least alcohol kicked your ass the next day. A booze high was bought and paid for immediately. Cocaine was a credit card you paid way down the line, and Brad, a natural debtor, knew himself well enough to stay away. Looking around at the crowd of people for whom he'd been buying drinks, Rinehart said, "I think I want to close out the tab, let's go to Cibar."

"But everyone is here because of your invitation."

"They'll be fine." He nodded at the bartender. "Close it out, I'll pay it tomorrow." To Brad he said, "I'm going to go like I'm heading to the men's room. Meet me outside in five."

Brad made his way back to Julia, kissed her goodbye on the cheek. "Looks like I got babysitting duty," he explained.

Rinehart slumped in his corner of the cab. "I'm sick of taking care of the bill all the time. It makes me wonder who my friends are. And I object to snobbery directed against people like waiters."

"Oh." This was odd. Rinehart was an unlikely advocate for the servant class.

"I guess my mind is on a girl I met."

"*Really.* Don't tell me you're going out with a waitress. Not that there's anything wrong with that."

"She's not exactly a waitress." The cab passed into a swath of light that illuminated the backseat. "She works at Strings."

Brad attempted to conceal his surprise but felt his widening eyes betray him. "She's a stripper?"

"She is a stripper," Rinehart said, in a tone that introduced a defensive correction, "but I met her at the gym." Coked up and contentious, he was still staring at Brad, daring him to dis-approve. "What do you think of that?"

"Hey, that's great. Good for you. Everyone should go out with a stripper once. I mean, I haven't done it myself yet."

"No, that's not what this is about, this is not mere novelty." Rinehart seemed pained. "This is the real thing. I've never felt anything like it before. As soon as I saw her, as soon as our eyes met, I realized that we had this connection that went way beyond such trivialities as income and occupation."

For a moment Brad surprised himself by experiencing something close to envy. Rinehart kept talking. "She was shy about telling me her job, too, like she thought that was going to be a deal breaker. Do you realize that most of the guys who go out with her want to go out with her *because* she is a strip-per. It's that novelty thing that you so wrongly assumed applies in my case. She's looking for a guy who would prefer that she *not* be a stripper. That's me."

"You're not giving her money, are you?"

"Not more than I can afford." He grinned. Thirty-eight years old, he had confided in Brad last year that his portfolio was worth more than ten million dollars. The way the stock market had gone since that conversation, by now Rinehart was probably worth thirteen or fourteen, and he was expect-ing another seven-figure bonus in March. He could afford to peel away a few grand here and there to finance happy hour for his friends, and what for a stripper? Clothes, car, a new apartment? The possibilities were worrisome. Anyone in Rinehart's position had gone through college studying too hard, sacrificing his social life and all that it would have taught him. Rinehart had spent the rest of his twenties in the dedicated service of GSR Investments, working eighteen-hour days, working weekends—still no social life. Professionally

it had paid off. Socially he was a case of arrested development, an angst-ridden twenty-three-year-old with enough real
money to finance the ill-considered choices that, at twenty-
three, Brad had been too poor to make. "I think this is a really
special relationship."

Sober, Brad would have managed to reign in his sarcasm,
but now he said, "Sure, you two have complementary interests. You like naked beautiful women, she is a naked beautiful
woman. You have a lot of money, she wants a lot of money.
With so much in common, how can you lose?"

"I forgive you for saying that. So when you wake up tomorrow and you realize you were an asshole, don't bother calling.
Just remember, I forgive you." Still, Rinehart stopped speaking. He was moving his lower jaw back and forth as if trying to
dislodge a piece of food from between his teeth.

They turned right onto Fourteenth Street, toward the grav-
itational pull of Cibar. "Look, I'm sorry," Brad finally said. "I
shouldn't have said that. I'm sure you and she have a special
connection."

"All she needs is a little help, a little cushion until she
lands on her feet and gets a regular job."

"How does she list *Strings* on her résumé?"

"I'm glad you're asking about her résumé, I appreciate
that." Rinehart suddenly wore his dealmaker persona, lowering
his voice, imbuing it with urgency, and underscoring his points
by chopping his right hand against his knee. "It shows a sensi-
tivity to her plight. I think that bodes well, because I'm going
to ask you for a favor. See, I think she'd be perfect in an up-
front field like corporate communications. She is like the ultimate client-facing person."

"You think she could do my job?" Brad had always suspected
that Rinehart didn't fully comprehend the political intricacies

and doublespeak artistry of writing a good press release, but to have it confirmed so crudely was something of an insult.

To his credit, Rinehart realized that this time he was the one to have spoken out of turn. "No, no, no, not at all. But she'd look good beside you in meetings, you'd be a good *mentor* for her. You're hiring, right? All you dot coms are hiring. And you're growing your department."

Brad nodded. A few weeks ago he had boasted to Rinehart about his mandate to hire three new PR employees in advance of the June IPO, so there was no point denying it now. "Even if I could get her in, she wouldn't make what she makes at Strings."

"I'm taking care of that. I'm trying to push her to go legitimate, that's all. But she's no receptionist. Way too smart for that. You'll see. With what she does now I can't really introduce her to my parents."

"Is she Jewish?"

He shook his head. "That's another problem, aside from the whole stripper thing. But I'm telling you, man, I'm in love. This has got to work out, and I don't mean just for me. Also for Sierra." Too late Brad turned his smirk toward the window. "That's not a stage name!" Rinehart nearly yelled. "Her parents actually named her that. They were flower people or something, she can't help it."

"This is why we haven't seen you these past two weekends, right?"

"She's amazing. You should see what she does to the poor schmucks who go in there. She makes them think she really likes them, but the whole time she's in love with me, so it's okay. She's a master of manipulation. That's one of the reasons I think she'd be so good in your field."

Brad shook his head. "I don't know, it's a little more than

manipulation. It's actually quite complicated. It takes talent."

"I'm not saying it doesn't. Of course it does. You're a very smart guy. Look, just talk to her, give her some career advice. Let her at least come in for an interview."

"Actually," Brad said—something about Rinehart's sincerity had finally whetted his curiosity—"why wait?" Through the bulletproof partition he told the driver there had been a change in destination, and recited from memory the intersection for Strings.

11. Job Interview

ALONE IN THE CAB AT THREE A.M., BRAD FOUND HIMSELF IN a test of wills against his cell phone. What a strange evening, and he had to tell someone about it, anyone. He wished he had Julia Dorsey's cell phone number, maybe she'd let him share a little more than news, but alas.

He had met Rinehart's stripper girlfriend, Sierra. He had sort of interviewed her for a job actually. The whole situation was comical. He would include it in the novel he would write someday after he settled down; some people might find it amusing. But told as fact at three a.m., via a drunken phone call, the anecdote would not necessarily reflect well on Brad. He knew that. Not everyone would approve of his even going to Strings. Mayor Giuliani himself was trying to legislate the strip clubs out of business. Not everyone would appreciate the absurdly tender way Rinehart's eyes glazed over when Sierra shook her glittered tits for Brad. You had to know Rinehart to get that. He might have been showing off his new Porsche 911 ragtop, tossing you the keys so you could take it for a spin around the block to confirm that, yes, your envy was justified. Perversely magnanimous, Rinehart insisted that Sierra give

Brad lap dance after lap dance while he slapped down the twenties, beaming, and once shouting, "Better you than someone else!"

Two or three times a year Brad found himself hanging out with a friend at a strip club, getting lap dances, convincing himself that, hey, this stripper wants to see me in real life. And a couple of times since high school he had unwisely gotten himself physically involved with a friend's girlfriend. But never had the two elements—lap dances and friend's girlfriend—come together like this for the space of five or six sequential songs, and never while the other guy watched. If Sierra thought the situation was odd, she didn't let on. As she danced for Brad, placing her hands on his shoulders and leaning into him, letting him feel her weight, lowering her nipples within inches of his eyes, nose, and lips before doing a little push-up that revealed again her whole body, his eyes falling to the narrow strip of cloth that covered her must-be-shaved pussy, Rinehart sipped his Jack and Coke and, when Brad looked up, mouthed, *Isn't she great?*

"I'm so glad to meet you," she said to Brad. "Rinehart has told me so much about you." He felt her fingertips on the back of his neck, a brief massage. Her nose was nearly touching his. Her breath smelled of peppermint and lip gloss. "You're the marketing guy, right?"

"Public Relations, actually. Rinehart gets the two very distinct functions confused sometimes."

"Don't worry." Smiling, she ran her index finger along his jawline. "I know the difference."

Though the music was loud, neither he nor she had to yell. At that nondistance everyone is a lip reader. "We do have a large and growing marketing department at AllMinder. If that's what you're interested in, I could make some introductions."

"That's okay. I think I'd like PR." She turned around, placed her hands on her knees, and pressed her ass into his lap, grinding it in circles. Only the embarrassment of Rinehart's leering approval spared Brad an erection. Then she bent over. With hands sporting manicured red fingernails she slapped first her left buttock and then the right, producing a good clapping sound. "I spend a lot of time at the gym," she explained. "Part of the job. You like?" Brad nodded. The waistband of the thong was merely a besequined string. The floss portion, gauzy and insubstantial, disappeared completely between her cheeks.

Facing him, again she squeezed the back of his neck. "So Rinehart says you guys are expanding?"

"Well, yeah. My department is looking for some good PR professionals." He had to squash this whole notion that he could hire her. There was no way he could explain to his colleagues why Sierra was the best person for the job and how he had met her in the first place.

Sierra squatted between his thighs, resting her forearms against them for support. Brad worried that perhaps this blowjob position would finally be enough to offend Rinehart; but no, a glance confirmed that he still wore a creepy proud grin and swayed his head to the music. Sierra gave Brad a practiced expression of vacant longing, as if mugging for the camera in a porn shot. She was one step ahead of him. "I know you probably have doubts about me, and certain preconceived notions about whether or not I can perform the job." All of this without losing her lap-dance smile. "Go ahead, ask me some interview questions."

"This would violate every principle of HR procedure I've ever been taught."

"Oh, are your HR people here tonight?" She glanced left

and right as if to spot them taking notes destined for his employee file.

"No," he admitted.

"Well, ask me some questions so I'll know you're taking me seriously. I don't think you can have this kind of treatment once we start working together."

Rinehart interjected, "Brad is strictly professional. That's one of the reasons I'm sending you to him. I trust him not to sexually harass you. Go on, Brad, ask her some questions."

"Why do you want to leave your current job?"

"I've got enough money saved up. This was never a career. This was just a way to get to New York. You can understand that, can't you? Or were you born here to a rich family?" She ran a finger down his nose.

"I've been here since graduating from college."

"And where was that?"

"Duke."

"Good school, Duke," she said. "I've got a master's in English literature from UCLA." In her near nakedness she plopped right down on his lap and threw an arm around his neck. Brad felt like some sort of perverted Santa Claus. He glanced at Rinehart and again was relieved to find him still smiling. Sierra said, "And I've been interested in putting my education to use. I've been interested in PR ever since Rinehart suggested it last week."

"Last *week*." Brad looked at Rinehart. "You gave me the impression she had an abiding interest in it. It's *not* an easy job, not something you just pick up in a few days."

"She's smart." Rinehart tapped a finger against his temple. "She's got it up here."

Indeed she was smart. Brad knew she was playing him. She seemed to detect that there was no way he could say no to Rinehart. "Look," she said, "I know I'd have a lot to learn, but you can't have any doubt that I'm up to the challenge."

Rinehart said, "You know that, man, you know I only go out with the smart ones!"

"Hey." Sierra placed a finger under Brad's chin and turned his face back to hers. "Don't look away while I'm sitting in your lap. You'll give a dancer a complex."

"Sorry."

She stood again and danced before him, running her hands all over his body, and then all over her own body in all the places she knew he wished he could touch. A pro. These girls were all pros. He had never walked out of a strip club with enough money even to pay a cabdriver. The doorman would kindly point him toward the nearest ATM, usually just a couple of doors down, some twenty-four-hour convenience store owned by an immigrant whose personal financial ethic would never, never permit him even one wasteful, foolish visit to that strip club down the street, but whose sons were probably, unbeknownst to him, regulars.

Sierra was about five eight and not exactly skinny, but hard all over. In the office she would be a constant disturbance, a walking storm, causing everyone to behave inappropriately, from the techies who were going to slaver after her without discretion to the married wolves like Jonathan Scarver who would stop by frequently "to see how things are going." Neither the special treatment she would enjoy nor her obvious lack of PR experience was going to go unnoticed by Brad's female colleagues, many of whom would resent him for hiring a women whose job until that point was to exploit the fact that she was naturally built *almost* like a Barbie doll and whose surgical enhancements put her over the top. He would have to beat them away with her UCLA master's degree.

No, no this wasn't going to work at all. He was not going to hire her. He had to tell Rinehart: no way, man.

"It's only four hundred dollars for a private room," she whispered into his ear.

That was a proposition he had never accepted. He'd heard there was no sex, at least not at the four-hundred-dollar rate, but there were rumors of upsell attempts to eight hundred, and what else could be going on at that price? At that price, hands-off ejaculation seemed the least you had a right to expect.

"Too rich for my blood," he said.

She threw a glance at Rinehart and he slapped his all-powerful credit card down on the table. "Oh, what the hell," he said. "I want you two to get to know each other. I'll pay for it."

"Great." She clapped, grabbed the credit card, and started tugging at Brad's hand. "Let's go."

Brad yanked his fingers away, pulled himself up from his armchair, and leaned over to Rinehart's ear. "Come on, this is too much. This whole thing is not a good idea."

"I know, that's why we have to get her out of here." Grinning, he stood to make his argument. "That's why you're going to hire her next week. Line her up with some stock options in a pre–IPO Internet company. In the meantime I'd rather have her dancing for you than for these other losers." He waved a hand at the crowd of mostly white young men.

"They look just like us," Brad pointed out. "Thanks anyway, but if you want to pay for me at least let me pick another girl."

"You wouldn't rather be back there with Sierra?" Rinehart's eyebrows rose.

"I mean, she's great and all, but she's *your* girlfriend. It's too weird."

"Don't worry about it. Just take her back there and ask her some marketing questions then. Don't look at her body, if that's how you feel."

"Rinehart, I am in PR."

"Whatever. The four hundred bucks will be good for her. Management here likes to see that." Rinehart put both hands on Brad's shoulders. "Every great success has its doubters in the beginning. So the role you're playing, I appreciate it. I consider it necessary. Later when it turns out you're wrong, remember what I said, don't even bother calling to apologize. I forgive you in advance."

"I'm not taking her to a private room."

"Fine, I'll go. C'mon, Sierra, it's you and me." Rinehart grabbed her hand and started to walk away. "You," he said, looking back at Brad, "have her in on Tuesday or Wednesday for an interview, okay?"

In that moment, while Rinehart's finger was pointed at him and Sierra was gazing at him with a smile so beautiful that it actually competed with her perfect body, Brad found himself saying the word, "Okay."

"Deal," Rinehart said. "Thanks, buddy."

Now from the back of the cab, cruising down Second Avenue, he wanted to call someone and share that his clothes were flecked with glitter where her body had touched him, and that he could still smell her perfume. What a great story, how his socially immature but wildly successful investment banker friend had cajoled him into pretty much promising to hire his stripper girlfriend and train her in the ways of dot com public relations. Yes, that was a good story, and he wasn't so drunk that he couldn't tell it, was he? But who was there to tell? At this hour, no one in the eastern time zone. Certainly not his parents, he had learned his lesson there.

What about someone in one of the tardy time zones where the night was younger? Tons of people, six of them programmed into his cell phone. Brad scrolled through the list until he came to: "George! Glad I caught you. I gotta tell you, man, I think this whole damn Panama pipeline shit is crazy. It's a scam. This is not how deals get made, George. Some PR guy's golf caddie slash handyman slash landscaper uncle does not call him in New York asking if he knows anyone on Wall Street who can put a deal together to finance the bypassing of the Panama Canal. It just doesn't happen that way, man—"

George launched into a defense of the scheme. Right now we must occupy the same drunken plane, Brad realized, because everything he's saying makes sense.

A few minutes later he found himself saying, "Okay, look, get me the guy's name and the name of his company. I'll do a little asking around. I'll find out if there's any legitimacy whatsoever."

In the morning, on his way to work, he dropped off his pants and shirt at the dry cleaners. "I've got some glitter on these things . . ."

12. Bridge Financing

BY MID-FEBRUARY, EXCEPT FOR ONE SMALL PROBLEM, THE IPO was still on for June and was almost certain to be the kind of success that would turn Jonathan Scarver into an NBA team owner, a philanthropist, and finally an immortal bronze statue in the new Scarver wing of the Alderman Library at UVA, his alma mater. Students would hang leis around his neck after Bahamas parties. Mardi Gras beads in February. Have some fun, you stern old man. They would never know he had in fact spent plenty of time in the Bahamas after making his fortune and had gone to Mardi Gras once or twice too. In life he had not been so grim faced. But no matter. Beginning with those two perfect kids up in Westchester whom he hugged and kissed every morning before driving to the train station, generations of Jonathan's descendants would find their lives already bought and paid for by Dad, Granddad, Great-Granddad, and finally that bronze bust in the library.

That future was hardly more than a dozen weeks away. Jonathan Scarver, Brad Smith, the accountants, and others were spending more and more time with the underwriters to determine the company valuation based on long-term projections of exponentially increasing site traffic and, therefore, ad revenue. The buzzwords of the day were still *eyeballs*, *ad impressions*, and *click-streams*. The experts of the day were columnists, online and print, who had taken it upon themselves to categorize and rate sites. Sometimes it seemed that half of Jonathan's job was taking those people out to dinner, during which he would laugh at their every writerly attempt at wit while he explained the vision of AllMinder. Best way to get a good article out of it was to follow dessert and coffee by soliciting strategic business advice from the stuffed and tipsy columnists. Often enough their ideas held up in the sober light of morning, and he would pass them along to the product development group.

Jonathan's schmoozing skills were also going to come into play in the days and weeks immediately after the IPO, when he would present the AllMinder vision to institutional investors at road show after road show. He was thinking that not just Brad but also the new girl, Sierra the body, should accompany him on those trips. Brad had already scheduled late June interviews for Jonathan with *Forbes*, *Fortune*, and *Newsweek*, and Sierra would be welcome at those too.

"Great hire, Brad, and I don't just mean because she's hot. Where'd you find her?"

"She came highly recommended by someone I trust."

"I swear she looks familiar to me. I can't figure out where I've seen her before, though. Where'd she work?"

"Just a little non-Internet company, a restaurant actually. But keep that under your hat, I don't want people holding that against her. She's got a master's degree in English from UCLA."

That was good enough for Jonathan. He was glad Brad had the balls to hire someone without direct Internet experience. Experience was overrated anyway and often led to inflexibility;

this was one point on which he and Farouk Kharrazi agreed. How else to explain his own role as GM?

Weeks from his potential billionairedom, he was never for a moment not working. Ideas would sometimes awaken him in the middle of the night: the site needs a new piece of functionality that does X. Afraid to go back to sleep, afraid that he would not remember the idea in the morning, he would leave the warmth of his bed, and sleeping Olivia, and go downstairs to start the coffee. From his home office at one end of the living room, he would fire off an e-mail to his direct reports, adding Sierra to the list to make sure she felt included and knew he was a great guy, and as a signal to her potential detractors that she had his support. "Just thought of something . . . please look into . . ." While he was up he would begin responding to other e-mails, and soon the windows would brighten with dawn. At dinner, at the movies, and yes, even asleep, Jonathan was always the GM of AllMinder, willing to take a call, suddenly needing to make a call. He made no distinction between time in the office and time spent away from it. He worked twenty-four hours a day. So the occasional lengthy lunch with the Biz Dev folks, the occasional late arrivals or early departures, did not trouble his conscience; nor did they bother anyone else. He was probably on his way to charm some writer or analyst whose positive feelings about AllMinder would mean a higher market cap, or perhaps he was a little hungover from having done that last night. Onward, upward, aspiring to bronze bustdom.

Yes, in mid-February everything was absolutely perfect except, except—there was only enough money in the bank to make payroll two more times.

The money had been flowing out at such a rapid rate that Jonathan and his accounting staff had found little time to analyze it. To launch some kind of time-consuming audit now might mean coming to the end of that second payroll without any more money and having to send everyone home, losing the IPO opportunity. Internet companies simply did not, in February of 2000, lay people off. They did not run out of money. So Jonathan, though slightly embarrassed, was not worried. If Farouk Kharrazi and the other investors wanted to recoup multiples of their investment so far, they would have to keep AllMinder afloat until the IPO, after which the company would have enough money to spend itself to profitability.

He sent an e-mail to Farouk Kharrazi, trying to sound as casual as possible. "Appears funds may be inadequate to reach IPO stage. Suggesting safety round of bridge financing to ensure continued viability . . ."

How best to explain AllMinder's imminent destitution?

Development costs were higher than anticipated because of several legitimate reasons, which Jonathan could tick off on his fingers with a straight face. For example, the marketwide short- age of Vignette StoryServer programmers had their hourly rate up to nearly $350. Everyone knew that. It would be unwelcome news to Farouk, though, that Jonathan had overruled his chief technology officer, Rick Stevens, and on his own initiative hired an even more expensive upstart Vignette StoryServer consulting firm that—no one could ever know *this*—just happened to be owned by his wife's sister's husband and in which Jonathan him- self had a secret twenty-percent interest.

Odds of anyone guessing the connection were slim, Jonathan's wife being a good Connecticut Catholic girl and her sister's husband being a lapsed Hindu (loved steak!) child of immigrants from Madras. ABCD was the term they used to refer to people like Raj: American Born Confused Desi. It sim- ply would not occur to anyone that Jonathan Scarver and Raj

Gupta were in-laws, and he sure as hell wasn't going to tell. As far as everyone else was concerned, Gupta Technology, Inc., was just another H1B visa factory that brought India's best and brightest developers to the United States, sponsored their visa applications, signed them to long-term exclusivity contracts that probably wouldn't hold up in a US court if only the indentured servants knew to sue, or could sue without losing their jobs and hence their visas, leading to pretrial deportation. Raj Gupta billed them out at four hundred dollars an hour, paying them only fifty of that. For Raj and Jonathan the gouging was easy to justify: Farouk and the other board members got a great site; the developers earned a decent wage and were well on their way to green card status; and Jonathan and Raj were better able to provide for their families.

Olivia Scarver had required some persuading. She had warned that Raj was charming but unethical. If the familial connection ever came to light, she argued, there would appear to be a conflict of interest. The general manager must avoid even the merest whiff of impropriety. But Jonathan countered that his secret investment in their untested firm would lend him not less but more authority in overseeing them, and was therefore beneficial to the company. Should he ever become dissatisfied with Gupta's performance, he would not be limited to discussing it at the conference table. He could go straight to Raj's house and complain over a couple of Taj Majals. For that kind of influence, it made sense that AllMinder was paying more than the going rate for StoryServer developers. And if deadlines were ever in jeopardy, Jonathan was sure that he could guarantee late-night and weekend performance, the threat of deportation being an effective motivator. Naturally overtime would be billed to AllMinder at time and a half.

"I've never heard of them," CTO Rick Stevens had complained. "Hiring these guys, especially at these rates, just doesn't make sense."

"Do you have anyone else lined up?"

"Well, no, but—"

"Time to market. Time to market is so critical. I see the rates as an investment."

"These guys have a weak portfolio," Rick countered, "not to say *no* portfolio, not in this country anyway. I wouldn't be surprised if this is their first job as a team."

"Don't be so American-centric," Jonathan scolded gently. "We're not the only ones who know how to write code, you know."

Rick was a realist, the no guy. He once told Jonathan that he was tired of going around stating the obvious: no, you can't design and develop several pieces of major new functionality in three weeks; no, you can't skip QA. He might as well have been passionately asserting that two plus two equals four when the required sum was six or seven. "I'd rather see us outsource the job to an experienced team from some known entity like Cambridge Technology Partners."

"India produces some of the best technologists in the world," Jonathan said, repeating a common dinner party boast of Raj Gupta's.

"Cambridge has plenty of Indians, if that's what you want. Besides, what about Russia? Russia produces great technologists. Should we hire the next Russian that comes through the door? Cambridge is the way to go."

"If I didn't know you better I'd think Cambridge was promising you a kickback," Jonathan said, continuing before Rick could deny it: "A guy I met at Internet World last year recommended these guys highly. I can put you in touch with him if you like." Had Rick taken him up on this, Jonathan would have delayed delivery of the nonexistent name and number until Rick gave up asking.

But Rick saved them both the trouble. "Don't bother. You seem determined to hire these guys, but as your CTO, I gotta tell you, they're not worth these rates."

Later Jonathan recounted the incident over dinner with his wife, sister-in-law, and Raj. "He did not for one second suspect I have any connection to Raj," he said. "Truth is, I did the right thing for the company. Rick just doesn't understand that time to market is everything. We need to go public and do our getting while the getting is good."

Among his small audience Olivia alone seemed immune to his enthusiasm.

At work Jonathan and Raj kept their guard up. Passing in the hallway, they would nod politely. It was, Jonathan thought, not unlike his relationship with the vice president of human resources. He and Barbara Lubotsky were certainly careful at work to acknowledge each other only within the context of their professional relationship, despite spending a couple of afternoons per month in a room at the Mayfair Hotel, a dignified little rendezvous spot on Forty-ninth Street on the West Side. Only in e-mail did he and Barbara ever discuss it at work, and then only obliquely, even though e-mail, of course, was quite safe.

He lowered his guard with Raj in e-mail too. They would allow themselves to trade a little bit of the glee that comes from getting one over on the world. Even then they were subtle, but a practiced snooper and good reader like Steven Bluestein, his science fiction book face down beside him, would find suspicious sentences such as this one, which Jonathan wrote to Barbara: "I'm looking forward to our off-site meeting . . . is it my turn or yours to get the room?" Also this one which Raj sent to Jonathan: "You and O going to be there tomorrow?" Could O be Olivia,

Jonathan's wife? If so the note was all the more odd for having been sent on a Friday. That Jonathan, Raj, and their wives were getting together at all was strange enough, and on a Saturday?

Jonathan's reply: "Looking forward to seeing you both there. I can assure you that your steak will be grilled to absolute perfection, partner. And we'll wash it down with some Cristal I borrowed from the AllMinder launch party."

It was troubling enough that the GM was guilty of petty looting, but never mind the Cristal. Steven found it more interesting and more odd that Jonathan was grilling steaks for one of the vendors, who, word had leaked out from accounts payable, was charging upwards of four hundred dollars an hour for Vignette StoryServer programmers. Considering there were five of them, that was eighty thousand dollars per week, and there was talk of keeping them on for another six months at least—more than two million dollars. Was that "partner" merely a nod to the westernness of grilling steak? Or was it to be taken literally?

From the beginning Steven had known something was not up to par about the Gupta employees. Though they were intelligent enough, they seemed to be winging it. Their methodologies were unorthodox; they went at every task with wide eyes, talking about how this would be "good experience for us," implying that they had never before, say, co-branded a site. But that couldn't be right, could it? Rick Stevens would never have agreed to hire them. Steven Bluestein was going to monitor the situation carefully. Within weeks he would learn that Jonathan Scarver secretly owned twenty percent of the firm he had hired. Every week, one day's worth of pay to Gupta Technology went straight to an account in his wife's name. Steven Bluestein was outraged.

And let's see what Jonathan is up to in his e-mail. Here's one to Kharrazi . . . We're almost out of money?

13. A Visit from the Tycoon

JONATHAN EXPECTED AN IMMEDIATE RESPONSE TO HIS e-mail announcing AllMinder's financial problems, but by the following morning, with no call yet from Farouk, he had begun to allow himself to fantasize that perhaps he would be spared the screaming lecture. And why shouldn't he be spared? The anticipated value of AllMinder on the open market must have made the bridge financing seem, even to Farouk, like a bargain.

Jonathan delayed his commute to arrive in time for a ten o'clock dentist's appointment. Reclining in the examination chair with the latex covered fingers of a pretty hygienist in his mouth, he heard his cell phone buzzing. Farouk? His eyes rolled toward the end of the room, where his sport coat, containing the cell phone, was folded on top of the counter.

"Only if it's really important," said the hygienist, without removing her fingers from his mouth. Her goggles exaggerated the size and blueness of her eyes.

Not wanting to seem at anyone's beck and call, Jonathan waved a dismissive hand in the direction of the phone.

But it vibrated again and again. It was a subtle sound, a

mellow cousin to the whirring tooth polisher, but for Jonathan, accustomed to instant communication and never out of touch, it was torturous. Throughout the examination, his anxiety about the incessant, desperate phone calls grew until he could hold himself back no longer. He sat up and rinsed the blood from his mouth into the porcelain drainage bowl. "I hate to be such a dot com guy, but I'd better get that." The hygienist arched her eyebrows and sighed, her mask hiding a scowl.

Jonathan picked up the phone—on the line, Maria Massimo. That's how he learned Farouk Kharrazi was in the office, having flown in overnight in response to his e-mail. Kharrazi was clearly audible in the background. "You are Jonathan's personal assistant? *I* never authorized a personal assistant for anyone. Even I *share* a personal assistant. Do you have him on the phone?"

"This will only take a minute," Jonathan whispered to the hygienist, pressing his palm into the mouthpiece. "Hello?" he said.

Kharrazi spoke as if he had just unmasked a crook and discovered: "Jonathan!"

"Hi, Farouk. What brings you to town? Wow, all the way from California. We weren't expecting you."

"What brings me to town? As if I don't have the right to take a crap on your desk if I want to. What brings me to town is, you just asked for more money. What I'm asking is, where all the money we already gave you has gone. Can you tell me?"

"Yes, yes I can. Of course I can." With a chuckle Jonathan explained that he was in the dentist's chair and would head straight to the office as soon as he was done. "Then you'll see it all makes sense."

"You know, some dentists have Saturday appointments."

How nice it would be to tell him to fuck off. Didn't this

guy understand that the GM works twenty-four hours a day? But beggars can't always afford honesty. "You're right, I'm sorry. Of course I should've looked into that. When it's time to go again, that's what I'll do. Sorry, Farouk."

"Hurry!"

He hung up the phone. The hygienist seemed to feel vindicated. The big important phone call for which he had interrupted her work had obviously been an ass whipping. Leaning against the wall, goggles around her neck, eyebrows raised, she said, "Ready now?" Suddenly this routine teeth cleaning with its attendant discomfort, the indignity of such unbecoming facial contortions in front of a condescending but attractive dental hygienist whom in another setting, a bar perhaps, he would have been trying to impress, was an occasion Jonathan never wanted to end. Being in this chair was infinitely preferable to facing Farouk Kharrazi across the table in the glass-walled conference room while AllMinder employees walked by wide-eyed even as they pretended to be minding their own business. Why did Kharrazi have to be so irrational? Sure, we were out of money, but so was nearly everyone else, and that money was well spent. It had bought us lots of eyeballs and positioned us well for a successful June IPO.

It wasn't all Farouk's money anyway. Just seventy percent of it, and most of *that* from his publicly traded Kharrazi Enterprises, in which he owned a majority interest.

Until the recent dot com boom Kharrazi, at fifty-three, was relatively young for a billionaire, but now these kid CEOs of profitless companies were beginning to crowd him out. AllMinder was his bid to get in on the action, to back something that he knew to be patently worthless but which, if he timed it right, might double or triple his fortune. That was Jonathan's card to play: Look, if you want to make the June

IPO we're definitely not going to be profitable by then, so we have to boost the other metrics that informed Internet investors consider—the traffic, the eyeballs—and to do that you've got to spend money. It wasn't going to go well, but what was Kharrazi going to do, fire him? Not this close to June. That would suggest instability. The investment bank would advise against it.

His tenuous job security and his newly clean teeth were his only consolations as he walked to AllMinder.

"Any cavities?" Kharrazi asked him in a tone that would have been mocking had it not also been ferocious.

"No, no. I'm all set for another six months."

They sat down on either side of the conference table. Against the wall, silent, stood Farouk's bodyguards, a couple of no-necks in expensive suits baggy enough to conceal a small arsenal.

"That thirty million was supposed to last you through June. Now I hear in an e-mail—in *e-mail*, not even the courage to pick up the phone, not even the foresight to mention it to me at the board meeting *just two weeks ago*, as if maybe you didn't know then, which if you didn't, you're incontinent—" Farouk paused as if unsure of that last word. Not without effort Jonathan refrained from correcting him: *You mean in*comp*etent?* "Now I hear that it's not going to last through March?"

"I know, I'm sorry."

"Sorry?" Kharrazi's face was livid then blank. He spoke softly. "I know it's stressful here living in the city, and people make bad decisions under stress. In the cars they are always blowing their finger and giving you the horn. I walked around the office. You bought everyone new chairs. I know how much those chairs cost. One thousand dollars. I know that because my employees at Kharrazi Enterprises asked for those chairs and I told them no, absolutely not. Comfy work environment leads to complacency and a counterproductive sense of entitlement. You give them donuts, they want eclairs. The eclairs arrive late one day, and suddenly they are all complaining."

Jonathan sat straighter in his thousand-dollar chair. It was time to start taking up for himself. "As soon as I realized the money wasn't going to last, I said we have to inform you guys immediately so that you can either give us some guidance or, my recommendation, give us more money. See, Farouk, it's not like we're wasting it. At this point we either grow or we die. The market is filling up with competitors in our space, and time to market is likely to be the key differentiator between who lives and who dies. We need to be there first, and we need to be the best. We need the most eyeballs and the highest brand recognition, and all of that costs money." He looked at the two bodyguards, hoping in vain to detect subtle nods of agreement, then back to Farouk: "Our market cap when we go public is going to make any money you give us now look like peanuts. That's the pot of gold at the end of the rainbow. This is not the time to be penny wise and pound foolish."

In ordinary times none of this would have swayed Farouk Kharrazi, but these times were not ordinary. How much of his gray-faced rage, Jonathan wondered, arose from feeling that the admissions standards of the Billionaire's Club had been relaxed after he had already joined the hard way? "You idiot, I can't just give you more. Don't you understand the concept of share dilution?" Farouk turned to his security detail. "He doesn't understand the concept of share dilution!" They shook their heads. "If I give you more, it dilutes the other investors' shares and they end up owning less of a percentage than what they contracted for. They won't have it."

"I did think about dilution," Jonathan said. "Everyone will just have to give in proportions equal to their original investment."

"No! You can't ask them for that. We would all have to go back to the negotiating table and *that* would delay the IPO, and you would run out of money again! You thought you could go back to the well and pull more money off the tree?"

"Look, what do you want, my resignation?" The tone was more smug than Jonathan had intended.

"Yes! I'd love to have it. But I can't. That too will delay the IPO. Plus I would have to go back in front of the board and explain myself. I'm the one who convinced them not to replace you with a Harvard MBA. 'He's the founder of the company,' I said. 'He's passionate about it, *I* don't have an MBA and look where I am.' At the same time, Jonathan, no one else can make an investment in the company before the IPO." Farouk paused, staring down at the tabletop between his clenched fists. "I have no choice but to have Kharrazi Enterprises loan you the money. It will be on Kharrazi's books as a loan. It will be on your books as a loan. No equity."

"Fine. That's fine. That makes a lot of sense."

Jonathan was glad to have kept the new floor renovation a secret. As irrational as Kharrazi was about the bridge financing, there was no telling how he would react to the necessary upgrading of the work environment. Besides, hadn't Kharrazi from the outset been vocal about granting Jonathan broad spending powers to build up the business? Jonathan was going to hold him to that. Once you've been given permission, it is a mistake to keep asking for it. And Jonathan had decided that the AllMinder floors needed to look like a dot com rather than like the accounting firm that had been the previous tenant. With the extra money that Kharrazi was going to loan to AllMinder, Jonathan could afford to proceed with the renovation. The return on investment would come in the form of increased employee loyalty, which would translate into higher quality work, a better site, more ad revenue, and a higher market cap. More money for everyone, including Farouk Kharrazi. No point in giving Farouk the option of shooting himself in the foot.

"Farouk, despite these problems, we are making remarkable progress. I want to show you around, you'll see how well our recruitment program is doing, even in this competitive environment." He took a risk. "I personally think it's the thousand dollar chairs—just kidding."

Ever one to take pleasure in surveying his domain, Farouk agreed to the tour that Jonathan already planned to conclude at the Public Relations cubicles, where the codger billionaire would be impressed enough with Sierra to forget his anger.

14. A Career Change

REBECCA, THE ONLINE AD SALES COORDINATOR WHOM BRAD had met on her first day, approached him in the kitchen, where he had gone to choose a bagel from the free basket that arrived every morning. "Does this mean I don't get to work with you on PR stuff?" She seemed less fresh now, less optimistic, having discovered that online ad placement and reporting was at once complicated and boring. Not like exciting PR, she must have thought. "Now that you have someone?"

"Oh, no. I'm sure you and Sierra can still work together. I'll come up with something." He wasn't intentionally lying, but neither was he wracking his brain to come up with some PR project that would involve Rebecca. Over time she had become less friendly toward him, which was just as well, for Brad was still determined not to make the rookie mistake of getting involved with someone from the office.

"Because I could go work somewhere else," she said.

"And miss these bagels?" Brad winced at the microwave clock. "Oops, time for yet another meeting. We'll have to talk later."

He had begged Rinehart to please coach Sierra on how to

dress. He feared she might show up in clothing that was merely decorative and, like wrapping paper, meant to be torn away to reveal the gift of her tanned, lotioned, glittery body. Perhaps the right (no, the *wrong*) song would trigger spontaneous undress and gyration. We could not have that in the workplace, so *please* Rinehart, please. And either Rinehart had come through or, Brad now suspected, Sierra had followed her own instincts. If anything she had been overdressed for her official interview, and would have looked more at home among the suited women of GSR Investments than she did among jeans and casual skirts, the wide range of acceptable feminine attire in the dot com world. Barbara Lubotsky had been pleased. "I have to tell you, Brad, I was skeptical at first. Usually when people want me to interview someone they know, there's too cozy a relationship, or someone's trying to do someone a favor. But I was impressed with her background, and impressed that she worked her way to New York waiting tables"—the agreed upon lie. Strings was not on Sierra's résumé. She, Brad, and Rinehart had conspired to list as her most recent employers three downtown restaurants that had recently gone out of business, one after the other. In ordinary times, working for, say, a pharmaceuticals company, Barbara Lubotsky might have objected to letting AllMinder risk pulling this person out of the notorious alcohol and drug infested food and beverage industry, but she had a hiring quota to meet and at least Brad had brought her someone with a legitimate master's degree and an obvious measure of determination. Only Sierra's gym bag, which she parked at her desk all day and carried out with her every night, hinted at interests outside work.

One of the newer Biz Dev guys, apparently with a better memory for faces than Jonathan, did pull Brad aside. "Dude, I'm pretty sure I've seen your new PR girl at Strings. Did you know that?"

"Look, that was just until she got on her feet. She came out here from California, didn't have a job." Not true. Brad knew that she had gleefully danced her way through several major cities: Los Angeles, Miami, Montreal, and now New York. "You can see how it might happen. She needed the money."

"She's got the bod too."

"I really respect her for getting out of it," Brad said. "Thing is, it might hurt her here if people find out. Do me a favor."

The Biz Dev guy mimed zipping his lips. "No problem."

Rinehart knew about the dancing gigs in those other cities, but he didn't know Sierra's true age, believed her story that she was only twenty-four. Her passport, which she had to supply to AllMinder as proof of her work eligibility, showed her to be twenty-eight. Considering the value that Rinehart seemed to place on what he thought was essentially a generation gap, Brad guessed that Sierra's lie was sensible and showed her to be a good judge of character. After some consideration he resolved to keep the information to himself.

Brad and Sierra sat at adjacent workstations and spent a lot of time chatting through the opaque partition. He was able to keep his flirting within bounds, more because of her relationship with Rinehart than because of his rule against dating someone from the office and his obligation as her supervisor to maintain a professional standard of conduct. Sierra was now a regular at the Rinehart happy hours. She and Brad would space their departures ten minutes apart, meet on the street corner, and share a cab down to the chosen bar. Julia Dorsey, glass in one hand, cigarette in the other, would harangue Brad with risqué conversation that over the course of a few drinks would become quite pleasant, and she would often wonder, sometimes too loudly, *what* Rinehart saw in Sierra, whose boobs were clearly fake and who—something about her wide smile, her frequent pats and squeezes—reminded Julia of her one visit, several years ago with her boyfriend of the moment, to a strip club.

Sierra tended to arrive at work early, and Brad found himself coming in a little earlier too, to enjoy some time alone with her in that open work environment before the rest of the crowd showed up with their cups of coffee and their egg sandwiches and started checking their e-mail. The desktop support guys, who sometimes seemed to be mere rumors, ghosts, made regular appearances at Sierra's desk to make sure everything was going all right. "No troubles?"

"Nope, still fine. Thanks for asking."

This was an unexpected advantage to sitting beside her, the speed with which the support specialists responded to all reports of problems within hello distance of Sierra.

Unsurprising disadvantage: frequent visits from other males. Vlad Morovsky, the dim bulb from Product Management, often stopped by to engage in the kind of banter he thought might win her away from her wealthy boyfriend. A second-generation Russian who lived on Staten Island, he complained to Sierra about his commute, bragged about his satellite dish at home, and claimed to be relentlessly pursued by several women. "God, there's this one girl, Patricia Lopez, Spanish girl. She wants to get married and move into my place at Staten Island but she says I have to go to Catholic class. I keep saying, no way, I'll see a movie with you, I might mess around a little bit. But you can't move in with me." His unintentional punchline: "I'd have to kick my mom out, and I can't do that. It's her house!"

Brad's own stories, he was pretty sure, were more interesting. He told her all about his Uncle George, beginning with the wild teenage years, skimming over the promising but abortive Vanderbilt interlude, and moving quickly into the juicier period of drug-inspired thievery, the grand theft auto conviction, and now the Panama Canal investment scheme. "So I do a little investigating. Actually it was the night I met you that I promised him I'd do that. I was on my way home in a cab when I called him. Anyway, I discover that this all-important guy who has the Panama Canal connection has already been imprisoned for fraud once. Ten years ago he solicited investors for some new kind of motorized scooter. He claimed there was a factory and everything. He even had what he said was a prototype. He made off with more than ten million dollars, most of which was never recovered."

"So what'd you tell Uncle George?"

"I told him what I found out, and he said—" Brad laughed. "He said he knew all about that, and the charges were trumped up. It was an international conspiracy masterminded by the CIA to keep him away from the Panama Canal. He said the guy fears for his life. The international oil and shipping interests are out to get him."

Sierra was not solely a listener. They had lively conversations about Scarver and Kharrazi, Sierra giving her Strings analysis of each. Scarver's the kind of guy who would grin ear-to-ear just to be talking to a nearly naked woman. She's seen it a million times, bug-eyed family man at Strings. Kharrazi's the kind who covets your body with a predator's appreciation, as he'd admire a sirloin for a second or two before beginning to devour it. "I actually prefer it," she said, "because you know where you stand."

"And what do you think of your new life in general, now that it's been a few weeks?" She tells Brad how wonderful it is to reclaim her mornings after so long in the "entertainment business," and if she thinks that's a euphemism, she doesn't let on. She had forgotten the sight of thousands of people striding the avenues and cross streets weekday mornings with a collective sense of noble, rather than base, purpose, the men freshly shaved rather than sloppy drunk and the women conservatively dressed, as Sierra herself is now. "I can't tell you how cool it feels to stand in line at a breakfast cart."

"But don't you find it hard making so much less money?"

"I've got a lot in the bank."

Brad didn't ask.

"Besides," she said, "aren't we all going to be rich in June?"

There was no irony in her question and none in Brad's reply. "Now that we're going to be *around* in June." He shared the secret news of the depleted coffers and the Kharrazi Enterprises loan. Forty million bucks.

If her clothing was not a holdover from her recent past, some of her gestures unfortunately were. She sometimes gave the men her lap-dance smile. Vlad Morovsky and his ilk took it as a sign of sexual interest: after years of getting *no* attention from *any* woman, suddenly the best one in the office wants me. And she did nothing to correct this assumption when she leaned close during conversation and touched their shoulders, as if about to suggest a four-hundred-dollar trip to a private room. As her supervisor, Brad knew he should correct her. He told himself he'd get around to it as soon as he could figure out how to broach the subject, but he was in less of a hurry than Barbara Lubotsky would have liked, perhaps because he relished Sierra's impropriety when he was its beneficiary.

Finally he took the indirect approach. On the phone in a conference room he described the situation to her benefactor. Rinehart took no offense. "I know, it's her training. I'll talk to her."

"Just don't mention I said anything."

"Don't worry." She is Rinehart's Pygmalion project. He is making her over in the image of his future wife, and says as much. "By the time I'm done with her, she's going to be a classy Hamptons socialite. Mrs. Sierra Rinehart. But I might change her name to Sarah. Sierra . . . Sarah. It works, it's subtle, and Sarah Rinehart, that's perfect."

15. The Rebound Guy

THE COMMUTE FROM THE EAST VILLAGE BACK TO HELL'S Kitchen, where Nicole still worked at the Film Center Cafe, was a pain sometimes, but more often than not it was improbably, undeniably beautiful, beginning with the hurried descent through her building, five floors down to street level. She took the F train to Herald Square and from there the Queensbound N/R to Forty-second Street. Often while in motion she found herself thinking, *I will remember this moment, I will never forget this moment.* Impossible, and the foreknowledge of her eventual forgetfulness, the way the details drop away, even names and faces, was the only depressing thing about being so alert and engaged with life. If I ever get Alzheimer's, somebody please put a pillow over my face. The bustle of Times Square. "And then I get off at Times Square . . ." she explained to her family, most of whom had watched the New Year's Eve ball drop on TV and some of whom had actually been to Times Square. They were amazed to think that somewhere so extraordinary as Times Square was, for Nicole, just a place she passed on her way to work, as they might pass a supermarket or the Air Force Academy. Her relatives didn't have to know that Times Square wasn't cool. Her East Village roommates hadn't been there in *years*, they liked to say. What for? To see *The Lion King*? Go to Madame Tussaud's Wax Museum? Both of those tourist landmarks were on her left as she walked west on Forty-second Street. She passed the multiplexes; the Internet cafes; the street sellers of incense, comic books, and counterfeit Rolexes; and the downright crazies who fanned out from Port Authority like PR agents commissioned to affirm the tourists' preconceptions: *We saw this one guy wearing a garbage bag!* Perhaps because she wasn't a native New Yorker, Nicole was secretly susceptible to all of this. She loved the tourist area but knew enough not to admit it in stylish company; and she loved Hell's Kitchen, resented the misguided effort to rename it the pompous-sounding Theater District or the bland Clinton. You don't want to remember your hardscrabble early years suffering for your art in a place called Clinton. Hell's Kitchen is where you want to have gone a little hungry, felt a little desperate, where the radiator in your apartment was sometimes as cold as a sidewalk mailbox.

Rounding the corner onto Ninth Avenue, she saw the blue neon sign of her employer. The Film Center Cafe was only three blocks from where she had lived with Dale, and where, as far as she knew, he still lived. Sooner or later, she was sure, he was going to show up at the bar and ask to talk to her. She wasn't looking forward to it. She did not need him or, for that matter, any man. Having had a boyfriend since college, this came to her as a revelation: she was capable of generating the necessary contentment and the necessary conflict of life all by herself. What is it about finally concluding you want to be alone that makes it suddenly easy to find someone?

She met Ed Larsen in the Film Center on February thirteenth. He would later say that he knew right then he wanted to marry her. Except for such impulsiveness, he was apparently the Sensible Man, the Perfect Guy, who was supposed to exist only in legend. She was behind the bar that night, and he was a broad set of shoulders and a strong jaw at the far end, his eyes following her as she reached and stooped for bottles and rattled the martini shakers.

"You want another?" she asked when he had finished his beer.

"Sure. I can tell you're an actress, and that's not just a guess based on demographic probability."

"How so?"

"You were made to be on film."

What amazed Nicole about lines like these was the sheer audacity that it must have taken to deliver them, the deliverer's unflagging and unsupported belief that a few minutes of witty flattery would get you into bed. It must work sometimes or they wouldn't do it. Tonight she had a quick, self-deprecating retort. "I can tell you're not a producer, director, or agent, because they don't seem to think so."

With a flick of the hand he dismissed all doubts and obstacles. "It takes time. It's a matter of keeping at it and doing what you can to increase your odds. So who's the lucky guy who gets to take you out for Valentine's Day tomorrow?"

Halfway through her reply Nicole wished she could retract it. "Oh, I'm spending some time with one of my girlfriends. We'll probably get a bite and watch a movie." Why hadn't she been more clever or evasive? And why compound the error with: "Why, you want to take me out?" Meant only as light banter, her question, still in the air between them, instead sounded desperate and even a little slutty. Now he was going to pay up and leave.

But he didn't. "I'd take you out, but I've got a date."

She corrected him, and herself. "You'd *ask* me out."

And then the bar got busy. Before he left for the night, he gave her his business card, knew her name, and said he would be back. At first she didn't think he had left a tip, but before her indignation rose she found, folded under his beer glass, a fifty. If you're tending bar or waiting tables, it is hard not to like a two-hundred-percent tipper.

On Thursday, three days after Valentine's Day and still no Ed Larsen—there had been plenty of time for him to fulfill his promise to stop by—she threw his card away.

Friday he came back, this time with a group of friends. One of them pulled her aside. "Ed is pretty much in love with you. You know that, right?"

"He seems nice."

"He's a managing director at GB Franklin. His bonus last year, more than most people make their whole lives."

"Oh," said Nicole. "Thank you so much for the warning."

The line was repeated to Ed, who seemed to take it as a challenge. Their first date was dinner a week after Valentine's Day. On their second date he got her up to his luxurious midtown apartment, the walls of which were bare except just inside the front door, where he had mounted a framed quotation from John F. Kennedy: VICTORY HAS A HUNDRED FATHERS, AND DEFEAT IS AN ORPHAN.

"Are you an admirer of JFK?" she asked.

He shook his head. "I'm an orphan."

And suddenly he got a whole lot more interesting, this Oliver Twist made good. She thought she might change her mind and sleep with him that night, but she recovered her earlier resolve. The guy was rich, he was smart, and he was used to getting whatever he wanted. She didn't want to be had. It was still too soon after her breakup with Dale, and she was still enjoying her new aloneness.

16. The Acting Life

"How's the acting going?"

The question was a sure bet during any conversation with her relatives. Her skeptical cousin, a lawyer in Nashville, was the quickest to get around to it, her tone conveying a warm-hearted disapproval, graciously held in check. One of these days, after Nicole had put all this acting stuff safely behind her like some sort of drug addition, after she'd been sensibly employed at a real job for at least a few months, long enough to have tasted the benefits of security and routine, the cousin would tell Nicole how hard it had been to watch her throw away so many years of her life. Not just hard for the cousin, but hard for Nicole's poor parents, who hadn't raised her in a God-fearing home out in Colorado Springs only to see her debase herself in this apparently endless act of vanity. Thinking you could be famous. Thinking you could rise above your station, which was a perfectly good station, one that the vast majority of the world's people would have felt blessed to occupy. Casserole on the table, a grill in the backyard. Living in the most powerful nation on the planet. Our blessed armed forces indisputably dominant. The Air Force Academy itself

just up the road, a gold mine of levelheaded potential hus-
bands. We pass it every time we drive to the mall. Sit back in
your small town and enjoy the safety and superiority. Live
humbly and with decency. Go to the movies on Friday night,
go to church every Sunday. The cousin had at least partially
rejected that—after all, she too had left Colorado Springs and
was living in Nashville, a drinking, singing city which in the
family's book was no less ungodly than one containing a neighborhood called, unbelievably, *Hell's* Kitchen. An uncle had
said, "That's what I call truth in advertising." Nicole's cousin
tried to be a little more supportive. But her true opinion came
out in the phrasing of her ostensibly encouraging inquiries:
"Any acting nibbles yet? Been in anything yet?"

One Life to Live, several times, in the background of many
scenes. A children's play down in Greenwich Village, attended
once by a famous film director and his kids. She'd done her
best to impress him, but she was costumed as a dwarf, and so
far he had made no desperate effort to contact her via the
theater—"Get me that girl who played Dopey!" Nicole had
also done a commercial during which she shared camera time
with Sarah Jessica Parker, who called Nicole "sweetie." "She
did that wave thing, like on the show. She's standing right in
front of you, and she waves and smiles." Once, as an extra, she
got close enough to Robert De Niro that she could have
touched the mole on his face, and was tempted. Once one of
a famous clan of acting brothers got so close to her that she
had to slink out from under his arm, mentioning at the first
opportunity her then-boyfriend Dale Caulfield, whom she
upgraded for the moment to "my fiancé." She was of course in
SAG and AFTRA. That in itself was an accomplishment. You
couldn't just sign up for the Screen Actors Guild and plunk
your money down. Dale, in one of his acts of generosity for

which she supposed she had no choice but always to be grateful, had paid from his own pocket the cost of her joining the
unions. More than a grand each. And then he took her out to
dinner to celebrate. "I am so proud of you for sticking with it,
Nicole." That kind of support could imbue a doomed relationship with improbable longevity.

"So you definitely still need your job waitressing, right?"
the cousin asked. "I mean, it's not like you could support yourself acting, is it?" God, no. According to Nicole's most recent
tax return, she made $2,345.74 in acting fees during the entire
previous year. That was about thirty days as an extra on various sets. She spent $1,600 on Willa Bernhard's class, $860 on
a head shot and prints, more than $500 on mailings, and
roughly $1,000 on assorted opportunities to meet and perform
for agents. As she waited on people who sometimes—was this
her imagination?—seemed to find it humorous that she was
the perfect embodiment of a cliché, the waitress who wanted
to be an actor, she kept herself going by imagining that someday these same people would nudge one another when she
walked by with her entourage: *Look, it's Nicole Garrison!* But
so far she was a not-for-profit actor.

"So that's pretty much where I am," she would tell her
cousin.

"Have you given yourself a deadline for success, or anything?"

"No."

"Well . . ." In the pause before her cousin's next word,
Nicole heard that maddening, gracious reticence—disapproval on a bitten tongue—and longed to hang up the phone,
a gesture that, when reported, would be taken as a slight
against the whole Garrison family. But she couldn't because—
and this is the irony that killed her—it wasn't how she was

raised. My family inspires me to rebel but then manages not to allow it. "I suppose as long as you're happy," her cousin concluded, "there's nothing I can say."

"That's right."

"But I know I'd definitely set a goal for myself and say, 'If I don't make it by this date, I'm going to do something else.'"

"The trouble with that," Nicole said, "is you'd always wonder if maybe you would've made it the *next* day or the next week or month, if only you'd stuck it out."

"I suppose that's right. I don't suppose people in your line of *work* are looking too hard at the odds. Like those old people who spend their entire social security checks on scratch-off lottery tickets."

Nicole was not insulted. That was the smartest thing her cousin had said in years. That was exactly right. Anyone who seriously considered the odds, anyone who, sadly, *lived* by the odds would run straight to law school, like you, you miserable, unhappy attorney, desperately seeking a husband at happy hour, when you have time for happy hour, and otherwise driving home to your two cats.

"I can tell you think I take no chances," the cousin said. "I'll have you know that I'm seriously considering leaving my job to join a dot com. I do make okay money now, but I'll have to work my ass off for a few more years before I make partner. And even then it's not the *big* money. I want the big money."

This was a difficult time to be committed to what just a couple of years earlier would've been considered perfectly lucrative traditional career paths, like the cousin's, to say nothing of being committed to paths that had always been considered whimsical and vain, like Nicole's. The doubts attendant to the latter choice were exacerbated now because everyone else seemed to be living so well, getting so many stock options, attending so many fancy launch parties at places like the SoHo Grand. And the job market was so welcoming that practically anyone, even an actor, could walk in off the street, having done nothing but audition and wait tables, and get a job that would transform her from someone who desperately collects twenty-percent tips into someone who graciously doles them out. Oh, the satisfaction of being a little too generous to the food and beverage class! "An actress," the dot com HR people would think to themselves. "Hmm. Let's put her in charge of all product demonstrations at trade shows. She's our, she's our, umm, she's our director of product evangelism and will start at ninety-five thousand per year, plus options and bonus." One of Nicole's fellow University of Colorado graduates had founded an Internet company and now was "worth," as they say, more than two hundred million dollars. Back in college he'd gotten aggressive with her on their first and only date, and that is how she remembered him now—a groper, someone she'd had to push away and whose eyes briefly glinted with rape before he caught himself and insincerely apologized. Now he lived in a Tribeca loft and supposedly partied regularly with Lenny Kravitz. And here was Nicole living in one room of a dingy East Village apartment—the bud vase still its only decoration— wondering if she should follow her cousin's unspoken advice. Ed Larsen, rapidly becoming her *de facto* new boyfriend, encouraged her in this line of thought; and yet he said, para- doxically, that her acting was one of the reasons he was attract- ed to her in the first place. Then why, she wondered, even come close to suggesting that she give it up, unless he didn't believe she could make it? It was a simmering point between them, which had yet to come to a boil.

There were times when Nicole thought Ed and her cousin were right, and she felt like a vain and silly fool for having pursued something for so long that had not yet panned out. And might never. If only she did not have this desire, this compulsion to be an actor, she could have a normal career and a regular schedule on into marriage, kids, retirement, and grandchildren. "Maybe you could get a job where they'd be kind of flexible, if you still wanted to go on auditions," Ed said. Fortunately it was a phone call, so she was able to hang up on some pretense, once again postponing what seemed an inevitable confrontation.

Every week she did a mailing to agents, casting directors, and anyone who had advertised relevant auditions in *Backstage*. To the agents and casting directors she sent postcard versions of her head shot, on the back of which she would let them know that she had recently appeared as an extra on this or that television show or movie, or had a speaking part in this or that low budget independent that will be rejected from all the festivals and that you'll never see mentioned in print again. To the producers and directors who were holding auditions for these doomed projects, she sent her full-size head shot and résumé. A couple of times a day she would step out of the Film Center Cafe and, standing on the sidewalk with her cell phone, check her voice mail; and a couple of times a week there would be a message from one of these postcarded directors or producers. Usually they sounded no older than twenty-five. "We'd like you to come in for an audition." An audition, even for a doomed movie, was hope. A mailing was hope. And so week after week Nicole staved off despair.

17. Bright Future Redux

LATE MARCH, BRAD FELT A TAP ON HIS SHOULDER AND turned to find a grave faced Jonathan Scarver.

"What's up, boss?"

"I need to see you for a minute. How you doing, Sierra?"

"Fine, Jonathan." She gave him the lap-dance smile. Brad suppressed a wince. "Just working on a corporate positioning piece."

Brad followed Jonathan to the conference room. What could be the problem? Was he in trouble? Two days earlier a peripheral acquaintance, someone from Rinehart's e-mail list, had sent to the entire group a photograph that showed an Anna Kournikova look-alike taking it up the ass. Brad had deleted it immediately, but maybe someone had seen it? Had someone complained to Barbara Lubotsky?

Across the conference table Jonathan broke into a smile. "It's bonus time, buddy, and you've done a great job. As a director you're eligible for up to twenty-five percent of your annual salary, and you have qualified to receive all of it. For you that's twenty-seven thousand dollars." He pushed an envelope across the table. "That explains everything. It'll hit your account via automatic deposit on Friday."

"Whoa, all right." Brad was nodding, reading the letter. "Thanks."

"Don't thank me, you earned it. Thank you."

By investment banker Rinehart's standards, this wasn't much of a bonus—Rinehart would get mid-seven figures this year—but it was more money than Brad had ever received in a lump sum, and he was already thinking to himself that, as the years rolled on, his bonuses would only increase. His future was full of beaches, blue sky, and light green margaritas. He was invincible. He was going to buy some new clothes, maybe find someone to take out to dinner. This was great! Maybe get a better monitor for his workstation at home; maybe that would motivate him to stay in and actually write instead of just getting drunk and talking about it. Julia Dorsey and crew still had a spot open in their Amagansett summer house. Maybe he should peel off five grand for that and become one of those New Yorkers for whom the summer workweek is merely a period of recovery and anticipation. Or maybe he should do the smart thing and put it all into these skyrocketing Internet stocks.

"Trust me," Jonathan said, "the way things are going, when we go public, that's going to look like chicken feed."

And they spent the next thirty minutes encouraging each other's fantasies of riches and trading stock tips. Mail.com could only go up. VerticalNet, now there was a winner. And don't forget eToys. It was a wonderful time to be alive. Not for them their fathers' long years of tedious toil, the measly pension, the factoring of social security payments into their retirement plans. Not for them the frugality of their underpaid high school teachers and college professors. They were going to be richer than even the most successful movie stairs. Very likely Jonathan Scarver would join Farouk Kharrazi on the *Forbes*

400, and Brad—well, no need for that. A mere few million would suit him fine. Hell, that was even enough for a wife and a couple of kids.

For the rest of the day as he considered his future he tried to imagine himself as a gracefully aging bachelor. He could see the aging part, but not the graceful part. He'd wind up like Uncle George but with money, and he wasn't sure that would be an improvement. He'd just crash fancier cars. He'd still be a drunk old bastard making late-night phone calls. At the same time, it was hard to imagine himself with a wife and kids, though now he was confident that someday he would be able to afford them. He'd seen the commitment vanish from too many ostensibly solid relationships. And could he have sex with only one woman for the rest of his life? He'd sooner give up drinking. But forget that, what about the commute? He never wanted to be one of those guys who had the train schedule memorized and knew exactly how long it took to get from their desks to the platform at Grand Central. He imagined with distaste the sight of himself rushing to the elevators beside his fellow commuter Jonathan Scarver. No, no, no. He would never be able to say with a straight face, "Actually, I get a lot of reading done on the train." Or, "For my money, the best brand of lawn fertilizer is . . ." Hell, lawns were dangerous things. You could chop your foot off with a mower. Fuck that.

18. Near Meetings

THE GUY NEXT TO BRAD AT THE BAR HAD JUST MOVED TO New York from Saint Louis, arriving in advance of his girlfriend to find an apartment and "send for her," is how the newcomer thought of it, feeling a bit nineteenth century and English: *After establishing myself in a suitable flat, I sent for my fiancée.* Except he had found in their price range no rooms with a view. And scratch the fiancée part too—he hadn't yet asked her to marry him, something he would get around to when he could afford the ring.

He still couldn't believe he had ever lived in Saint Louis. It was marriage that had taken him there. In fact all his moves since college—except this one to New York—had been undertaken with his ex-wife. Too passively he had followed her career, and when the divorce became final he found himself lost in the Heartland, in a city he would never have chosen and about which he felt no curiosity. She used to pretend to fluff his chest like a pillow, his wife, and then one day she couldn't look at him without clenching her jaw, and everything he did was wrong. Compared to someone else she'd met, he was an embarrassment, didn't have enough money, hadn't done enough with his life. Well, he wasn't done yet. Love passes, unfortunately. Love passes, thank God. The only way to make up for lost time and show himself a little respect was to dive into Manhattan. What a great excuse he had now to do that, a divorce!

His girlfriend—for against all advice he had jumped right back into a relationship—was at a similar point in her life, and for similar reasons, having moved to Saint Louis with a boyfriend who promptly dumped her. She had always wanted to live in New York too, and so the two lovers, each on the rebound, each wary of the other yet undeniably in love, agreed that together they would not simply flout the advice of family and friends—*Don't get involved*; *Don't make any major life decisions while you are still recovering*—but flout it as dramatically as possible. Not only did they get involved, they shacked up, and not just in Saint Louis but in another world entirely, New York City. Crazy fools, but happy. How exciting it had been to plan for it! To sit in a Saint Louis coffee shop with an overpriced copy of the Sunday *New York Times* and declare that their intended destination was the most important city in the world, to look at the Arts section and imagine being able to *walk* to those plays.

Every week, from their respective places of employment in Saint Louis, they would simultaneously log onto the *Village Voice* Web site, call each other, and discuss the apartment listings. It was going to be impossibly expensive. No, not impossible. We'll eat Ramen noodles like in college if we have to. The alleged impossibility of it was the bar you had to clear to get there. It kept out the uncommitted; the worthy would find a way. They sat down together and made hypothetical budgets, working it out so that they could eat in decent restaurants twice a week and see a play once a month. Both sets of parents and most of their friends reacted as if to news of a suicide pact: *I urge you not to do this. You're not ready. You really want to move to New York?* There was no converting the nonbelievers. A person either got it or not.

At the age of thirty-one, enjoying the sweet pang he felt for his absent girlfriend, looking forward to her arrival next week and feeling that life was about to start over again, he looked at Brad Smith, whose name he would never know, whose story he would never know, and he nodded. Brad returned it and they both went back to their drinks. I bet that guy has lived here all his life, thought Saint Louis. How great to have grown up here; that must give you something that we transplants can never hope to have. Later he would meet a New Yorker born and bred who surprised him by confessing anxiety over whether or not he would have had the guts to move here from somewhere else. "I'm envious of you, because you *know*. You're the small-town guy who came to the big city. I'm here by default."

Bonused Brad was watching the attractive female bartender, wondering, How is it that I aspire to both ends of the socioeconomic spectrum? How can I want to live like Rinehart—a multimillionaire in a top-floor luxury apartment—and also like this bartender—probably just scraping by in an East Village share? How can both lives be so appealing? The twenty-seven thousand, minus taxes, was still warm in his bank account. A check was on its way to E*TRADE; it was time for Brad to become an investor. Compared to what was coming, that bonus was like the first drop of water on your forearm, heralding a rainstorm.

Speak of the devil. Rinehart clapped his shoulder. "Hey man, sorry we're late."

Sierra was right behind him. "Hi, boss." Even in front of

Rinehart she still gave Brad her lap-dance smile. Hell, maybe it just *was* her smile.

The plan was to have a few drinks and then go to a party in Tribeca. The guy no one knew was from Saint Louis tore his eyes from Sierra and stared into his drink, but the throb of his jaw betrayed the effort of that discretion, and a few minutes later he was gone, having slipped back into the city, one of whose gifts to her inhabitants is the option of escaping from one's self.

At the party Brad found himself observing a conversation between Dale something, who was a creative director for some Internet design shop, and a woman he apparently had known in school. "You know how in all those movies about college friends getting together, they're always really successful in these various fields. They're sort of like the A-Team of professionals." Dale turned to bring Brad into the conversation. "Am I right? What do you do?"

"Corporate public relations." And so the conversation went. Brad heard more than he wanted to know about the difficulties of working on the services side of the Internet economy. "I mean, these people want their site designed yesterday, and you're like, 'Let me check my calendar, oh, I'm sorry, yesterday was yesterday.'" He heard how impressed the guy was with Sierra's thong, which was clearly visible through her dress as she leaned over to skewer a shrimp. Before Dale could go too far, Brad said, "Yeah, she's a good friend of mine." He was surprised at how true that rang. Sometime over the past couple of months she had gone from being a favor he was doing for Rinehart to being a plain good hire, with a remarkable ability to read a room and know who was happy and who needed some extra care. ". . . used to live with my girlfriend . . ." Dale was talking about his recent breakup, advising Brad to avoid actresses at all costs, "unless they're rich as hell."

Noticing that Dale's classmate had extricated herself from this conversation, Brad decided to follow suit. He finished his drink and announced that he was going to get another one. "Can I get you anything?" he asked, having already checked that Dale's glass was nearly full.

"I'm fine, thanks."

And at the bar, Julia Dorsey, a drink in one hand and a cigarette in the other. "Well, well," she said, rising on her toes to kiss his cheek. "It's the man I don't want to spend the rest of my life with."

"Promise?"

They chatted for a while and then, though they drifted apart, kept looking up from their current conversations to check for each other.

Rinehart pulled him aside. "Give it to me straight, how's Sierra doing at work?"

"Great." Brad glanced at her across the room, where she was talking to Julia. "She's really assimilated well."

"It's not like she was some freak to begin with."

Brad didn't bother disagreeing, although privately he considered Sierra a former freak whom he had helped to transform into a PR professional. The final measure of his success in pulling that off was the now widespread rumor—and spontaneous, not even started by Brad, though he wished he had thought of it—that Sierra was a trust fund baby. That's where the money came from to buy all of those expensive professional suits and the Manolo Blahnik shoes mentioned so often on *Sex and the City.*

Brad found himself listening to the creative director again, who was recounting a recent conversation with a cabdriver. "The guy was twenty when he came over in 1950, so that makes him seventy now. He was going on and on about how much he used to get laid. I asked him if he ever wound up with a wife and kids. He said, 'I got a cat, a landlord, and three bartenders.' Those are his dependents!"

Brad said, "A man who stuck to his guns." He felt warmth at his side: Julia, standing too close on purpose, leaning into him a bit.

An hour later they spaced their exits a couple of minutes apart and met on the curb, Brad's arm already up for a cab.

And the next morning, true to her talk, Julia did not hang around discussing where they should eat brunch and what movie they should see afterward. She got up, groaned at herself in the bathroom mirror, and said, "All right, I'm getting the hell out of here."

If his head were clearer, and if he weren't destined to become so rich on this AllMinder IPO that he was already losing his ambition for other achievement, Brad would have spent the morning making notes and writing. Instead he did some stock research on the Internet, and decided to place his first bet, a small one, just part of his bonus—a mere five grand—on eStamps. If past performance were any indication, that five would be worth twenty-five before the summer was over.

19. Father Knows Best

WHAT A SHOCK WHEN THE LONELY NAYSAYERS, THE worthless and ostracized technology bears, finally had their day: Friday, April fourteenth.

At nine o'clock Maria Massimo led the construction crew to the floor that, when the four-million-dollar renovation was complete in just three months, would house the client-facing employees of AllMinder. Already Jonathan, Brad, and the others had picked out their workstations on the architect's floor plans, and between nine and nine-thirty they strolled through their future home to witness the commencement of construction. The workers were tearing out the walls.

And then the disastrous day of trading began.

Neither Brad nor Sierra could reach Rinehart to get his professional assessment of what was happening with the market. Rinehart was probably holed up in some war room meeting or trying to talk some guy in from a ledge. Maybe Rinehart himself was on the ledge, his back against the building, watching the action on the sidewalk through the goalposts of his Brooks Brothers wingtips. Brad and Sierra, and a few others in the general vicinity of their workstations, kept a close watch on the market, refreshing their screens every few seconds to get the latest twenty-minute-delayed quote. Among the companies hit hard by the bloodbath was Kharrazi Enterprises, down twenty-eight percent by midday. eStamps would finish the day down only seven cents, to $3.68, but there was little consolation in that, considering Brad had bought it at $9.37 a few days ago. Already three companies scheduled to go public next week had announced that they were going to wait until the markets stabilized. What does this mean for the AllMinder IPO and for our future riches? "I don't know yet," Brad told all who asked.

"But you're the PR guy."

"I know, and I haven't consulted with Jonathan or Farouk or anyone yet. As far as I know, we're still on." Thinking of his own investment in eStamps, he added, "Things have got to improve by June anyway. We'll probably be fine."

When he got a moment, Brad called Jonathan. "If it's not too late, you might want to consider postponing the renovation project."

"Don't you think that would be an overreaction?" But there was fear in Jonathan's voice.

"I don't know. I mean, we're getting our work done on a plain old nonrenovated floor. Maybe we should hang on to the cash."

"I think we'll be fine. This is just one day of trading."

Brad's father phoned. "I am not going to say I told you so."

"But you told me so. I hope you're okay?" Brad worried that his father, in an uncharacteristic moment of daring, might have made an ill-timed tech-heavy investment last week, say in something foolish like eStamps, and might now be faced with a significant decrease in total net worth, a contraction of his retirement horizons.

"Are you kidding? I've been totally in cash for the past three months."

Brad did not conceal his sigh of relief. "I'm glad you invest conservatively."

"One of us has to. How much did you lose?"

"Not too bad in actual cash. I didn't have a high percentage of my money in the market." No point in mentioning eStamps specifically. "But if we don't get to do our IPO, I've lost future millions."

"I hope you haven't been counting on that."

But already Brad was regaining his optimism. The same people who were selling today had been buyers yesterday, and tomorrow would be buyers again. The market would go back up, if only because it was too tempting, and there was no other place you could put your money and hope for the double- and sometimes triple-digit returns that had funded the nation's—and especially New York City's—years of gluttonous consumption.

Sierra finally got through to Rinehart after lunch. Among her excited whispers, Brad heard, "I love you too." After a few minutes she looked up and said, "I'm transferring him to you."

"I don't know what to tell you," Rinehart said. "It sucks."

"Do you think it will recover?"

"Maybe, but let me put it to you this way. The Japanese market, which could do no wrong throughout the eighties, still hasn't recovered from its 1989 crash. It's been more than ten years and they're still not there. So what we're seeing here, it might not even be the crash. It might be just the beginning of the crash. This could be the first hill on the roller coaster. We might have barely begun the descent. It's impossible to estimate time of recovery."

"Do you think we'll go public?"

"Your underwriters would be crazy."

"I disagree."

"Who's the money management professional here?" He didn't wait for an answer. "I have to go."

In Jonathan's office after five, Brad found the general manager looking like hell even as he made an effort to continue the rhetoric that only yesterday had sounded perfectly sensible. "I honestly believe that the old metrics still do not apply," Jonathan said. "Despite what is happening today. It'll go back up. Things will be on track." For the next fifteen minutes he peppered Brad with questions about the PowerPoint presentation that Brad and Sierra had created for his post–IPO road show. Brad answered the questions as if there would indeed be an IPO in June, after which Jonathan would travel the country, going from road show to road show, delivering his spiel about how many eyeballs we were getting.

Because we were still going public, weren't we? We could not have mistimed it so perfectly, scheduling the IPO just a few weeks after the market crashed and could no longer support us. It would be too much to say that we were on our way to the party, could see it up ahead, through the doors the beautiful people dancing, the bouncer smiling at us, and then, when we were only a half-block away, so close we could see flashes of blond hair and martini glasses, the whole thing blew up.

Brad and Jonathan, and many others at AllMinder, had left great jobs in established industries to stake their claims to a pile of Internet cash which was there for the taking like gold in the California creeks of 1849. In sensibility, Brad thought, the Silicon Alley and Valley people were the forty-niners' direct descendants. In Silicon Valley they even occupied the same blessed land.

Jonathan had his online brokerage account on the screen. Brad resisted the urge to inspect the balance. "I should've sold yesterday," Jonathan said.

"We all should have."

"It's going to work out, isn't it?" The question wasn't rhetorical; it was a plea.

Brad touched his fingers to his temples, caricature of a psychic, and closed his eyes, the better to see the future. "Yes," he said. "One way or the other."

Jonathan shook his head at the red in his portfolio. Brad was thinking, We are the world's newest fossils; they should freeze-dry us and stick us in a museum somewhere. Here was Jonathan, a guy who had played well in the froth of the Internet economy, rising to the top spot in a high profile dot com well before his experience had prepared him for the job. Now he presided over a 150-person organization that made no money but had what he and Brad called a "great corporate culture." Free bagels and cream cheese every morning. Free catered lunch every Friday. Razor scooters for transportation around the office. A goddamn pinball machine in the lobby. The whole place felt like a playground, and the thing is, *it had to feel that way!* If Jonathan hadn't done that, it wouldn't have felt like a dot com, and all of his people would've started going elsewhere, looking for the work environment that most closely resembled a trip to the arcade. Even as great as it was to shoot a few balls on the way to the bathroom, the technologists were *still* being wooed away by rival companies and by headhunters with promises of riches and fun elsewhere. Massages, some of these places offered! So there was no point in knocking Jonathan about the games, the bagels, the pizza, any of that. As long as the NASDAQ was willing to reward investors based on nonmonetary metrics—eyeballs, click throughs, site ratings—it didn't matter. Farouk Kharrazi didn't really give a damn about the size of Jonathan's Razor scooter budget. Only if the market didn't recover would these extras come to represent to Kharrazi the height of what he still called incontinence.

Brad had the sense that the crash was anomalous and would soon be forgotten. Rinehart was wrong; what did he know? This wasn't Japan. Just because their market hadn't recovered didn't mean that our market wasn't going to recover. The NASDAQ was like a buddy who was guilty of an isolated social gaffe, an uncharacteristic lapse of judgment committed by an otherwise dependably polite person, who, mortified, would endeavor never to do that again, and so it was only right that we would forgive and forget.

Wrong again. Over the next few months it would become clear that the NASDAQ market had a personality disorder that no amount of hope and good intentions could overcome. There would be the promises to improve. There would even be brief dramatic improvements—hundreds of points in a week; once in a *single day*—but the downward trend was dominant. No one at AllMinder, especially not Brad Smith, could have imagined that in less than a year the NASDAQ was going to log its five-year low, down more than sixty percent from its high in March of 2000.

Jonathan was gathering up his mule load for the commute home, zipping up his computer bag, placing papers into his brief-case. He would walk to Grand Central like some modern day hunter-gatherer carrying skin purses full of machinery and documents rather than weapons and animal flesh for his family. "I've got to try to catch an early train tonight. My daughter's in a play."

"Oh, that's nice." Brad checked his watch. It was almost time for happy hour.

Part 2

20. Nicole's Choice

FOR SOME THE CRASH WAS A VINDICATION. THANK GOD Nicole had not taken some dot com job back when she'd been briefly tempted. She was relieved now too that her cousin also had resisted the urge to leave her partner-track position and go for what she was now denying she'd ever called the "big money." "Let me tell you something, I saw this whole crash coming," she said. "I never once seriously considered leaving my career for something that was so obviously a bubble."

If she was an insufferable attorney in Nashville, well, at least she was an employed one. Nicole preferred it that way. Let my relatives succumb to their blood and upbringing and be safe, and I will take the chances with my life: you can live vicariously through me. She could never have taken herself seriously while discussing, say, spam policy or whether the site should accept animated GIFs in ad banners—not that she didn't know the jargon well enough from having waited on tables of dot com people back when they liked to talk loudly in restaurants about their work. She could never have sat through a user interface review knowing she was missing perhaps the one audition that might have been her breakthrough.

And so for Nicole there was a certain relief in the lengthy crash that by now, midsummer, had postponed so many IPOs and closed so many profitless companies. Now it was possible for Nicole and the rest of the non-Internet class to believe they had missed nothing after all, and to congratulate themselves for not having abandoned their true callings for stock options that would have turned out to be worthless. Already the dot com backlash had made its way into *New Yorker* cartoons. It was over, and all who for one reason or another had not switched careers to join some now defunct Internet company were engaged in the largest collective schadenfreude orgy in history.

And yet somehow this downturn wasn't that much fun. It did not leave Nicole, or anyone for that matter, untouched. There was a negative shift in the mood of the city. Possibilities seemed more limited, not just in the dying dot com world, not just on Wall Street, but in general. Week by week Nicole's tip numbers were dropping.

Throughout the summer she had auditioned diligently, had done everything right. After each audition she walked home practically skipping, sure that she had won the part; and she did get plenty of call-backs. There was never a time when she was not waiting on at least one yes or no; there was always at least the possibility of a yes. "If I get this part . . ." she liked to say to Ed, giving that sentence any number of hopeful endings, but he seemed less and less interested in her ifs.

In spite of the hope, in spite of the call-backs, she never got the part.

"Don't worry," Ed Larsen would tell her. "If it doesn't work out, maybe you'll wind up getting married to a handsome young rich managing director at GB Franklin, and you'll be fine." He meant it to sound reassuring, but in comments like that one she began to hear her cousin. Perhaps he thought he had a chance to cast her in the role of suburban wife and mother. Soccer mom. "I'll get us a big house up in Westchester. It'd be fun to have some kids, wouldn't it?" He didn't wait for her to answer. He knew she couldn't even think about having kids right now. "There are some theater opportunities outside of New York, you know," he said.

It was a measure of how low she felt about her acting prospects that she let that go, did not rise up in a flailing rage to tell him *you completely misunderstand me, you just don't get me!* Unintentional insults are the worst because they are so honest.

There was a lot she liked about Ed. She enjoyed his money, of course, but she had turned down rich guys before. She liked the way he had set up that "I'm an orphan" comment with that JFK quote in his apartment. But most of all she liked the fact that he was so confident in everything he did and that the world rewarded his confidence. Ed walked down the street with an air of bestowing himself—*all you lucky people . . . here . . . I . . . am!* When he raised his hand for a cab, one seemed to appear immediately, out of nowhere, the driver risking life, limb, and license to screech over from the far side of the three-lane avenue. When he drove her to the Hamptons for the weekend, traffic seemed to part for him. Once he was there, parties formed in his vicinity. When he walked into a restaurant, the maître d' immediately began to fret: how best to keep this obviously important man happy?

This arrogance offended some who could never hope to achieve it, but Nicole admired it as a kind of constant theater, the illusion of everyday stardom. He was ignorant in a way and therefore blissful in a way. For Nicole, whose self-esteem depended on the often careless remarks of directors and agents and Willa Bernhard, Ed's aura of invincibility made him almost irresistible. At the same time, she knew that if she entered his safe and secure world she would risk losing herself, and someday, too late to recover the time she had sacrificed, would resent him for having charmed her into complacency. Perhaps the most his confidence could give her was the confidence to leave him. If he could do that for her, drive her away, then perhaps she would love him more in later life— having lost touch with him completely, wondering what had become of the orphan guy with the JFK quote, the millionaire who had helped make her post-Dale (thank God) summer of 2000 so bearable—than if she lived with him in a house in Westchester, taking care of the kids, doing the laundry, and begging for his support in allowing her to do community theater, rehearsals for which would be unmissable, requiring him to take earlier trains home, forgoing happy hour with his buddies, where he probably flirted inappropriately with the young office chicks and maybe even trotted out some Dale-like line about how his marital relationship had run its course. Harboring the paradoxical notion that she should break up with Ed precisely because in many ways he was so perfect— as her attorney cousin liked to point out, "Don't be a *fool*, Nicole"—she joined him for dinner one Friday in late August at a small, exquisite restaurant in SoHo, twenty seats, all very close together and all occupied.

She was not prepared for what he had to say.

"Nicole, let's talk about the future." The waiter, a thin blond man, was standing right there. Nicole vaguely recognized him, probably from some open call audition somewhere. She would have preferred that Ed wait until the guy was out of earshot, but Ed seemed to give no more thought to speaking his mind in front of a waiter than to speaking it in front of a dog. "I mean, I think it's great that you've come to the big city and thrown your hat into the ring and tried to be an actress. I wouldn't have done it. I don't have enough faith in others to let them determine how high I should go. It all has to be in *my* control." He made fists on the tablecloth. "That's why I'm in the field that I'm in, and frankly I think it's why I've been so successful. But you, I really admire you for this; you had the courage to give it a shot. Almost everyone you see out there walking around, they all imagine they could be actors. They go to movies and they come out thinking, 'I could do that.' I know I've thought it. But the rest of us, we don't pursue it because we're too reasonable and sensible, and there's something sad about that. Not you. And I think that is just so cool. You were willing to spend your whole twenties in pursuit of this unlikely dream."

She didn't know what to say, could not count the number of times he had just insulted her. She would need to play it back repeatedly over the next several hours. *Whole twenties—* what did that mean? Was he reminding her that in December she would turn thirty? No need for that; she thought about it every day.

He mistook her silence for receptiveness. "I want you to know, and to never forget, how much I admire you for trying. It's one of the reasons I was attracted to you at Film Center in the first place. But if my investment advice consistently turned out to be sub-par, after a while I might begin to think I'm in the wrong business. Maybe then I'd try to be an actor," he joked. "A movie star."

"What are you suggesting?" That he looked like a leading man—perfect suit, full head of hair, broad shoulders, cleft chin—was suddenly not a point in his favor. She felt the years of commitment and preparation in her right hand like a club. If he stayed on this path she was going to clobber him.

"Now, don't get sensitive," he said.

"What do you mean, 'don't get sensitive'? How about if you don't get cryptic. Subtlety is not one of your strengths, so don't even try. Say what you want to say."

He touched a finger to his lips to signal that she was being too loud. At nearby tables a few heads turned. He had been fine with the waiter and probably a few nearby diners over-hearing his opening salvo, but he blushed that she would return fire with commensurate indiscretion.

In a quiet voice he said, "I just think there comes a time when you have to evaluate your career trajectory relative to your career goals and see whether or not you're on track, and either make adjustments to the trajectory or to the expected outcome. Consider this. How much money do you have in the bank?"

"Enough for rent, utilities, and groceries."

"That's what I mean, that's no good."

"You know, you might think you're being friendly, or even avuncular. You're being paternal. Big difference."

"And credit card debt? How much there?"

Here she paused. That was hitting low, especially after she'd increased her debt just last week on the occasion of Ed's thirty-eighth birthday. A three-hundred-dollar wool sweater that had seemed to worry him as soon as he lifted it by the shoulders from the box. "I don't want you spending this kind of money on me. I mean, thanks and all that, but still, where'd you get the money?" Credit card, she admitted, much to his unconcealed disappointment. Rather than accept graciously that she had added to her pile of debt in order to buy him something that he might actually have considered buying for himself, something he could wear up in the Hamptons without some snob thinking, Banana Republic—three hundred dollars, an amount that she suspected most of Ed's former girlfriends would consider insignificant, the price of life between breakfast and lunch—rather than thanking her for her sacrifice and her thoughtful effort, he had instead lectured her about the importance of paying off her debt. Normally she was not extravagant with her card. She did not go out and buy rounds of drinks with it or expensive shoes. And yet over the past eight years she had managed to run up a few hundred dollars each year, usually in acting-related expenses (head shots, class fees, mailing costs) which seemed to get away from her. Don't forget to pile on a few incidental expenses related to leaving Dale. Oh, and there was that sofa she had left behind in his apartment; she'd bought that with plastic. She looked forward to her first windfall as an actress—not even windfall, really, to her first mere regular salary—so she could feel the relief that would come from paying off the card and finally living debt free. She owed six grand, but she wasn't going to say so aloud. "Let's not talk about my finances in public, if you don't mind."

"It's just, when you get to your thirties—"

"I'm not thirty yet. Ed, this whole discussion is making me extremely uncomfortable. I really feel like this is none of your business."

"Hey, it's only because I love you." He reached out and held her hand captive on the table. She wanted to pull it away, but he held it so tightly that to do so would have caused a scene, and very likely she would have knocked over her water glass. "I'm trying to help. You've got to look ahead. What are you going to be doing in your forties? Still waiting tables? Still waiting on that crucial phone call?"

She began to cry, tried to keep it quiet. "I *am* going to make it."

He was shocked that she was taking his well-intentioned interference so poorly. "Oh, no, honey, I didn't mean to sound harsh. I'm such an idiot sometimes. I actually mean for this to be a very happy conversation."

"Doesn't seem like it." Keeping her head down, she honked her nose into her napkin.

He let go of her hand. "Honey, shh. Maybe you should excuse yourself to the bathroom. People are looking."

"I don't know why I haven't been able to make it as an actress. I've been doing everything I'm supposed to do." Her face was beginning to break down. "Everything all the books say and everything Willa says. I don't know why I have no agent, I don't know *what is wrong* with me." The touch of his hand on her shoulder gave her no consolation; she shrank from it as if he were poking a wound. He retracted his arm to his side of the table.

Compensating for her volume, he whispered, but in a desperate tone now. He seemed to sense finally, too late as far as Nicole was concerned, that he had crossed some personal boundary of hers, and now this whole evening was in jeopardy. He lapsed into fast-talker mode. "I'm not telling you you should quit acting. I mean, who knows? You never know when an actor is going to hit it big. Remember the 'Where's the beef?' lady from those Wendy's commercials? I think she was like eighty something. I bet she had a normal life in the meantime though. I bet there was a point in her life when she reckoned with herself and said, 'Time to get sensible.' See, Nicole, I think you can have a real job, get the benefits, the health insurance and the 401K and so forth, and you can still go on auditions. Maybe not as many as now. Maybe you just go once every couple of weeks instead of every day. Maybe you're not going to acting class every single week, or you skip it if work runs late. You go maybe once a month to keep your toes in the water. Why are you so upset?"

The effort of crying silently caused her throat to ache. Her back was heaving. All she could say was, "Where's the *beef?*"

"That just popped into my mind, I'm sure it's not the best example. But you know what I mean. I'm only telling you this because I love you, and I think it's important that we come to some sort of understanding about shared goals and so forth because . . ."

He was tapping her on the shoulder, trying to get her to "Look up, Nicole, look up."

Her face was wet with tears and snot, but she did as she was asked. She felt like the ugliest person in the world. No wonder she never got the part. Maybe if a script ever called for someone naturally hideous. That would be her equivalent to the old woman's "Where's the beef" break. Nicole said, "I have to go."

He grabbed her wrist. "Oh, no, you don't."

With his free hand he reached into his inside jacket pocket and pulled out some sort of charm perhaps that was going to make her overlook his astounding lapse of tact. It was a velvet ring box. After all he had said, a goddamn velvet ring box. He put it right there on the table between them. Then he sat back and folded his arms, smug, smiling, sure that he had her now. It was the same ignorant bliss that had first attracted her to him. He had no idea how unforgivably he had just insulted her; he thought the ring box would make up for it. This guy actually believed she would be eager to open it and thrilled about what she would find inside: a great house up in West-chester with top-of-the-line appliances, the security of never having to worry about money, no more of that ridiculous East Village share (at nearly thirty, a share!), and no more of those degrading, fruitless auditions.

"Well?" he said, pushing the box closer to her. "Aren't you going to open it?"

In a state of disbelief she reached over her water glass, lifted the box, and brought it toward her. She opened it. As she suspected. An engagement ring.

"That's two carats," he said. "And the other three Cs are impressive too."

"The other three Cs?"

"Color, clarity, and cut. You don't know that?" He clapped his forehead in mock shock. "I could've saved thousands!" Now that he felt like he was back in control of the situation his voice had risen again to its usual confident jocularity. Let the neighbors hear him. A few of them, sensing a proposal in progress, were paying attention. What a relief that this was not, as it first appeared, an argument that threatened to disrupt the atmosphere, but an actual will-you-marry-me, a good story to tell at work.

"What I was saying, I think we should come to some sort of agreement about our goals together because—Nicole—" There in the restaurant, down on one knee. After suggesting that she had wasted her life thus far, down on one knee. After comparing her to the "Where's the beef?" lady, down on one knee. Nicole's tears dried up on her suddenly red hot cheeks. "Nicole Garrison, will you marry me?"

She said nothing. Her lip hitched up in an unbecoming sneer. This was one of those forks in the road. This was one of those moments when you were either true to yourself or you were not, when you decided between pleasing others or pleasing yourself.

"Come on," he whispered, "don't leave me hanging, work with me here, people are watching."

She shook her head, and with no thought to volume or to the spectators, she said, "I could never marry you." It sounded more bitter than she had intended, and louder. Suddenly she was projecting her voice as if in Willa's acting class.

Ed whipped his blushing face around at the other tables. By the speed with which everyone went back to their food it was clear that they had all partaken of the scene in which he was suddenly, perhaps for the first time since his childhood orphan days, the oaf, the fool.

She shrugged, her eyes welling again with tears.

"Nicole, look, can we get through this together and then talk it out for real outside maybe? Do me a favor—say you'd love to marry me, give me a big hug and a kiss, everyone will clap." He raised his eyebrows and nodded yes yes yes.

"I guess I'm just not good enough to perform that scene. Maybe the 'Where's the beef' lady could have pulled it off."

"Nicole, you took that entirely the wrong way. That was just to illustrate a point. You took *everything* the entirely wrong way."

"You shouldn't have done this in front of people." She was perfectly audible to their silent, attentive audience, the other diners, a few of whom held forkfuls of food in midair as if they had been zapped by some sort of freeze ray. "Was I supposed to feel pressure? Was I supposed to be more likely to say yes just because we're in front of all these people?"

Having already lost in the court of public opinion, Ed gave up his attempt at discretion and raised his volume to the level he had planned to use to order drinks for the house to celebrate his engagement. "Nicole, look, I know it's a big thing, it's overwhelming to be presented with a ring this valuable and a proposition this life-changing by a guy like me." He touched his hand to his chest. For a moment she thought he was going to fish a card from his shirt pocket to remind her what a bigshot he was. "Everything I said came out wrong." He looked around at his uncomfortable, silent audience. "I love her, folks! Nicole, I understand you need time. Just take the ring home and think about it."

"I don't intend to think about it."

"Be reasonable."

"I am *not* reasonable and I have no intention of ever trying to *be* reasonable. I will *not* give up my career."

"What career?" he asked his neighbors. "Eight years she's been at this and still no Broadway debut or soap or anything." Turning back to Nicole he said, "I'm not saying it's your fault. I really think you have to be born into that industry. They're all related. Hollywood is like the fucking Appalachians, they're all inbred. They should remake *Deliverance* and set it in Beverly Hills. But never mind all that, my point is, what career?"

She stood up, leaving the ring on the table.

He stood up. "You're being overly dramatic."

"Spare me the acting advice. I'm perfectly in character and this is exactly what I would do in a scene like this." She marched past him toward the exit, yanking her elbow from his grip. One of the other diners made a crack about not knowing this was "a dinner theater place," but Nicole didn't hear him, for by then she was gone, her arm in the air to hail one of those roving yellow escape pods that at any other moment would have been a plain taxi. The embarrassment, the weight of the "dinner theater" remark, fell on Ed alone. His ears burned red.

He sat back down and waited for her inevitable return. "Geez," he said in a stage whisper for the benefit of the eaves-droppers around him. He was confident that some were on his side, knew the value of the four Cs and the house in Westchester, and that they thought he was handsome. Probably any other woman in the restaurant would have accepted my proposal. I am a goddamn millionaire.

He turned to the waiter. "Drinks for the house." A meeker voice than he intended. "On me. I'm sorry, folks."

The waiter began taking orders. Ed declared, "Can't even propose to someone in this city anymore!" He was surprised that the line drew no laughs, and that some couples declined his free drinks.

He ordered the filet mignon. The waiter removed Nicole's place setting. As Ed carved his beef, the ring box open beside his bread plate, the diamond sparkling, he could not resist a sort of Lot's wife glance back toward the front door to see if his future wife was rushing back to him in beautiful contrition and acquiescence. She was not. Soon enough he would feel no more emotion about that than would a pillar of salt.

21. Kharrazi Redux

ON THE TRAIN INTO THE CITY JONATHAN WAS AWAKENED BY his cell phone. He grunted into the mouthpiece, then cleared his throat and tried again for the civil alertness that would support his repeated assertions that this was the time of day when he did his best thinking; on the train he was planning out his strategy for solving any number of problems. "Yeah, hi, Maria, yes it's me . . . No, of course I'm not asleep—"

"Farouk is here again." She whispered as if to keep from being overheard by the military patrol that was Kharrazi's security entourage.

"What do you mean 'here.' Here in New York?"

"In the office. In *your* office, actually."

Jonathan felt ambushed. He was sure he had not left anything incriminating on his desk and that he had locked down his workstation so no one could go through his e-mail, which included hotel and timing correspondence with Barbara Lubotsky, how-are-you! notes from old college buddies and ex-girlfriends he had tracked down via UVA's online alumni directory, and plenty of other notes that had nothing to do with making Farouk more money. If Kharrazi was looking for ammunition to use against him in the one-sided shouting match that would ensue as soon as Jonathan walked into the office, he wasn't going to find it. "Please tell me this was not on my calendar, it's not something I just spaced about."

"No, this is a surprise visit . . . Apparently we didn't tell him about the new floor renovation?"

After the usual delays that are to be expected with any construction project, the renovation of the new AllMinder floor was finally nearing completion. Jonathan had started signing checks. Accounting had appropriately included them in the monthly close, which was reported to Farouk Kharrazi in accordance with standard operating procedure. Why was Farouk even going over those line items personally? After a moment Jonathan said, "He shouldn't be concerned with that sort of thing anyway. That is way below his radar."

"Jonathan!" Maria whispered. "Don't you think you should have told him? He's really pissed!"

He wanted to lay into her, make it clear that she had not been hired for her business acumen but for her phone voice and the general pleasantness of her disposition—though that did seem to be directed toward the men only, AllMinder's women complaining that toward them she was bitchy and full of attitude. He caught himself: no point in turning on the lower ranks just because the higher ranks have turned on you. This was between Jonathan Scarver and Farouk Kharrazi, period. Besides, if things fell to shit he'd need Maria's support later. He might even need her testimony. He said, "That decision was mine to make within the parameters that I agreed to when I took the job."

"He says the new floor looks like Hollywood. He's going around looking at everyone's computer setups. He wants to know how much it all costs. He says we paid too much for everything. He keeps talking about fifty million dollars. Do you know what he's talking about?"

The loan. The growing loan from Kharrazi Enterprises to AllMinder was up to fifty million dollars. "We have a high burn rate. He knew that getting into this."

"Wait, right now he's yelling," Maria reported. In the background Jonathan could hear Farouk's growl. "He's saying what moron decided to rent another floor *and* renovate it. He's saying he gave approval only to replace the water fountains and upgrade the bathrooms on *this* floor. Not a whole full-scale goddamn architectural project and to get the movers in here to relocate everyone back to this floor." Maria still whispered. "How much did it cost, he wants to know."

"It was only a little more than three million." Actually closer to four. "A bargain." He thanked Maria for the warning and began formulating his arguments. He gave it up, realizing there was no more point in that than in preparing a counterstrike against a hurricane. Best to board up the windows, wait it out, and hope you would still be standing when it was over.

As recently as April, Jonathan's golden future had seemed but a few weeks away. Hell, he had marked it on his calendar: the IPO date. Back then it made sense to renovate the floor. That the project had commenced on the day of the actual stock market crash was a bitter coincidence and would make him look foolish to Farouk with his 20/20 hindsight, but Jonathan still felt that he'd made the right decision at the time. You had to proceed. If you were a leader, you had to stay the course. You couldn't pull the plug at the first sign of market jitters.

That was a philosophy to which Kharrazi apparently subscribed as well, for he had peeled away not just that initial forty million dollars in loans from Kharrazi Enterprises to AllMinder, but also, in July—again by necessity, if he wanted to keep AllMinder open—another ten million. In the meantime Kharrazi Enterprises stock had lost eighty percent of its value and was now trading at around ten dollars. Kharrazi's personal stake in the company was now worth only $1.3 billion. Poor guy.

By the time Jonathan made it to the office Kharrazi was pacing in one of the glassed-in conference rooms like an enraged primate at the Bronx Zoo. You wanted to press your hand against the glass, make some kind of connection. He was grunting into his cell phone and banging his meaty fists against the table so hard that his Palm Pilot hopped a quarter inch into the air. When Kharrazi saw Jonathan, his eyes seemed to turn red, as if in a cheap snapshot. He waved him into the conference room. If he attacks me, will his two no-neck bodyguards restrain him? Or will they hold me down?

"Sit," he said. Jonathan did as he was told. Kharrazi paced, hands locked behind his back. A trial lawyer.

"Tell me, when you came to my house for dinner, did you steal my silverware?"

"Of course not."

"When a man is walking down the street and you see his wallet in his back pocket, do you run up and hit him on the head and take it?"

"Farouk, I really don't see the point in these rhetorical questions."

Kharrazi sat down and said, "I've walked around the new floor. A lot of time, energy, and money went into it. It looks ridiculous. It is the perfect symbol of excess. I am goddamn tired of being treated like a rich wife that you take to the dinner and you take to the play *with my own money* when I come into town and you fill my ears with sweet talk that things are great, and oh, by the way, honey, I need some more money.

Meanwhile, while I am gone, you are whoring around town with every little tramp who has initiative enough to put on some makeup and wear bright shiny costume jewelry, because you are so stupid, such an easy mark, that you will give her some of my money. This—" He waved the blueprints of the renovation in the air. "You had an architect come in and redo the floor! I'm amazed!"

"It was important," Jonathan said. "We have high-level executives coming in from other companies. It's important that the place look professional."

"Oh, top executives like, say, *you?* Real smart guys, as smart as *you?* You should put in a playground—oh, wait a minute, you already have. Since when does pinball belong in the business environment? It doesn't look professional. It looks like a playground. If I'm some top executive, when I walk in here, I don't think I'm going to do business with you. I think you and I are going to ride around the floor on those god-damn"—searching for the word—"*laser* scooters."

"Razor." Jonathan pinched his forehead. "*Razor* scooters."

"Retard scooters is what they are. What happens if someone breaks a leg? Is our insurance going to cover that? What about the lawsuit? Forget the scooters. What about that pinball game over there? When I walked in, I saw a kid playing pinball. I said, 'What do you do here?' He said, 'I'm a Vignette StoryServer consultant.' Some Indian guy. I said, 'Then get the hell back to work!' I should not have to tell him that. I should not have to get involved in the operations of the company at that level. And then I walked around, and I see your CTO—your CTO!—playing at a basketball hoop that is screwed into the wall. There is a court and everything, with the lines of tape on the floor! I said, 'Can I see you a minute?' Do you know what he told me?" Kharrazi closed his eyes and ran a hand down his face and spoke slowly, as if each word caused him great pain. "He told me, 'Just a minute, let me make this shot.' Well, in case you guys have forgotten, I am the guy who has loaned this company fifty million dollars to keep things going."

"Farouk, look, the basketball hoop, we use sponge balls so it doesn't disturb anyone." Before that was out of his mouth it already sounded stupid to Jonathan, and he wished he could take it back. "It's just a little hoop like a kid might have in his room. It's just a good way to blow off a little steam, and as for the floor renovation—"

"Which I did not authorize."

"You authorized me to run the company. I thought we needed a floor renovation. Keep in mind the context in which we made that decision. Things were different back in those days. We needed to look like a dot com. We needed to look like the future. We had high-level executives—" He decided to drop that. "The place needed to inspire confidence."

"Let me make one thing very clear. I am the only high-level executive you should be worried about."

"It was the culture of the time. Please understand."

Again Kharrazi wiped his face. He seemed to hope that the next time he opened his eyes Jonathan would have vanished in a flare of spontaneous combustion. "I'm sick and tired of people telling me that I should understand their culture. By my culture, I am supposed to pick my sword and cut your head off!"

Jonathan's eyes dropped to Kharrazi's waistband. No scabbard. Even without the blade, though, Kharrazi seemed ready to attack. Perhaps one of the bodyguards would pull the weapon from inside his sport coat and wordlessly provide it to Farouk. Jonathan glanced through the glass to see if there were any witnesses. Just Maria. She was pretending not to listen, but her posture was unusually straight and her ears were red. Everyone else who passed through the lobby, seeing what was happening in the main conference room, hurried on through, the better not to be conscripted into battle by either of the fighting men.

Kharrazi sucked in a deep breath and kept going, his hands in the air, face livid. "For nearly eighteen months now I have poured money into this place in anticipation of an IPO, and now I feel like I'm eating a dead horse. Everything you tell me is about to be done turns out to be months from being done. And now *also* I find you—" Kharrazi's mouth turned down as he referred to notes on his Palm Pilot. "Now *also* I find out that you threw an IPO party at some fancy hotel on the day we were supposed to go public? And you invited *vendors* and not me? Vendors are blood sucking thieves! That is their nature! That is how they exist. They don't need a party. They should be throwing *you* a party, and you should be throwing *me* a party."

"We had the space reserved, Farouk. We'd already put the deposit down. People were looking forward to it. Some people had already arranged for babysitters. We thought we might as well go through with it. It might seem weird that we invited the vendors, but look, not so long ago resources were tight all across Silicon Alley. We needed to cultivate good relationships with them. We needed preferential treatment, so we gave them preferential treatment. It could've turned out to be a smart thing to do."

"How much did this party, this vendor extravaganza, this giveaway of my money, cost?"

Jonathan wasn't sure. He knew that the bar itself rented for a few thousand dollars, which had not sounded like a lot at the time. There had also been a hefty per-head fee for the top-shelf liquor, and he had invited staff members and vendors each to bring a friend. Some brought several friends. Along about eleven o'clock that night, when everyone was good and liquored up, it had seemed the thing to do to open up the party to nearly any well-dressed person who happened to approach the door. *Come on in! You heard of AllMinder? That's us! I'm the general manager, which is sort of like the CEO!* The maître d' was standing beside him, keeping count of the additional guests to add to the final bill, tens of thousands of dollars. "It was a few thousand," Jonathan told Kharrazi.

"Of course it was more than that. You think I am an idiot?" Kharrazi wiped his face again. For a moment he seemed unable to close his mouth and yet unable to speak. Finally the words came: "Forgive me, I have been too harsh with you. You are not a thief after all. You are mentally handicapped. Forgive me for yelling at you. It is like yelling at a retard when he stabs your sofa and pulls out the stuffing. I am going to call my household staff and yell at them for not cutting your meat into bite size pieces for you and for giving you sharp objects instead of plastic plates and the paper spoon!"

Jonathan had had enough. *If he's going to fire me, fine, but I don't have to subject myself to this kind of verbal abuse.* He stood up.

"Where the hell do you think you're going?"

"Why don't you shut us down?"

"What do you think are the odds that I haven't thought of that?"

"Well, all I can say in my own defense about how I've run the company is that I did my best within the context of the time."

Farouk said, "I'm not going to shut you down." He pounded his fists on the table. The Palm Pilot jumped. The bodyguards stood by, passive and expressionless. Jonathan considered sprinting for the door of the conference room. Farouk Kharrazi yelled, "I would shut you down if I could, but I *can't!*"

22. Bringing Everyone Up to Speed

BRAD SMITH, RICK STEVENS, BARBARA LUBOTSKY, AND THE other senior staffers and aids to Jonathan had all done walkbys during Jonathan's meeting with Kharrazi, and they had all assumed the worst: we are without a GM; in the interim Farouk Kharrazi himself will be our GM; it will be hell.

But when the meeting was over, Jonathan calmly asked them all to join him in the conference room. His was not the demeanor of someone who had just been fired, or whose company was about to be shut down.

"I know some of you probably saw me having a shall we say *spirited* discussion with Farouk today. He still believes in AllMinder and knows that we have the right product at the right time. He disagrees with some of the things we have spent money on. But he and I are on the same page regarding what we have to do. In fact, we're so on the same page that he asked me to handle this meeting. He declined to attend. He's out there walking around among our employees, which kind of scares me, so let's make this kind of quick so I can go run interference."

Brad said, "He's going to shut us down, isn't he?"

Jonathan broke into a smile. "You guys are looking at a financial genius, if I do say so myself. He *can't* shut us down. He can't let the *other* VCs shut us down. Why? Because Kharrazi Enterprises has a fifty-million-dollar loan on the books to us, and if he shuts it down they have to write it off and take the charge in their quarterly earnings. It will hurt their earnings per share. That will further depress their stock and kill some acquisitions that he's trying to do that are totally unrelated to us, *and* reduce Farouk's personal fortune. So the irony is, all of the money that we have *squandered,* which is the inflammatory term he insists on using, is going to keep us from going under. He has no choice but to keep us alive so we can float that debt. So thank God we spent all that money. If we had spent less, if we had any money left over, he could reclaim it and then shut us down. We are, however, going to have to reduce our staffing levels and do some good old-fashioned layoffs."

AllMinder was going to have to drop seventy percent of the headcount and keep only enough warm bodies around to maintain the site in its current form. "I'm still going to want to see some development, of course," Jonathan said. "And rest assured, all you people here in this room are considered critical to the operation. You are the keepers of the"—forking his fingers at his own eyes—"the vision of AllMinder. You all have the option of staying until the end, be it good or bad. It's the middle managers and lower where I think we're fat."

"You mean the people who actually do the work?" Brad asked. A bit too much sarcasm in his tone. He tried to make amends. "I mean, I guess we'll all have to step up and do some of the tasks we've been depending on them to do, that's all."

Jonathan said, "I think we still need to maintain our strategy team—we're the visionaries—and yes, also some doers."

"How are the bonuses looking for next year?" Brad asked. "Has Farouk said anything about that?"

"The bonus plan is still in effect, and in fact I think we're going to be looking into a retention bonus plan paid out quarterly going forward."

Barbara Lubotsky said, "Seventy percent, huh?"

"There's no list yet, and no exact target number, but yes, about seventy percent. Start thinking about your departments. And don't say anything to anybody, because I don't want everyone suddenly jumping ship."

Before the meeting adjourned Jonathan again asked everyone in the room to keep the upcoming layoffs a secret. No one honored his request. Brad felt he owed it to his one direct report, Sierra, at least to give her a hint. Later that afternoon he confided to her that things weren't looking good for the long-term future of the company. "Even the short-term, actually," he said.

"What do you mean?"

"Well, I can't imagine that Farouk is going to be able to tolerate the kind of money drain that we've become, not when the potential for an IPO windfall seems to have vanished. I mean, there are *no* IPOs these days. If we had gone out last March, we would've been a billion-dollar company, at least for a few weeks. Today? They'd laugh at us."

"Farouk seems pretty nice," she said.

"You've got to be kidding."

"While you all were in your meeting, he stopped by and we chatted for a bit. Jonathan introduced us once, back when I first started, so I guess he felt comfortable with me."

"Yeah, I bet."

She let that go. "He seems like a smart guy."

"Look, this is a Business 101 situation. He was stopping

by to see if you were doing any work and if you were necessary to the company." She seemed sufficiently alarmed. "Please tell me you were actually doing something and that you didn't say you had any time on your hands to help him with anything."

"Don't worry," she said. "I don't think he was trying to entrap me or anything."

Brad shook his head, willing himself to say nothing more about it.

Other managers also let their direct reports know that something was up. Rumors of impending layoffs swept the company. All work that was not absolutely necessary for the day-to-day maintenance of the site simply stopped, and anyone walking through the company could see, on almost every computer monitor, the unmistakable formatting of résumés. Activity on the basketball court increased. Trick shots were developed. Organized H-O-R-S-E contests became a constant feature of the floor near Brad and Sierra's desks.

The first AllMinder entry appeared on FuckedCompany.com: "Rumor has it that you'll soon be able to call it NoMinder.com. That's right, those fucks are almost done."

23. Sierra Advances

THAT NIGHT AT A FASHIONABLE INDIAN RESTAURANT called Tamarind, Sierra Hamilton sat across from Farouk Kharrazi, whom she had met for the second time earlier that day while Brad and most of the other senior staffers were in an unscheduled, hastily called meeting with Jonathan, which Farouk had declined to attend. He'd spent half an hour yelling at Jonathan in the conference room, Sierra knew—everyone was still talking about it, instant messaging about it, "What does it mean for the company?"—and suddenly the basketball court beside her desk cleared out, Vlad Morovsky and Art from Biz Dev scattering like birds before a storm. She felt a presence behind her, saw a shadow on her monitor. Turning, she saw Farouk himself staring at her screen.

"You are actually doing something productive," he noted. "And just a few feet from the basketball court!" He seemed pleased when she told him that she never played basketball at work—or anywhere else for that matter. He said, "One of the things I like to do, to really find out what is going on within a company that I'm financing, is to skip the top levels. Forgive me, but they're all full of shit anyway. They say what they think

I want to hear. I like to find the truth from someone they would not ordinarily let me talk to. I am interested in your ideas about the company and how it is run, and what you have observed. So I would like to take you out to dinner tonight to hear what you have to say. Okay?"

The guy was worth more than a billion, they said, even with the recent drop in his stock. The way he was looking at her now, she had seen it before. This wasn't about her work-related ideas. If she accepted the invitation tonight, her job would be to justify his overture, justify his lust, by turning out to be as smart as she was beautiful. No problem.

"Sure, Mr. Kharrazi."

He waved away the formality. "Farouk. Please."

Now the only question was how to get out of a previous engagement with the relatively impoverished Rinehart, with his paltry fifteen or so million. Not that fifteen million wasn't enough, but Rinehart had begun to bore her with his drinking and to worry her with his cocaine use. The girls at Strings always said you can't date a customer. But where else do you meet people? Rinehart's trajectory of success—and of life—seemed unsustainable. Why hitch yourself to a falling star? Farouk Kharrazi by contrast seemed an unstoppable force of his own making. She liked that he made the other men run quivering from the basketball court, liked the massiveness of his goals, his successes, and the way his fortune reduced antagonists to petty carping behind his back while still rendering them servile before him.

Now about that Rinehart excuse. She couldn't tell him she was working late. He would call and berate Brad for making her do so, and Brad, defending himself, would dispute her story. She couldn't tell him she was not feeling well. He'd want to come over with flowers and send out for chicken soup. Most of all she couldn't tell him the truth, that *the* Farouk Kharrazi had asked her to dinner so that he could hear her expert opinions about how best to run AllMinder. He'd know what Farouk was up to; he'd know what *she* was up to. In the end she settled on a weak "girls' night out" excuse. She hadn't seen her friends from Strings in a while. A couple of them were off tonight, she said, and they wanted to go party. In his acceptance of that she detected a barely concealed glee: now he'd be able to go out and get drunk with Brad. "Should I transfer you to Brad so you boys can go out and have fun?"

"Oh, sure, I guess. I'll miss you though."

So now here she sat across from Farouk, telling him that she thought the fundamental premise of the company was unsound and needed adjustment, and that there was no question Jonathan was more interested in being liked than in being a leader. Farouk was nodding. "I can tell you, you are right about that. You are a smart girl."

She had long been able to detect what men needed to hear and then simply to say it. "You know I really admire what you've accomplished with your life. You must have seen and done so much."

"Thank you. I appreciate that." For just a second his eyes were glossy. "You'd be surprised that this actually intimidates people when really it shouldn't."

"No, it should give them comfort, because they can depend on your knowledge and superior experience."

"One thing I've learned, and I want to give you this advice because you're at an age where you can make this mistake or not, you should keep your standards high. You're at such a young age that you could find yourself involved with someone who really doesn't have any original thought in his head."

Sierra said, "I know. It's scary. I think that's why I've always been attracted to older men. I've been sort of casually seeing this guy who's thirty-eight."

He smiled. "That's perfect for you. Me, I'm too old. I am in my late forties."

"Late forties! Come on, I would never have guessed it. Besides, late forties is a man's prime . . . as I'm sure your wife would agree." She nodded at his left hand. "I see a telltale band of platinum."

"Yes." He looked at his wedding ring sadly.

She hesitated.

"What?" he asked. "Go on."

"Someone once said that a man marries a woman hoping that she'll never change, and a woman marries a man hoping that he *will* change, and both are disappointed."

He nodded. Again the brief glossiness in the eyes.

"But you know what, Farouk? I'd never try to change a man. That's one of the reasons I think I'm different. People are what they are, by their nature. You can't get mad at them for being true to themselves." His face downcast, he knuckled the corner of an eye. "It's a lonely position you're in," she continued. "Having to be the leader all the time, having to be the smart one, the one with all the answers and the fat wallet, because as much as people need you, they resent you."

Farouk pinched the bridge of his nose and closed his eyes. "Forgive me. It has been a rough day. I'm just surprised that you understand."

"I'm sorry. I've spoken too freely."

"No, no, it is refreshing. When you have as much money as I do, there is an isolation. There is a dehumanization." He aimed a thumb over his shoulder, where his bodyguards drank ice water with their backs to the bar. "If I don't have these guys with me? Chances are I'm walking along and I will be attacked by someone I fired ten years ago for gross incontinence."

She couldn't help herself. She laughed so hard that wine came through her nose. "I'm sorry, I'm sorry."

"What?" he asked, confused. "What is it?"

"Gross *what?*" And when she explained to him that the word he was looking for was *incompetence* and that the one he had used meant the inability to control one's functions of elimination, a darkness came over his face, and then it lifted, and he began to laugh. He doubled over, holding his side. The maître d' rushed over. "Is everything all right!"

Red-faced but unable to speak, Sierra and Farouk nodded.

"I've been saying that for years!" Farouk finally said. "No one told me! They were afraid! You see what I have to deal with?"

And so the evening went. Sierra read him perfectly, gave him what he needed, gave him every reason to fall in love with her. Every few minutes one of them would say something like the chef here clearly was not incontinent, and the laughter would begin again.

She even—this was a risk—confessed her recent stripper past. That would turn some men off, but it was best to get it out on the table early to avoid any subsequent charges of inadequate personal disclosure. "For reasons you can understand," she said when she was finished, "I never told that story at AllMinder."

"And why should you even have to tell it?" he said. "Those clowns would probably hold it against you, so you were right to keep it to yourself."

Farouk had never seen the inside of a strip joint, except for brief scenes in some movies, "a pair of detectives talking to a pair of, you know," he said. But he assured Sierra that he did not disapprove of exotic dancing as a business. There was nothing wrong with parting a fool from his money; that was perfectly ethical. "I do it myself all the time. It's the nature of business. I actually admire you for doing it, and for getting out."

After dinner he gave her address to his driver. On their way to the Upper East Side, with one of the bodyguards in the front seat and one following in a different car, Farouk and Sierra agreed that this special connection they felt for each other must remain hush-hush, at least until he had a chance to mull it over. "My marriage," he said, shaking his head, "it's breaking up. I want you to know it's not because I'm in love with another woman. At least that was true until tonight. Or maybe it was only true until the first time I met you, back when you first started and Jonathan was showing me around."

She touched a finger to his lips. "Think before you say anything, Farouk, because I've got to tell you, the way I feel right now, I'm going to want to hold you to it."

"I'm glad to hear it. I've never had a night like this. Not in a long time. We must be discreet while I'm still married, to be respectful of my wife. But I *must* see you again."

"Let me ask you something," Sierra said. "Isn't your wife American? And couldn't she have corrected your word usage like I did?"

He suddenly looked angry. "Yes, come to think of it. Yes, she could."

In front of her building she leaned back into the car to kiss his cheek. She allowed him to pull her back inside, hugging her to himself, the strength of his embrace betraying a need that went beyond the physical, though that was obvious too. "You didn't answer my question," he said. "Can I see you again?"

She touched his nose and smiled, a gesture that said, Of course you can, you rich old man.

24. Holding the Company Together

"I KNOW THERE'VE BEEN A LOT OF RUMORS FLOATING around," Jonathan told the assembled multitude at the Monday Morning Meeting. "Some of you may have seen me in the conference room with Farouk Kharrazi. We're both very passionate about maintaining the vision of AllMinder, and the vision, let me assure you, remains the same. Yes, despite what you might have thought, Farouk and I remain good friends." He chuckled. "No, we were not about to kill each other. Yes, Farouk is intent on supporting AllMinder and still sees us as a viable business going forward. As for layoffs, I know there have been rumors. I really can't say anything except that at the moment there are no plans for layoffs. Basically, anything I say to you might turn out to be untrue, in which case I'll look like a liar. So I ask you to please bear with me. Thank you for doing that, thank you for being here. I can assure you that Farouk knows this is a temporary market condition, and the key for us all is to be prepared to take the company public as soon as things settle down. We are fully funded into 2001. And as for a certain message board out there"—referring obviously to

FuckedCompany—"all I can say is, those are just rumors, and I encourage you to ignore them."

Jonathan looked over at Brad, who nodded his approval. He had delivered the agreed upon spin well enough, and people seemed to be buying it. For personal reasons people wanted, *needed* to buy it. The employment market, which last March had been so hot that anyone could land a high paying Internet job—witness Sierra—was now so cold that no one could, not even Brad with his years of high-profile PR experience. Sure, if he wanted to take a pay cut, if he wanted to do for some other company what Sierra was doing for AllMinder, if he wanted to work in some sort of grunt capacity, giving up the most enjoyable part of his job, the crafting of communications strategy, and instead become someone's worker bee, then yes, he could find a job. How did he know this? He'd posted his résumé online with the various job search sites, and every couple of days he read the descriptions of the positions available. The job titles should have read Primary Whipping Boy, PR Grunt, Coffee Runner, and the like. It had been months since Jonathan had pointed out a new AllMinder employee at the Monday Morning Meeting.

So for Brad there was no rush to leave. He was still getting a paycheck that the job market was telling him was inflated, and he was getting pretty good at two or three trick shots on the office basketball hoop. He could bounce the little sponge ball off the air ducts and sink it eighty percent of the time. He was considered a top H-O-R-S-E competitor. The forthcoming layoffs, about which Jonathan had just pleaded ignorance and optimism, would not touch him. Brad knew this because he and Jonathan had gone over the roster together, discussing who should stay and who should go. Sierra, unfortunately, was on the go list. He had gently suggested to Rinehart that this might be the case. "I mean, for all I know Sierra and I *both* are going to be gone. There are no guarantees."

Rinehart told him not to worry. "It'll be good for her to experience some kind of rejection. She'll come out on top."

"I don't know, it's a pretty tight market."

"Well, you know she comes across great in an interview." Oh, that night, the glitter . . . mere months ago, but under the influence of a different mentality and the expectation of endless money, plenty of twenties to buy dance after dance.

It wasn't just the miserable job market that kept Brad on board. There was also the memory of that twenty-seven-thousand-dollar bonus back in March, which Jonathan had implied would be repeated next March, only a few months away. He was still a director. He was eligible for that bonus, assuming the company still existed. Naturally it might be a little lower next year. Now that everyone had stopped hiring, retention tools no longer had to be so powerful. But March of 2001 was far enough away that conditions might improve, and near enough that he might as well wait it out. He was halfway there. He had already earned half of whatever his March 2001 bonus would be. If he took a new job he would forgo that bonus, and very likely his new employer would not offer one in March but would wait until an entire year had passed. Might as well stay. The excitement of the forthcoming workforce reduction was going to make the next few weeks disappear painlessly, and then there would be the regrouping of survivors who would nobly carry on with the hopeless AllMinder mission. Next thing you knew, it'd be Christmas and New Year's, and then there'd be only a few weeks to go until he'd once again be Bonused Brad.

Under the assumption that his employment would continue, and in expectation of that sizable March bonus, Brad did not modify his spending habits. He still hung out with Rinehart at places where you handed the bartender a twenty for a pair of drinks, and she stood there waiting for you to cough up more. Except for breakfast every morning, cereal and milk, he could not remember the last time he had prepared a meal for himself—no, wait—it was about a year ago. Home with aches and a fever he had been the influenza gourmet, heating a can of soup and smearing a spoonful of old jam that was probably still okay onto a slice of bread that wasn't quite moldy. All of his money was going to bars and restaurants.

He and Julia were still fucking too. The sex itself was emotionally affordable, but it had begun to require occasionally some pre- and postgame activities that came perilously close to Brad's idea of dating. The damage to his wallet was similar. Julia was particularly fond of trying newly opened restaurants. She liked the fresh buzz more, he suspected, than she liked the food. And if she agreed to go to one that had been open longer than a month, it must have been in business for years, famous enough that even her mother back in San Diego would have heard of it. That she insisted on paying her share saved Brad the embarrassment of having to fold his wallet and go home. On the other hand it forced him to stay and plunk down half of the bill as if he too were making a quarter mil, her rumored salary. At least splitting the check allowed him to maintain to himself and to Rinehart, and anyone else who asked, that they were just a couple of friends out sharing a meal. "She always pays half. Certainly this is not dating." Brad didn't even bother to clear his dresser top of the business cards he had collected over the past year or so, though he did offer that few of the women had come back to his apartment. "These are mostly women I met in bars and promised to e-mail but never did." Julia recognized three names from the pile.

But somewhere along the way they had dropped the King and Queen of Irony act, and now they spoke honestly about whatever was on their minds, the events of the day. A contentious race for the U.S. Senate. The mayor's prostate cancer, his estrangement from his wife. Undercover police shot an unarmed Haitian immigrant in a bar on Eighth Avenue. Had the stock market finally bottomed out? Under the right circumstances the conversation would turn personal. It was to Julia that Brad first confessed his qualms about his "social drinking," he called it. Julia said, "Not to sound like a government spokesperson, but in your case 'social drinking' is to alcoholism as 'passing away' is to death." He also told her that he wanted to write a novel. "You should," she told him. "Why don't you just go out one night a week? Cool off some. Get to work on what you really want to do."

He was thinking about that advice—cool off, buddy— while he watched Jonathan continue spinning before the assembled employees of AllMinder—too many now to all be here in person. Some chose to stay at their desks and call in on the speaker phone.

"Well, that's certainly true," Jonathan was saying in response to some question. "Recent market conditions have not been favorable to companies like ours. What does that mean for us? Well, nothing in the short term. We're getting an additional round of financing. Farouk is committed to AllMinder. Bonus plans are still intact, and so everything needs to continue normally. Everyone needs to still get here on time, you're still getting a paycheck, and everyone needs to work a full day. I realize I'm talking to the wrong group here, since you are all here and it's the start of the day, but if you could pass the word around I would appreciate it. I want to ask you all to do me a favor and limit your online job searching to after five p.m. Or you can also do it before eight in the morning. It just doesn't look good when I'm walking a prospective partner through the office and you're all on HotJobs or playing basketball, you know?"

That was supposed to be at least half a joke, but no one followed Jonathan's nervous leading chuckle. "When the time comes, I know we'll have a very successful IPO. So please consider this nothing more than a little bump in the road, not a roadblock. Any concerns or questions, feel free to come to me or of course to Brad, our PR guy, he's up to speed on all this stuff."

25. Simmering Resentment

DURING THE MONDAY MORNING MEETING STEVEN Bluestein stayed in the back, leaning against the wall, clenching his jaw at Jonathan and all the other senior staff who were involved in this conspiracy of misinformation. Brad Smith, who rarely spoke at these meetings, nevertheless was, Steven suspected, the chief propagandist, the one who invented Jonathan's lies. The most pathetic thing about Brad, as far as Steven Bluestein was concerned, was that he didn't even know everything there was to know, hadn't a clue, for example, about the Gupta Technology kickbacks or the Barbara Lubotsky–Jonathan Scarver affair. The layoffs really pissed Steven off. Even though he was not on the list, the fact that others were, and that they were being lied to, infuriated him. He also knew that the only reason Farouk wasn't shutting the company down completely was to keep Kharrazi Enterprises from having to write off those loans. Farouk wasn't committed so much as cornered.

AllMinder had shown that it could not make money. The NASDAQ had shown itself to be a legalized Ponzi scheme. It was enough to make a guy want to post all of this on FuckedCompany.com. All of this, plus the Gupta Technology kickbacks to Jonathan. The Barbara Lubotsky afternoon delight sessions. Brad's alcoholic womanizing. The fact that Sierra used to be a stripper. No, he'd let that slide, he liked Sierra. He wouldn't even post that Kharrazi was in love with her—that seemed real, seemed almost sweet. FuckedCompany would love to post it, even if it weren't true. Chronicling the downfall of dot com after dot com, allowing people to post rumors and slander anonymously, FuckedCompany ironically seemed to be the only prosperous Web-based business in existence. Lots of eyeballs and run by just one guy, apparently, so maybe he could actually support himself by ad revenue alone. Steven Bluestein monitored that site every day; it had even begun to compete with the fun of reading other people's e-mail.

And how could Brad lie to Sierra like that? They sat right beside each other; they talked all day. They worked together. And he had put her on the list? Well, that might be a career-ending mistake, as Brad would soon find out.

In the ongoing correspondence between Sierra and Farouk, Steven saw a whole new side of Kharrazi. The guy could get downright sensitive sometimes, and thoughtful. There was nothing overtly sexual about the notes between these two, who were not yet lovers, Steven guessed; and yet between the lines the notes were full of tension and longing. The two seemed to be falling for each other. In e-mail Kharrazi freely alluded to his marriage problems in a way that assumed prior knowledge on Sierra's part, so they must have discussed it whenever they were out having dinner together, which apparently was often. This was pretty serious. Farouk was surprisingly candid with her about the business too. "I wonder," he wrote, "if a pure e-commerce play can work at all. Never mind how this one has been boondoggled. The only good thing he did was hire you. I am impressed with the positioning statement you made. Unfortunately, we may have to liquidate. I worry that seventy-percent layoffs might be useless. We might have to shut it down. That is confidential. I miss you. I have a table reserved for us at Tamarind next Tuesday." Oh, to be a fly on the wall when Farouk finds out they've put her on the list for termination.

Jonathan was still up there spouting bullshit. Steven raised his hand.

Jonathan called on him. "Yes, Steven Brownstein?"

Once again Steven let slide the miscoloring of his name. "How sure are we about there being no layoffs?"

"There are absolutely no plans for layoffs."

"Have there been discussions? I mean, what constitutes a *plan* for layoffs? Are you formulating a plan?"

"No."

"I guess I just ask because I don't see how we can continue to operate at this level of headcount, considering that we make no money. Especially when you factor in that the stock of Farouk's publicly traded company, Kharrazi Enterprises, is in the toilet."

Stepping forward, arching his eyebrows, Jonathan adopted a condescending tone. "Fortunately these are not questions that you as our systems administrator need to worry about. I don't know how to say it more clearly. There are no plans for layoffs."

Steven *Blue*stein clenched his jaw and backed off. FuckedCompany was too good for these guys. He had to think of something else. Later in the day he still seemed so visibly bitter that CTO Rick Stevens stopped by to ask him what was up.

"Oh, nothing. Everything's fine." Except for the layoff list, he did not say. Except the whole reason you were forced to hire Gupta Technology was so Jonathan could get his twenty-percent share. And by the way, don't tell Barbara Lubotsky anything you don't want her to tell Jonathan while she's lying naked in bed with him at the Mayfair Hotel one of these afternoons. And finally, listen, if you have something to communicate to Farouk Kharrazi, don't go to Jonathan. Go instead to Sierra, who is an ex-stripper and technically has a boyfriend who's best buddies with Brad—that's how she got the job. If you want to communicate with Farouk, she's your go-to girl. Mention it in such a way that she will seize upon it as valuable information, and she will pass it along to Farouk either in e-mail or over a romantic dinner. That's how fucked up we are, Rick; that's why I've got this angry lockjaw. I've got so much information, there are so many lies that my head is about to explode. And Maria Massimo won't even look at me. She's got her damn Mr. Green giving her big screaming Os all the time, and I'm at home surfing porn sites and jacking off. I haven't had an actual piece of pussy since 1996. It's a good thing I don't own a gun. I'd be tempted to bring it in here to facilitate some honest discussion. But no, just kidding, ha-ha, that's an overreaction. I'm going to think of something else, something that will hurt a whole hell of a lot more than a post on FuckedCompany. But right now the only thing I can say to you is, "Oh, nothing. Everything's fine."

That seemed to satisfy Rick Stevens. At least it sent him on his way, chatting with other techs at nearby workstations, perhaps in an attempt to normalize retroactively his uncharacteristic visit to Steven. You don't really visit Steven. Steven just keeps things running. As long as he's got his science fiction books he's low maintenance.

Steven was more and more obsessed with Mr. Green. He imagined a broad shouldered Wall Street guy with a big swinging dick, treating Maria like a little animal, nothing more, and who at the same time made her love it. She embraced the indignity of being used. She seemed to use him right back. When he wasn't around, she dated from her regular stable of studs, whom she called only by their first names: Eric, Steven, Simon, etc. No "Mr." for them. She did fuck an "Ensign," though, one of the thousands of U.S. Navy sailors in town for Fleet Week. "It was all about the uniform," she wrote. "Once he took it off, he really did nothing for me. Then when he put it on again, I was like, oh, that's why I did him." She seemed so damn loose, a warm horny little club scene girl. She was all over the place. Steven imagined she'd do anyone who bought a few drinks and an appetizer.

Why not Steven Bluestein, then? Forget fuck, she won't even look at me unless there's something wrong with her computer. Thinks I'm the desktop support guy, and I'm so desperate to get close to her that I cannot bring myself to turn her away, would rather demote myself just to be the one who gets to sit in a chair that's still warm from her ass, put my hand on the mouse, and feel her presence over my shoulder as she observes my miracle, usually the simple correction of some dumb user error. Her smell reminded him of a department store's cosmetics section, through which he could pass as if invisible, without being hailed by any of the aggressive employees, because *he* obviously wasn't looking to buy anything for his girlfriend, since he obviously didn't have one, at least not one who needed to keep herself pretty in order to deserve him.

He loathed Mr. Green. He wanted to tell Maria, Look, this is no good, you need to clean yourself up. Most men won't forgive you for your sordid past and your consistent record of sexual misjudgments, the fact, frankly, that you are such an easy lay that you should be charging cash rather than just alcohol and a little food. But I will protect you. I will send you to therapy. I will help you end this relationship with Mr. Green, who gives you lots of "big screaming Os," as you like to call them, but damages your self-esteem. I will make love to you, and you'll see how easy it is to be satisfied with one man. But of course he could none of this say to her without revealing that he knew about Mr. Green, and how except by reading her e-mail?

Steven's general frustrations about Maria, the fear that he was inadequate for her—worse, invisible to her—contributed to the increasing hostility he felt toward Jonathan Scarver. People needed to know the truth about the state of the company. People had real decisions to make about how to continue to pay the rent and buy groceries. To give them no warning, to suggest in fact that things were fine, was to set them up for one of life's great sucker punches: sudden and surprising unemployment.

How could Scarver stand up there and tell people that there were no plans for layoffs and suggest that the IPO might still somehow be on? Technically, he supposed, it wasn't a lie. There were going to be layoffs, Scarver was going over the roster right now, but there wasn't an actual *plan* yet. It reminded Steven of something Bill Clinton said in response to a question about Monica Lewinsky: "It depends upon what the meaning of the word *is* is." None of Steven's colleagues had the advantage of Steven's whole insight into what was really going on. It offended Steven's sense of justice, and he knew that he had to do something about it. How the hell to convey the truth without revealing that he had snooped to find it? Make copies of the e-mails and place them in everyone's snail mail box? No, too obviously an inside job. Cherry pick a few e-mails from Jonathan's account and forward them to the people they affected? Again too obviously done by someone who knew the system inside and out, someone exactly like Steven Bluestein. And so Steven kept thinking.

If Jonathan had asked him then, "Are you going to expose me as an embezzling adulterer?" Steven could have said, "There are no plans to expose you as an embezzling adulterer." He chuckled at that. I can honestly say that I have no plan yet, Jonathan, to harm you in any way.

But he was trying to think of one.

26. Look Who's Here!

"I HAVE THIS UNCLE, UNCLE GEORGE, WHO IS ALWAYS TRYING to come up with a get rich scheme, right?" Brad lit a cigarette for Julia, moved an ashtray onto the bed, and told her the Panama Canal story from the beginning. Listening attentively, she made no effort to cover herself, and he didn't bother sliding back into his boxer shorts. The fifteenth or twentieth time they'd done this (neither could have said with certainty), they were long past postcoital modesty. "Now it's a scheme to import a special kind of rare marble from Italy. 'A few boatloads, and pretty soon you've got an empire, you're a *magnate!*' he says. He called me about it yesterday. He's an alcoholic and a drug abuser or whatever, and he's always looking for the big score that's going to keep him from ever again having to open his eyes to the sound of an alarm clock. And it seems ridiculous when you talk to him. He seems like a scheming pathetic character from some old movie, trying to find a treasure map or tunnel his way into a bank vault. But the thing that scares me more than anything else about him is I can totally see his point of view. Actually, I identify with him too closely for comfort. I mean, this whole stock market thing. Last year at this time I thought this year at this time—September of 2000, for God's sake—I'd be worth millions. On paper at least. And look at us."

"What do you mean?"

"Well, what are we doing? I'm a month into thirty-four, you just turned thirty-one." He panned over her body, slapped his own slight gut. "We make it to the gym every now and then to offset the partying, but we are not among the blessed ageless. In five years, we're going to look five years older, and neither one of us is close to doing anything with our lives really."

"Define *anything.*"

"You know. Marriage, kids."

"I want those things. I just haven't met the right person yet." She began to pick at a cuticle. "Definitely time to get the nails done."

"I *don't* want those things, so I'm not sure I even want to meet the right person. She'd have to not want those things. The problem with us is we're too into the moment. We can't look ahead. I drink too much, I don't read enough. I was an English major in college because I wanted to write novels, not press releases. You want a Bloody Mary?"

"Twist my arm."

He put on his boxers. In the kitchen he made the drinks. It was Saturday afternoon, and she had been here since eleven a.m., having stopped by on her way home from the gym. They would probably get a bite to eat and then go their separate ways for the evening. Over time these after-sex discussions when the walls were down had become therapeutic. It was a comfortable arrangement, and perhaps precisely because neither participant was asking for permanence, both felt that it might last a very long time.

"What's wrong with being in the moment." She was in the kitchen with him now, cinching his robe around her waist. "I'm not much of a deferrer. You're not meant to be married, Brad. So what? Maybe that's fine."

"I was thinking about it, and really I don't think anyone should marry me. If I wanted to marry that person, if I really loved that woman, I'd honestly have to advise her to move on."

"I'll keep in mind," she said, "that if you ever marry a woman, you're not being honest with her."

"No, if I ever marry a woman, I will have reformed myself so that I'm worth it. I don't know, I'll stop drinking so much, and I'll maybe have that book under my belt." He took a drag on her cigarette and handed it back to her. "I'm really pissed off about this layoff list."

They had discussed the AllMinder situation at length. Julia had turned out to be a trustworthy confidant and the best kind of listener: slow to mete out prescriptive advice. She too was feeling the effects of the downturn. She couldn't move the enterprise-wide system software as quickly as she'd been doing at the beginning of the year, and the commissions had slowed accordingly, though not yet enough to keep her from suggesting the Union Square Cafe too frequently for Brad's taste, expediting the depletion of what was left of his bonus after the bad eStamps trade. Maybe she would have to move on to a new job, but Brad *certainly* would have to move on. They both knew this even though he was not on the layoff list. "Which of course makes no sense. Why do they need a PR guy? I'm not on the layoff list because I'm buddies with Jonathan and maybe because I know too much."

The conversation was interrupted by a knock at the door—strange, for no one had buzzed the apartment from the intercom outside the building. "I'm not expecting anyone." In case

this was a push-in robbery, Brad picked up an empty wine bottle for self-defense. Through the peephole he saw one of his
neighbors, and behind her—what are *they* doing here? He
opened the door. "Mom, Dad! What a surprise." Hugs all
around, while behind his parents his neighbor explained that
she had found them staring at the intercom outside. "They
seemed harmless enough . . ."

"So you let them in," Brad said, "well, thanks!" Too late he
remembered he was wearing only his boxers, was still holding
the wine bottle as if he'd just guzzled the last of it, and that he
must smell like smoke, booze, and Julia.

"Well," his father said, still smiling but his eyes darting
around at the signs of George-like dissipation, "your Mom
wanted to come up for the John Singer Sargent watercolor
exhibit at the Met, and we got cheap tickets at the last minute
on the World Wide Web. So we thought we might as well . . ."
He noticed over Brad's shoulder a bedraggled party girl
wearing the bathrobe they had given Brad for Christmas. She
was smoking a cigarette. "Hi there," he said. Without taking
his eyes off her, he said, "Brad, why don't you introduce us to
your friend?"

He backed into the apartment. "Mom, Dad, this is Julia
. . ." For some reason he couldn't remember her last name.
"Umm . . ." It was not that he didn't know it. He knew it well.
Dorsey Dorsey Dorsey! Part of her e-mail address even! He e-
mailed her two or three times a week! This was merely a case
of surprise-induced amnesia.

Julia pronounced her last name.

"I know that," Brad said. Nervous laugh. "Dorsey. I know
that. I just blanked."

His mother was already looking around the untidy apartment with an air of reticent disapproval. She waved her hand

back and forth in front of her crinkled nose. "I'm sorry," Julia said, "does the cigarette bother you?"

"Well, I guess I'm just not used to it."

Julia turned on the kitchen faucet and touched the glowing tip to the flow.

Mom walked into the bedroom. Brad was right behind her—"Mom?"—but too late. She stepped on the used condom. It glommed onto her comfortable walking shoe, which she had put on this morning in anticipation of seeing a lot of the city and covering at least a mile or two in the Met. She didn't notice the rubber. But the wet spot on the bedsheets lifted her eyebrows and repelled her back into the main room, the condom still glued to her shoe.

"What is *that*?" Dad asked, pointing down at it.

"What? Ahh!" She jumped as if the thing were a snake, shook her foot, kept shaking her foot, and finally the rubber splatted to the floor.

Everyone looked at it.

"Well, I guess you two are pretty serious," Dad said.

"Oh, not really," Julia said. "We're just good friends."

Brad gave her a helpless, agonized look. Why did she have to tell the truth? Couldn't she, under these desperate circumstances, pretend this was a real relationship? "I'm going to get dressed," Julia said, closing the bedroom door.

During her mercifully short absence, Brad apologized for the appearance of the apartment. "If I'd known you were coming I would've hired a maid or something." It seemed the wrong thing to say and led to a series of stunted attempts at small talk about cleaning products. Realizing he had been gesturing with the wine bottle, he finally set it on top of the television.

Julia reentered the scene fully dressed. "It was nice to

meet you two." She kissed Brad on the cheek, said she'd see him later, and walked out the front door, leaving the three Smiths standing there in stunned silence. Even as problematic as her "just friends" comment was, even as much as he planned to throttle her later for that, he would have preferred that she stay. He could have used her dismissive attitude to help steel himself against the disapproval he would feel over the next few minutes. He deflected a few pointed questions and then decided to absorb them and answer honestly. "No, I don't think there's anything wrong with two consenting adults getting together and having sex. I don't believe it is irresponsible. I think I'm doing pretty well in life. Any other set of parents would be proud of all the things I've done. Far from being a derelict sitting around doing nothing, I'm a productive member of society, I'm accomplishing something!" They didn't seem to buy it. "This just goes to show that it is totally impossible for anyone to please their parents. I don't want you to stick your noses in and try to make me behave like you want me to behave. I am thirty-four years old. Who else do you visit without giving them a heads-up? Who else would you do that to?"

Almost immediately he regretted every word of it. He should have learned by now, from their example, how to bite his tongue. He recognized that he was matching their indignation with his own, and with regrettably superior vigor and more venom than they deserved. He was a goddamn ingrate is what he was, had not even given them the courtesy of saying that he loved them. He did love them but could not blame his father for suggesting otherwise.

"That's not true," Brad said, again sounding angrier than he'd intended.

"You know who you remind me of, Brad? Your Uncle

George. Smart guy, charming guy, good looking back when he was your age, and he drank it all away in every bar all over the Southeast. He flushed away his potential from the inside out, sixteen ounces at a time. I guess it's easier for you to get to the bars without driving, so maybe that's why you're not challenging George's DUI record. If you count the one with the stolen car, I think he's going on number five now. Here you don't need a car, you just stumble down the block to the next watering hole. Or blow ten bucks on a cab instead of putting it in your savings account. And I know you don't put stock in the religion in which you were raised—"

"It's not *any* stock and not *just* the religion in which I was raised. It's all the religions. They all think they're the only one. Everyone religious thinks everyone else is going to hell, and that's bullshit. Some kid born in India is going to hell, but you're not because you were born in the Bible Belt and raised in the predominant religion of the region? And the irony is, that kid in India, he probably thinks *you're* going to hell, that he's the heaven-bound chosen one essentially because of the accidental location of his birth. I guess you could say that by being born where you were born, where the dominant religion just happens to be the right one, you were in effect chosen, but so could that Hindu kid, and I have a hard time buying it. And the other thing that drives me crazy is this glorification of the lack of ambition. Live a humble life and die. Well, you know what, I don't want to live a humble life. I don't want to be content. I think *that's* a waste. I think *that's* a sin. I kind of like that about George actually, that he's always looking to strike it big. I don't care if he never does, it's still admirable."

Okay, he regretted all of that too. Not that he didn't believe it. But why torment people who disagreed with him, especially his parents? He was not about to be an antireligious zealot. The very concept exceeded his tolerance of irony. People believed what they believed. You want to change their minds, give them a drug. It was just—there was something so obvious and irritating about his parents' disapproval this time. True, Mom had stepped on the condom, incontrovertible evidence of premarital sex. A sin in their book. So Brad at thirty-four, possibly halfway through his life, was supposed to still be a virgin? Ridiculous. The mere thought was getting him all riled up again.

"Look, let's pretend like we called ahead and you cleaned the place up and you aren't living like some rock star," his dad said. "And then we'll all go out to dinner tonight. Bring your lady friend, we'd like to get to know her."

When he called Julia to complain about her "just friends" comment, she said, "What, was I supposed to lie to your parents, pretend like I'm your girlfriend?"

He heard himself directing at her some of his familial frustration. She gave it right back, chiding him for his lapsed Christian guilt over having been caught, if not with his pants down, then wearing only his boxers after an undeniably bed-wrecking session of fornication.

"Don't forget to attribute some of it to the way you were waltzing around in my robe, *smoking*," he reminded her. "You had *reason* to guess that some modicum of tact was in order!"

"Look, Brad, I think you've got some issues you need to work out. I think we need to cool it for a while. Why don't we take a break."

"You honestly think you're breaking up with me? There's something to break off?" His sense of loss confirmed that, yes, actually there was.

27. Conciliation

THAT NIGHT HE TOOK HIS PARENTS OUT TO DINNER. THEY had spent the afternoon first at the Met and then browsing several famous midtown stores. During a cab ride Dad had apparently quizzed the driver on the business particulars of the job and wound up impressed with what these guys go through every day to make a living and to provide for their often extensive families back home in Africa or South America or wherever.

"That's why I never feel guilty blowing ten bucks on a cab to get to a bar," Brad said, unable to resist reprising that line of argument.

Dad couldn't resist, either. "Yeah, one interesting young cabdriver was a Christian . . . from Nigeria, no less. Not exactly the Bible Belt."

"Touché," Brad said. "Look, about what happened earlier." Since their somber departure from his apartment his face had been hot with the necessity of apology, and now he stammered out the words. He readily conceded all of his faults, even ones he thought were excusable. For example, that he worked at a dot com. He had been *so greedy* as to quit a perfectly decent, stable job; he had been George-like enough to hope for riches from a profitless company that now, served him right, was clearly in trouble. Icarus flew too close to the sun. Know your place, boy. He found himself repeating to them some of the platitudes and half-truths that he himself had crafted for Jonathan Scarver to deliver to the company. Farouk Kharrazi still believed in the vision of AllMinder and was willing to continue funding it to fruition. The IPO had merely been postponed.

Dad was nodding over a mixed greens salad. "What's your personal financial situation like?" he asked, not saying what he didn't have to say: You make a lot of money, more than you think; people like that cabdriver raise families of six on less money and do it well, making sure there is enough for Little League fees and immunizations and doctor's bills, or, if the kids are still back in some third-world homeland, enough for a trip to visit them there, bearing gifts. Brad said that things were more expensive in the city for someone with a PR-type lifestyle; it was tougher to get along. The frugal, virtuous cabdriver might as well have been sitting beside him in counterpoint. He conceded that he probably drank too much but pointed out that most of his friends drank even more. Somehow that didn't seem to make them feel any better. His joke—"Don't worry, my vanity will save me from alcoholism"—hit his parents' unified front like a bird against a plate-glass window and fell dead. They both looked down at it. "Come on." He attempted resurrection. "Sometimes two vices cancel each other out. Vanity . . . alcoholism. Ha-ha?" They weren't buying it. Throughout the afternoon leading up to this dinner, he had been wondering, Am I a bad person? Not the son they wanted? Does a yes to the latter imply a yes to the former? Of course not. This must be how George feels around the rest of the family whenever they come to check him into rehab or bail him out of jail. Perhaps there runs in the family some gene of prodigal recklessness. Dad's brother got it, and now I have it.

His parents were picking gloomily at their salads when his cell phone rang. He checked the display: Rinehart. Best not to answer it right now. He put the phone on vibrate and stuck it in his shirt pocket. When he refilled his wineglass, Mom placed a hand over hers. She made a point of asking the passing waiter for three waters.

Dad said, "Whatever you think about what you're doing with that girl we met this afternoon, what's her name, Julia?"

"Yeah, Julia *Dorsey*," Brad said. "And her middle name is Anne. She grew up in San Diego. I've known her for more than three years."

Dad ignored the unsolicited bio. "I mean, even if something were to ever develop that resembled something meaningful, you couldn't trust her, given how free and easy she is with herself."

"She's been a good friend, Dad."

"You need to be with someone who values herself."

"Oh, I think Julia does." Fearing that news of his falling out with her would only prove his father's point, that the relationship was ephemeral and meaningless, he refrained from reporting it. "She has to go visit a friend on Long Island tomorrow," he said. And then to change the subject, he added, "There are some really nice parts of Long Island. The Gold Coast is out there. Lots of celebrities. Lots of money."

Mom said, "The U–Haul stops at the graveyard."

Brad concentrated on buttering a bite of bread. He felt his cell phone vibrating and allowed himself a glance at the display: Rinehart again. Mom complimented the flavor of the bruschetta, said it was almost as good as that served by a place near their home in Atlanta. People who would or could never live in New York flew here determined to conclude that in their day-to-day lives back home they had it at least as good, probably better. The food, the theater, the museums. As a matter of policy Brad always allowed their remarks to go unchallenged. A New Yorker lands in Atlanta already determined to reach the opposite conclusion: Things are worse here, beginning with the bagels. You should see the bagels in New York!

"This is a good place," Brad said. "I know the owner." He was quick to imply that this wasn't where his paycheck was going. "Not that I come here that often."

"The waiter knows your name," Dad pointed out.

"Brad makes a good impression wherever he goes," Mom said, not unkindly.

We are not good at confrontation, Brad thought. If we were like Rinehart's family, God protect the people at the next table from all of our metaphorical dirty laundry flying through the air, and perhaps some actual food items, maybe even a utensil or two. If it got really bad, a fist. Rinehart had come back from Thanksgiving two years ago with a black eye, courtesy of his brother, for whom six months later he served as best man, making a cryptic reference during his toast to the groom's boxing skills and promising that the inevitable rematch would have a different outcome. But those were the Rineharts, not the Smiths. We do not come to blows. We Smiths value politeness and appearances and propriety. No one should get too uppity, and if they did, why, they'd learn their lesson. Like Icarus. Like jailbird Uncle George. And like Brad one of these days.

"Look, we're not good at confrontation," he said aloud.

"Why should we be?" Mom asked in a tone that was in fact confrontational, and somehow pleasingly so.

It was Brad who backed down. Later he would attribute

this to his training in being a Smith, to having begun life immersed in Smith amniotic fluid and then in Smith culture, including diet and activities. We have a disagreement about religion, but we are pretty much all the same people. Perhaps that's what irritates us so, that we recognize dominant in one another certain of our own traits that we have worked hard to suppress. Brad had managed to lose his southern accent, but there were certain words that gave him away, especially when he was tired or drunk, or, most tellingly, when he was nervous. Under fire—say, when Farouk was yelling at him: "Why should I keep a PR guy around?"—Brad's accent reverted completely, and he heard himself sounding like a shifty, obsequious, white-trash southerner with a smokeless tobacco canister in the back pocket of his Levis and his wallet chained to his belt, the kind of guy who looks forward to the state fair because next time he's going to win that big stuffed animal for his halter-top girlfriend. But it went beyond accents, of course: I know that within me lies ready to flower their sanctimony. Perhaps they harbor my alcoholism. Perhaps with us Smiths it is either one or the other. And if I ever have kids, what culture will I create for them but Smith culture? And years later I'll be sitting at a table like this one, but on the other side of it.

"You're right, there's no need to be confrontational," he said. "I'm sorry about earlier. I guess you just need to give me a heads-up that you're coming in, let me clean the place up a bit. I'd do the same for you."

"We have nothing to hide, you can come by any time."

"I have nothing to *hide*," he said. No one mentioned the condom, but it might as well have been resting in the bread basket. Brad refilled his wineglass. "I want to make sure you know that I love you—" Why was that so hard to say? "I'm really sorry."

"Well, we'll have to have a good talk about it sometime. Maybe you could come home one weekend? Why don't you look into airfares? Ours certainly was reasonable."

There was no need to bring him home to make him feel how far he had strayed from the dreams of his uninformed youth and the frozen expectations of his parents. He felt the weight of the discrepancy at all times, even without waking up once again in his boyhood room, the dresser top a forest of debate team trophies that Mom would have dusted in preparation for his arrival.

Chewing on a piece of bread, Brad shrugged and nodded. He did not verbally agree to the plan, something he would point out when it came up again in a few weeks.

The rest of the dinner went all right (Brad ignored two more calls from Rinehart) though Mom found that the marinara had too much salt, not like at the place in Atlanta, which Brad will have to try when he comes for his visit. Also there was a guy at church who was involved in renovating the Presbyterian Web site, and perhaps Brad could give him some pointers. "Sure," Brad said.

They walked out of the restaurant and into Union Square. It was still warm for September, and the college girls had yet to put away their summer clothes. Brad had to keep himself from whipping his head around as they passed.

Perhaps it was the sight of one of them, one of the younger ones, that made his mother think of his high-school girlfriend. "We saw Pamela the other day at the Sunday buffet at Western Sizzlin'! I forgot to tell you. She looked great. She was in Atlanta visiting her husband's parents, had both kids in tow. Darling little things. They'd all just come from church."

"That's great, I'm glad to hear it." That was Brad's parallel

life, his road not taken. That's what might have happened to
him if an Uncle George-like dissatisfaction that had been simmering within him all through high school, even as he won
debate after debate, had not boiled over during college, and
he'd realized: not for me. I can't live that life. At his first col-
legiate Thanksgiving break, he had dumped Pamela, who was
then a senior in high school and two weeks shy of being
crowned homecoming queen. His parents were disappointed
enough to mention it to some of the extended family, most of
whom shared their concern. What had gotten into Brad's head
up there at school? Only Uncle George, come to think of it,
had offered his congratulations and support, phoning it in
secretly: "Wise move, my man. Trust me. Don't tell your father
I called."

He watched Dad take pleasure in hailing a cab. The old
guy did it correctly, waiting for one whose roof number was lit
and then giving a quick raise of the hand, none of the indis-
criminate windmilling and jumping that characterizes the
attempts of less experienced tourists, and none of their beaming delight when the thing actually stops. Brad hugged both
parents, told them that he loved them, and agreed to meet for
breakfast at the hotel in the morning.

No sooner had the cab pulled away than he returned
Rinehart's four calls. Something was wrong, something was up
with Sierra. "Can you please meet me at Volcano?" Rinehart
pleaded.

At Volcano, Brad put his lips to the brim of a strong Jack
and Coke.

"We were supposed to go out tonight to Blue Ribbon
Sushi," Rinehart explained. "She loves that place, but she

called up with some excuse. It's like the second time in a week that she's canceled on me. Has she said anything?"

"No. Not at all." Brad was genuinely puzzled. "She seems happy with you, as far as I know. Did she give a reason?"

"She said something came up. You know how long it's been since I heard that? Not since I made my first million has a girl said to me, 'something came up.' I think she might be seeing someone else."

"Come on, she wouldn't do that." Not that Brad believed it, but it was the right thing to say. He kept himself from reminding Rinehart, "Hey, she's a stripper, what do you expect?" and then he thought: *Holy shit, that is exactly what Dad would say!* It came from one of those Smith traits that lay within him not so dormant as he might have wished.

"I've been calling her all day. I don't even think she's home." Rinehart held his head by the sides and spoke directly into his drink. "What if she went out of town?"

"See, it's tough for me to comment, because I don't know where you two have taken this relationship. I don't know what expectations you've set."

"Well, goddammit, I think it's safe to say we don't leave town with other people, if that's what she's done."

Rinehart suggested they leave Volcano and pop into Strings to make sure she hadn't gone back to stripping. "I mean, maybe with market conditions and all, she's worried about making a living. I've gotta let her know I am there for her, I will help her out."

While Rinehart was sitting there feeling resolute, Brad recounted what had happened with his parents and their surprise visit. Julia sitting there in a bathrobe, *smoking*. Rinehart managed to emerge from his Sierra preoccupation long enough to order a couple of tequila shots and wince at Brad's bad luck: "Wow, sucks to be you." After a polite interval, though, he brought the subject back around to the issue that most concerned himself. "She hasn't seemed that happy with me lately, man. I mean, I'm totally in love with her."

"Well, you know I think she's a great girl, but you are two different people. It's always tough."

"Look at me."

"What?"

"Look into my eyes." Brad did as he was told and was alarmed at the rage he saw there. Rinehart said, "You're fucking her, aren't you?"

"What? No!" It was hard to maintain eye contact, and yet if he broke it he'd be guilty. Even this pause was dangerous, a pause long enough to confirm that the skin immediately beneath Rinehart's nose was shiny, puppy wet. "Come on, you're wired."

"What if I am? That still doesn't mean you can fuck my girlfriend."

"I'm not, okay? I'm not." He touched a hand to Rinehart's shoulder, felt the tension there. "Obviously I'm not the one with her tonight, am I? No paranoia, please."

Rinehart raised his eyebrows. "Okay. Fine." He slapped Brad's back. "I didn't really think so, but I did catch a guy like that once. He totally buckled, admitted everything. I know I can trust you." Rinehart lifted his shot. "Do this with me and let's forget about it." Brad touched his own tequila glass to Rinehart's and threw the liquor against the back of his throat.

"All right," Brad said, "on to other subjects."

Rinehart said, "But I know it's someone at work. She's fucking someone at work."

"There's no one at work. I mean, everyone is interested in her, but there's no way she's interested in anyone else."

"Has to be work. My spies at the gym tell me it's no one at the gym. I was thinking maybe one of the trainers, but those guys really have no money. Even with their muscles, how can they compete with me?"

"First of all, it might not be anyone. This could all be in your head. And maybe money's not the most important thing to her."

"Trust me, money is important to her. If you're raised the way she was raised, dirt poor, you grow up with an appreciation for money. And I think she's in a relationship or starting a relationship with someone. She seems different. Distant. And she canceled a Saturday night date? What the fuck is that all about? You don't call me up on a Saturday afternoon and fucking cancel. You do that to the guy you're going out with when *I* ask you out." He laughed as if he didn't really mean it, but he meant it.

At Strings, Rinehart gave the bouncer a hug. No cover charge when you're with Rinehart. Inside he asked one of the girls if Sierra Hamilton had started dancing there again. Nope. "Well, as long as we're here," Rinehart said to Brad, "let me buy you a couple of dances. It's the least I can do, since I just accused you of screwing my girlfriend."

Brad went with it, not foreseeing that at breakfast his mother was going to say, "What is that on your neck? It looks like . . . is that glitter?"

28. What Goes Around

THROUGHOUT THEIR PROFESSIONAL RELATIONSHIP JONATHAN Scarver and Raj Gupta had been careful at work not to seem to know each other. In a nice touch, Scarver made a habit of getting Raj's name wrong in front of others, calling him "Ravi," and occasionally, just to really push it, "Sanjay." Playing the part of the humble contractor, Raj wouldn't bother correcting him. He left that to Jonathan's wincing colleagues. CTO Rick Stevens, though initially reluctant to hire Gupta Technology and still uneasy about their rates, nevertheless felt they deserved the courtesy of accurate address. "Can't you at least call him by the right name? The guy is head of the consulting firm doing most of your Vignette work, you owe him at least that respect. And by the way, StoryServer developer rates are coming down. With the layoffs coming and everything, it might be time to renegotiate our contract with Raj."

"I don't want to rock the boat," Jonathan told him. "I don't want these guys to lower the quality of their work because they feel like they're getting screwed."

"Hey, I'm only trying to help. You're the one who says Kharrazi's been on your ass about the burn rate."

"Kharrazi understands the value of what we're trying to do here. He knows there are some up-front costs that are unavoidable. It hurts him at the moment, that's all, but I can handle him."

Rick, who had seen through the glass walls of the conference room a red-faced Farouk Kharrazi flailing his arms and yelling at Jonathan Scarver, who slumped ever lower in his chair, was not so sure that Jonathan could "handle" Kharrazi. Survive Kharrazi, maybe, but even that was in question. In fact Rick had wondered at the time if maybe he should stay within view in case the discussion devolved into an actual fistfight, though he could not have intervened—Kharrazi's security crew. All he said now was, "Okay, if you say so." But he felt, as he often had in Jonathan's presence of late, that he was being snowed. He didn't think Jonathan was doing it intentionally. Jonathan just couldn't turn off the unrelenting positive attitude that had attracted so much seed money in 1999 and had convinced Rick himself to leave a solid job at IBM to work for a profitless Internet company with a "flexible" business plan and a "great corporate culture."

He was surprised later that afternoon when he saw Raj Gupta in Jonathan's office. I should be in there, he thought, especially if they're doing some negotiating. He would have to mention that to Jonathan later.

He would have been even more surprised at the conversation he was missing. "It's not that I don't want to keep the gravy train rolling," Jonathan was telling his brother-in-law. "It's just that, frankly, we're going to have to lay some of our own people off. If I'm going to get rid of regular full-time employees, it'll be hard for me to make the argument that we should keep you guys, especially at your current rates."

Raj would see the logic in that argument, wouldn't he? All

good things must come to an end. AllMinder had paid Raj and company more than eighty thousand per week—exorbitant even for February of 1999, when the deal had been struck. Now that kind of money was harder to overlook. Kharrazi's people had already been questioning him about it.

Raj, however, offered no shrug of resignation. Instead he leaned forward, his smile disappearing. "We have an agreement, Jonathan. We need to stick to it. Who else knows the system like we do? I mean, we built it. With all due respect to your regular employees, they can't do a damn thing to improve the site. What are your marketing people going to do? What are your ad sales people going to do?"

"That goes to my point. The ad revenue model that supports radio and television so well does not appear to be working for the Internet, and that's the problem, Raj. We have got to cut back on expenses, and one of our expenses is Gupta Technology. Look, we have a special connection, obviously. We're in-laws. I'm telling you, this issue is soon going to be out of my hands. Once Kharrazi starts looking at the books—"

"One of my people," Raj said, "was having a late lunch at a restaurant on Forty-ninth Street. The Mayfair Hotel."

"Really." Jonathan set his coffee cup down slowly. "I'm surprised he had time to get all the way up there and back during a lunch hour."

"Oh, it usually takes you longer than that, does it, when you go for lunch?" Raj let a few seconds pass. "While my guy is sitting there, who walks into the hotel but you and Barbara. He sees you check in, you get a room key, and you both go upstairs. Now I understand that a man has needs that perhaps my sister-in-law, your wife, can't or won't fulfill." Raj leaned forward. "But, Jonathan, does *she* understand that?"

Jonathan couldn't believe it. "You're blackmailing me?"

"Oh, no. I'm trying to help. This person that I'm talking about, he comes from a very religious background. He does not approve of what he saw. He was going to confront you directly in the office. I talked him out of it. 'Don't bite the hand that feeds you,' I said. But you see, if you lay him off I have no leverage."

"So keep him."

"But he shared the secret with some of his colleagues, all four of them in addition to me. I don't think that keeping him and firing the others would necessarily do the trick."

"You're blackmailing me."

"No," said Raj, getting to his feet, checking his watch. "I'm trying to help save your marriage."

29. That Explains It

DURING THE MONDAY MORNING MEETING BRAD LOOKED over at Sierra, who waved to him from behind her Starbucks go-cup. Jonathan was in full cheerleader mode, talking about what a great week last week had been for Biz Dev.

Brad found himself watching Sierra. Judging from her skin tone, she'd hit the tanning booth sometime this weekend. A sign of fresh romantic interest perhaps? As Saturday night had progressed, he had managed to convince Rinehart that her infidelity was all in his head, even as Rinehart had convinced him, over the same period of time, that it was not. Somewhere during the argument, they traded opinions, and though they walked out of Strings in apparent agreement, Brad now was secretly convinced that, yes, Sierra was up to something. He was divided three ways among his professional obligation not to meddle in the personal life of a direct report, his personal obligation to spy for Rinehart, and his commonsense inclination to keep his nose out of it altogether. Rinehart was a good guy; he'd done a lot for Sierra. He didn't deserve to get hurt. On the other hand, hey, sometimes things just didn't work out, and if Sierra needed to move on, so be it. But she could at least give Rinehart fair warning.

He felt like a complete idiot when, after the meeting, he found out from Sierra what she'd been up to all weekend. "I got a really cheap roundtrip ticket to Miami. I used to work there. I have a lot of girlfriends."

"Oh, when I saw Rinehart on Saturday he didn't seem to know that. Not that you have to check in with him, I assume. But he seemed worried."

She took in enough breath for an exasperated sigh but caught herself before she let it out. "I told him I was going to Miami."

"No biggie, it's none of my business."

On the phone with Rinehart in a conference room he said, "Why didn't you tell me she told you she was going to Miami. That explains everything. I don't appreciate being set up. You had me interrogating my own employee."

"Look, I didn't believe it, so I didn't mention it. Maybe now, maybe I'm more clearheaded and I see it's not beyond the realm of possibility that she actually did get a good last-minute deal on tickets to Miami, okay? I'm sorry. I'm going to try to make it up to her. I'm taking her out to dinner tomorrow night. Actually it was her idea."

Brad thought nothing more of it until the next day, Tuesday, when Farouk reappeared in the office and requested an urgent meeting with Jonathan and his direct reports, Brad among them, to go over the proposed layoff list. The meeting began with the following exchange:

Jonathan, kissing ass: "You look like you got some sun, Farouk. Looks good."

Farouk, king of the world: "I took the Kharrazi Enterprises jet down to Miami on Saturday. Just got back. I tell you, it is a wonderful place. Stayed at the Delano, that one owned by Ian Schrager. What a wonderful, wonderful weekend."

And during the rest of the meeting he waxed almost jovial, almost as if he had fallen in love. Sierra? Farouk and Sierra? She'd said the tickets to Miami were cheap. Maybe that was an understatement; maybe there had been no tickets at all.

Brad sincerely hoped he was wrong, because she was on the layoff list that Farouk was at this very moment perusing. When he gets to her name, I'll know by his reaction.

Sure enough. "Sierra Hamilton?" He chuckled at first, and then his voice turned brusque. "You are getting rid of such a talent?"

"You know Sierra?" Jonathan asked.

"She does fine work. She is a highly skilled public relations professional and exactly the kind of person that we need to keep around. Why the hell would you want to fire her?"

Never one to take the bullet, Jonathan said, "I have to defer to Brad on that one. It's his department."

"Well, the assumptions that Jonathan and I were working under," Brad said, trying to reel his boss's name back into this, "dictated that we had to get rid of a certain number of employees. You're right, she's great, but this just made sense in light of your headcount reduction goals."

Farouk was grinning, shaking his head no. "Brad, you'll be out of here before we part ways with Ms. Hamilton. Have you ever talked to her? Have you ever really sat down to listen to her ideas?"

"Sure," Brad said, "we sit right beside each other."

"But about her ideas!" Farouk suddenly yelled. He pounded a fist on the table. "We're trying to trim the fat, and you want to get rid of her? For what I pay you two clowns, I could hire four or five people at her salary. Let me tell you something.

Seniority is a stupid reason to promote someone or to keep someone, and lack of it is a stupid reason to lay someone off. It just so happens that I was able to talk to her—" He seemed to realize he had surprised everyone with this defense of an entry-level employee whose name he had no reason to know. Quickly he added, "In the conference room, I talked to her. I have not seen her outside of work, of course." And with that bit of protesting too much, he had confirmed it for Brad: *I, Farouk Kharrazi, am in love with her, I see her all the time, she's in love with me, you can't fire her. We're still sandy from our South Beach love junket.*

"Well, we were never exactly positive about laying her off," Jonathan said. "Right, Brad?"

Brad took the cue. "That's right. We actually would prefer to keep her and get rid of one of the Gupta Technology programmers."

"I don't know about *that*," said Jonathan. "Those Gupta guys are top notch. Raj knows what he's doing."

Rick Stevens's contribution so far: "Wow, you got his name right. You're suddenly showing him a little respect."

Jonathan ignored him. "So I don't think we can get rid of any Gupta people. But to keep Sierra we might be able to find some fat to trim somewhere else."

"Do it. If this company has any future, it's with people like Sierra."

She must have treated him to one hell of a weekend. I bet she *does* do fine work. A highly skilled professional indeed.

Later Sierra skillfully answered all of his Farouk-inspired questions about Miami.

"Where'd you stay?"

"Just some hotel."

"Not the Delano was it?"

"I forget the name."

"What'd you and your girlfriends do down there?"

"Oh, we just hung out."

"Where?"

"Places. What are you, asking me these questions so you can report the answers to Rinehart?"

"No!" Too emphatic, obviously a lie.

She smirked. "I'm going to see Rinehart for dinner tonight. Until then it's none of your business."

That evening Brad was having a margarita at Zarela when his cell phone rang. Rinehart, and it was only nine. Was he calling during the middle of his dinner date?

"Tell me where you are," Rinehart said. "I'll be there in ten minutes."

"Where's Sierra?"

"Don't mention her name to me!"

But of course when he arrived she was all he wanted to talk about. He was alternately angry and teary. After a trip to the bathroom, he was sniffing and rubbing his nose. She could've been the one. She was the kind of girl he could've married.

"Except," Brad reminded him, trying to be helpful, "not Jewish." That seemed to make him feel a little better, so Brad pursued that theme. "Think of all the complications you avoided. You have no disappointed grandparents now. There's no argument about how to raise the kids."

"She told me it's some guy from work. She tells me it's not you. I know it's not you, because she tells me he's got more money than I have. What about your CEO?"

Brad shook his head. "If he's got more money than you, it can only be Farouk Kharrazi." He took a long sip from the margarita.

For a moment the news seemed to lessen Rinehart's pain. For Rinehart that was respectable. Losing your girl to a *Forbes* 400 billionaire, what were you going to do? There was prestige in the loss. It wasn't like losing her to some guy like Brad, who would be living paycheck to paycheck right now if not for his rapidly vanishing small bonus.

But by the end of the night Rinehart was bitter again. They were hunched over cheeseburgers in a diner, Rinehart bug-eyed, sniffling, and chattery from his frequent trips to the bathroom. "She was so perfect. I guess I'm just going to have to make a whole boatload more money. I guess a mere fifteen million won't cut it these days in the bachelor department. It's really not all that much."

"Please."

"I'm serious. It's the wrong amount of money. I can't get married, because I can't afford to lose half. On the other hand some people might not think it's enough to justify a prenup. And then again, if I don't sign one, some people will think I'm stupid." He rambled on, talking about Sierra's commune childhood and her consequential appreciation for private property. She'd been raised a vegetarian too; and now you should see her rip into a sirloin. Blood on her chin.

Brad found himself suppressing the urge to offer too much unsolicited advice about how Rinehart should be living his life more carefully, more responsibly; suppressing the urge, he realized, to be his parents.

30. Nicole Rising

FROM THE DAY SHE'D WALKED OUT ON ED LARSEN'S proposal, leaving on the table the two-carat house arrest device, Nicole seemed to have turned some psychological corner that allowed her to be more aggressive in the pursuit of her career, and more effective. For years, and in fact for the rest of her life, she would be unable to explain what exactly Ed had done to her to have such a positive effect and how exactly she had begun to behave differently. But the results came quickly. For one thing, her attorney cousin was no longer able to get under her skin. "You *what?* You *stormed* out of the restaurant?"

"He viewed it as a deal, and I did too. I just didn't like the terms."

"Nicole, Nicole, Nicole, you've been waiting tables for how long now? You have no *skills*. That was your ticket."

"I have no skills, huh? Do me a favor, I want you to remember you said that. In ten years when you're a thick-waisted, well-fed law firm partner, you'll be able to tell people that, yes, your cousin is *that* Nicole Garrison, and you can share with them that you once said I have no skills!

Maybe if you're lucky I'll appear in your office someday and take you to lunch."

In September she was offered two supporting roles in independent films that were, unfortunately, scheduled to shoot simultaneously. After nearly ten years of being over-looked and tossed aside, she was in the unfamiliar position of having to dole out a rejection to a director who, much to her gratification, begged her to change her mind. The movie would not be the same without her, he said. "This is how much I want you. I'd be tempted to delay shooting if I could, but I can't. Why do you want to be in this other movie? Is it more lines, a sexier part, what?" She could not tell him that it was a better story, since he himself wrote the one he was shooting. "I felt more connected to the part," she lied. She expected never to hear from that director again, but he had mentioned her name to a prominent agent, Ray Bernstein, with the famous bicoastal Creative Management Talent Agency, who phoned her and asked her to stop by to perform her monologue.

Having prepared to perform her monologue only for *the* Ray Bernstein (pressure enough), she was stunned to find that Bernstein had also invited several of his equally famous col-leagues, whose clients included Oscar and Tony winners, and three or four twenty-million-dollar action heroes. "We generally all have to agree to accept a client," Ray explained. "I want my colleagues thinking about you in relation to their clients, so they're not thinking just about what Arnold will do next, but what Arnold will do next *with Nicole*."

Her cousin considered the monologue process inherently demeaning. "I can't believe you subject yourself to being judged solely on the basis of a quick reading—"

"Not reading, *performance*. It's usually some important,

revelatory scene for one of the main characters. But it can't be too well known, because ideally the agents will not have in mind some famous actor doing it. It would be a mistake for some guy to do De Niro's 'You talking to me' scene from *Taxi Driver*, because you don't want the agent comparing you to De Niro."

For Ray Bernstein and his prominent colleagues she pulled one out of her past, a monologue that she hadn't performed for two years, from Sam Shepard's *Cowboy Mouth*. She was loud, she was energetic, she wiped away an angry tear; even better, Bernstein did too.

When she was done, he turned to his colleagues: "All right, you sharks, get away from her, she's mine."

He signed her on the spot and began sending her out on auditions the next day. He seemed disappointed that her first break—after an audition, a callback, and a screen test—was coming from daytime TV. "I shouldn't even have sent you," he said on the phone. "*Love and Loss,* of all the cheesy shows, wants you as a contract player."

She could barely contain her excitement. She was walking west on Forty-second Street, toward Ninth Avenue, on her way to the Film Center Cafe. The noise of the crowd forced her to repeat herself, raising her voice. She plugged her exposed ear, the better to hear Ray. "I don't see anything wrong with that. Come on, Ray, I'd love it actually. That was Willa Bernhard's show."

"Who?"

"My acting teacher."

He'd never heard of her. "I'm not sure we should do it. It'd tie you up for too much of the year contractually. I don't want you to have to turn down any movie roles because of this. I really see you on the big screen."

"Fine, give me a contract for a major movie and I'll skip the soap."

"Well, there's no offer yet," Ray said.

"That's my point. I like the idea of a regular paycheck. Of being on the set every day. Eating in the network cafeteria. It all seems great to me, it's exactly what I've wanted. There'll be time for movies and stuff. But Ray, this will make me a working actor! I'll be able to stop waiting tables. Do you even understand what a milestone that is?"

With an avuncular sigh he relented. "Okay, fine, I'll let you sign, but I'm shortening the terms and strengthening our out clause. Even with those measures in place I'm not sure this is the right thing to do."

Before walking into the Film Center Cafe she called her attorney cousin. "Just wanted to apologize for flying off the handle the other day."

"Well, something good came of it, because you inspired me to go to the gym. I will not be thick waisted." Her voice softened. "I'm sorry too. It was none of my business to point out that you walked away from a life of leisure, and that you had no acting work and—"

"Actually . . ." And out came the *Love and Loss* news.

"Nicole, that's fantastic! Oh, I always knew you could do it!"

I can't believe she just said that, Nicole thought. Where's the tape recorder when you need one?

She told everyone else too. Mom, Dad, everyone at the Film Center Cafe, customers and co-workers. Back home she e-mailed Dale, who e-mailed back his congratulations. She e-mailed Ed Larsen, who did not respond at all. She imagined him still smarting from her rejection, embittered about it, and deciding that she, like everyone else who disagreed with him, was crazy and best avoided.

And of course she announced it to her acting class. Everyone *acted* like they were happy for her, and perhaps her success did give them all some reason to hope that maybe theirs was next. Willa seemed particularly proud, arms in the air, copper bracelets clinking. "This is the kind of thing that happens to people who are talented and work hard and are persistent," she announced.

Nicole recognized Willa's pause as her cue: "And who've had a great acting coach."

"Thank you. And I'm sure it didn't hurt to mention my name in the audition, did it?"

"It happened so fast, it didn't come up."

Willa's smile disappeared. "Well, no need, apparently." When the day's exercises began, Willa was particularly hard on Nicole, criticizing every choice she made, accusing her of not being in character. "Just because you land a contract part on *Love and Loss* doesn't mean you can get lazy." Willa tacked on a chuckle that failed to take the edge off the admonition.

During the middle of class, Willa delivered a gratuitous soliloquy about her time in the spotlight and all the things Nicole would have to watch out for, the mistakes she would have to avoid. Nicole nodded, outwardly receptive but, for the first time, feeling that she had surpassed her teacher.

"But all in all I think you'll have a good time," Willa said. "Enjoy it while it lasts. When I starred as Meredith McCallister during the show's apex, it was one of the most demanding periods of my acting career to date, and one that is still rewarding. I still get stopped on the street. People still want my autograph. And any day now they're going to write Meredith out of her coma, and I will be back on the show."

It came out almost like a threat. *My character's going to*

come out of a coma and give your character a McCallister kick in the keister! Steal your boyfriend, maybe poison you into a coma, kick you off the show!

Nicole said, "It would be great if we could be colleagues."

31. Brad Falling

THE WEEK OF THE FORTHCOMING LAYOFFS, WHICH HE NOW knew that he himself and the Farouk-fucking Sierra would survive, Brad reluctantly updated his résumé on Monster, Headhunter, and HotJobs—reluctantly because he still wanted things to work out at AllMinder. Hell, he was three months from the end of a year during which he had met all of his obligations and should once again receive, in March of 2001, a bonus equal to twenty-five percent of his salary. Even if that didn't happen, there was still the retention bonus plan that Jonathan had said would render smaller but more frequent rewards. As he searched the jobs boards for New York–based PR positions, he was careful to click away to something work related whenever someone approached his desk. Particularly Sierra. What was she telling Farouk about him?

Two years earlier he had found himself wooed by several different organizations. Jonathan had taken him twice to Sparks Steak House to explain why Brad Smith alone was the right PR guy for AllMinder. One time they'd dined next to Mayor Giuliani, who afterward came over to shake their hands. "I arranged for him to be here," Jonathan joked as hiz-zoner walked away. "That's how much we want you on board." Considering that Jonathan had managed to convince Farouk Kharrazi to hand over millions in startup costs, it wasn't hard to believe that he could command an appearance by the mayor.

This time around Brad's résumé generated little heat. Toward the end of the week he received a call from one recruiter, Greg Fray, and agreed to come in for an interview. Later that same day, walking by Jonathan's desk, he overheard Jonathan on the phone: "Yes, I'm returning Greg Fray's call, please."

So the apparently loyal Jonathan was also looking.

By Thursday the AllMinder FuckedCompany forum had more than a hundred posts. The level of vitriol was astounding. An anonymous poster called Brad a "boozing, womanizing, no-good PR guy, slime of the worst sort, perhaps the most superficial individual you'll ever meet." Jonathan was a "bung munching faggot." Farouk, whom Brad had never seen in a turban, was a "towel head." *I work with these people?* Brad suspected Steven Bluestein, who had become more and more shifty and bitter of late, scowling through the Monday Morning Meetings. Several times he walked by Steven's desk to see if he could catch him posting.

Sierra asked to speak to him. "In one of the conference rooms," she said, code for *this is private.* He followed her down the hall. In her suit she looked like an unusually beautiful business professional, but he still smelled the perfume of her former occupation.

"I know you've figured out that I'm seeing Farouk.

Rinehart called me drunk last night and rambled on about it. I know you told him. I want to say, I never meant to hurt Rinehart."

"Am I supposed to relay that message?"

"I've told him myself. But I just want you to know. And I realize how this looks. It looks like I go out with whoever has the most money. The truth is, I *do* admire money. I think a guy who can make millions must have something. The truth is, Brad, I *need* it. If you knew anything about me . . ."

As she continued he was surprised at the earnestness of her demeanor. She seemed desperate to explain herself, to ask forgiveness. She told him all about her childhood, living on a commune dedicated to the notion that there is no private property. Everything for everyone. Apparently that pertained to sex as well, even if you were a fourteen-year-old girl—and she said no more about it, leaving him to imagine the abuse. The accumulation of wealth, he realized, whether it was a roll of twenties in her garter belt or one of Farouk Kharrazi's credit cards in her wallet, was for her a form of rebellion against her hippie parents. "I had a shitty childhood. I just wish I was the only one who had to suffer for it. I wish you still liked me."

Had his recent disapproval been that obvious? He conceded to himself, yes, probably so. Since he'd made the Farouk–Sierra connection he had been unable to speak freely for fear that she would repeat whatever he said, and he couldn't help but wonder what lay behind any question she might ask him. Was she working for Brad still, or simply acting as Farouk's spy?

"I really like you, Brad. I really appreciate you giving me a break. I've learned a lot, first from you and now from Farouk. I never would've met Farouk if not for you."

"And you never would've met me if not for Rinehart. So in that sense you owe it all to him."

"Rinehart's got a drug problem, Brad. I can't be involved with someone like that. Farouk, he's so wonderful, and we are really, really in love."

"Hey, go with it, then. Of course, there's the wife problem."

"He's going to work that out." She folded her arms and looked down. "It would've ended, even without me."

He nodded. "I believe that."

"I just want you to know you can still trust me. I'd never say anything to Farouk that would damage you. Like the fact that you sometimes come to work with a hangover that makes you pretty much useless, I'd never mention it."

Brad nodded. Was she threatening him or expressing genuine concern?

She said, "Do you ever worry about it, Brad? You do go out an awful lot."

"Someday I have to quit, I know."

"You say the word, I can get you hooked up in rehab."

He shook his head. "Jesus, no. It's not like I'm Robert Downey fucking Junior."

"Sooner or later you'll wind up there. Maybe you're not ready yet." She let a few seconds pass, during which he surprised himself by not disagreeing with her. "I do think," she said, "that in some parts of the company there's been some pretty obvious wastefulness that Jonathan should've curtailed a long time ago." Suddenly she's a business expert, a Farouk Kharrazi MBA student. "And I do tell it to him like I see it. He really values my opinions. My opinion about you, besides the fact that you drink too much, is that you're talented and smart and we need to keep you around for as long as we can. We're going to need a good PR guy until the end, and if things get really tight, we could move you around. You're smart enough to pick up responsibilities that don't fall directly within your area of expertise."

"Well, I appreciate that." He was nodding again. This lap dancer has become my boss. Would she resent that he knew what she looked like wearing nothing but a thong and glitter? Find an excuse to get rid of him? Maybe that was the whole rehab thing: ship him off for thirty days, long enough for her to take over.

"Brad, I owe you big time for bringing me in here. It's been a great opportunity."

"Put in a good word about my bonus, would you?"

"Farouk and I were talking about bonuses the other day. People here seem to assume they're getting bonuses. There's a sense of entitlement. But a bonus should be for extraordinary work only. Instead everyone here considers it part of their salary. That's another thing about the AllMinder culture that Farouk and I feel we need to change. Not the elimination of bonuses but tying them to specific performance goals. Your goal might be, I don't know, three positive articles about us in the *Wall Street Journal*."

He was still nodding, still getting used to this new arrangement.

"With the layoffs coming—and I know I was on the list, by the way, and that Farouk made you guys take me off. I'm not holding that against you. I'm sure you were under a lot of pressure from Jonathan."

She waited for him to acknowledge her magnanimity. He said only, "It seemed to make sense at the time."

"That's because Jonathan asked for across the board cuts, more or less based on seniority. It's a stupid way to do it. Jonathan, I think, always seems to take the easy way out."

"You're really after Jonathan, aren't you?" He realized that she didn't want his title, the mere director of public relations. She wanted to be CEO, and Farouk was crazy enough and angry enough, and perhaps in love enough . . .

"I do think Jonathan has wasted a lot of Farouk's money. In Miami it took me a whole day to calm him down about the basketball goal and the pinball machine."

Jonathan had no chance against her. Brad wondered if he should give him a heads-up. But it was hard to imagine how the conversation would start and how it would play out. It might also be dangerous. He didn't want to wind up on Sierra's shit list, if he wasn't there already.

"So, do you forgive me about Rinehart?"

"Rinehart will be fine."

"If there's anything I can do. I mean, if you decide to say something to him about cutting out the cocaine."

"I'll keep you in mind," he lied.

And that was it. She was in charge now. Later that day Jonathan called him from the train on his way home. Apparently Sierra had marched into his office and announced that from now on she would be attending all senior staff meetings. Farouk, she said, wanted to be represented in those meetings by someone he could trust. "I've got a call in to Farouk," Jonathan said, "to ask what the hell this is all about."

"No, let it go. Sierra and Farouk. Do you understand?"

This was one train ride that wasn't going to put Jonathan to sleep.

Reactions to the layoffs Friday ranged from tears to high-fives. One of the victims was an hour away from giving notice anyway to start a new job in two weeks. If she had done that before getting fired she would have received no severance pay. Now she was getting six weeks. For Rebecca the online ad sales coordinator, who a few months ago had seemed so fresh and promising, today was her last day. She cried at her desk as she cleared it out, cried to her mother over the phone. "I guess I just *suck*," she said.

Everyone was meeting for drinks at noon at the dive bar across the street. Not wanting to subject himself to bitterness and irony and insincere promises to stay in touch, Brad passed.

And when he received Rinehart's happy-hour e-mail—Volcano, 6 p.m.—he declined that too. It was not just that he didn't know what to tell Rinehart about Sierra's new power within AllMinder, it was also that for some reason he didn't want to get drunk tonight. The last thing I need is one more night that I can only half remember. If I don't remember my own life, who will?

He spent Friday evening at home in his Gramercy Park apartment, sipping ice water and reading that novel he had bought months earlier at the Union Square Barnes & Noble. It was tough at first. He felt as though he were missing something. When his cell phone rang, he looked at the screen: Julia Dorsey. He imagined her standing on the sidewalk outside Volcano with the phone to her ear. It had been weeks since the surprise parental visit, and he hadn't seen Julia since. If he answered now, she would tempt him to hit the town, and they'd wind up hungover and naked in his bed tomorrow morning, Brad having read nothing, having written nothing. He did not answer. He turned off the cell phone. He could hear occasional shouting in the streets. "You guys take this cab, we're getting the next one . . . We're going to Lucky Strike." He longed to go down to Cibar and sit at the end of the bar, see what developed. Or maybe cab up to Thirty-sixth between Fifth and Madison to join Rinehart, Julia, and the usual crew of enablers at Volcano.

But tonight, no, he was staying in. And around ten o'clock, still sitting there reading, he began to lose his desire to go out. The next time he checked the clock it was 10:45. He refilled his water glass and kept reading. I want to turn the corner. I want to behave differently. If I'm ever going to write that novel, I must learn to protect my solitude and my brain cells.

The last time he had awakened on a Saturday morning without a hangover was months ago, during a visit to his parents' house in Atlanta. He woke up without one now. There was no Julia beside him mumbling about brunch in her cigarette baritone. His head was clear. He felt great. It was only seven a.m.

One of his computer files, called "New York Stories," contained notes and observations from the past couple of years. These he had long planned to work into the novel he was going to write if he could ever find the time. He opened up the file and began to fill out the anecdote Julia had shared with him that night at El Teddy's back in January. During an acting-class exercise, a young woman discovers that her live-in boyfriend has given his business card to another woman and has asked her on a date.

The next time he took a sip from his coffee he was pleasantly surprised to find it cold; in the excitement of his sudden productivity, he had forgotten to drink it.

"Hey there, Brad! How's it going!" Uncle George. Drunk, of course. "Listen, man, I've come into some money."

"Really? How'd you do that?" Brad was at work. He rolled his eyes at Sierra and mouthed *crazy uncle*. Weeks earlier they'd had a good laugh about George and his pipeline scheme. Now Brad hoped that George's intrusion, this evidence of the family problems that Brad handled so selflessly, would impress the newly powerful Sierra. Maybe she would put in a good word with Farouk. On the other hand, maybe she would consider him to be wasting time at the office.

"Don't sound so surprised!" George was suddenly very irritated. "Anytime I do something good, anytime something actually works out in my favor, people are shocked. They don't think I can do anything on my own."

"Not me. I consider you innovative and resourceful."

"Damn right!"

And then Brad listened with growing unease to the story of how George had "come into some money." Apparently he had been paid to travel to Mexico, pick up a car, and drive it across the border into the United States. The man he delivered the car to paid him five thousand dollars cash.

"Are you fucking crazy? Have you done this yet?"

"Once. No hitch. Five grand in my pocket that night. A lot less when I woke up, but there's always more where that came from."

"You want to go back to prison?" Sierra was listening closely now.

"Hey, I don't know nothing about no drugs, I'm just the driver."

"That won't matter. George, you've got to stop."

"See, my plan is do it a few times, and then I'm going to move to Mexico, the beach somewhere, and open up a jet-ski rental business. You wait, Brad. Your Uncle George is going to be king of the beach. I'm going to have plenty of money. I'm never taking off my bathrobe except to slide into my jacuzzi with three or four women."

"I'm telling Dad. We're coming to get you. We can't let you go back to prison."

"If you had helped me with the pipeline thing this wouldn't be an issue. But nooooo." He slammed down the phone.

Brad hung up his own phone and told Sierra about it. "You're right," she said, "you have to get your dad involved."

"But see, I haven't spoken to him since that weekend they visited." He had shared that story with her too.

"Then this is perfect," Sierra advised. "You can start communicating with each other again by solving someone else's problem. You don't have to directly address the issues that still exist between you."

"Dad thinks *I'm* like George."

It would take a week, and Brad's father would have to fly out to Arizona to collect his brother and put him back into rehab, but in the end Sierra's analysis of the situation would prove accurate. George's gift to Brad was not shares in a Panama pipeline but a little piece of common ground and mutually acknowledged familial responsibility. By phone Brad and his father discussed strategy and psychology at length, and Brad had to give Dad credit. Call the guy self-righteous if you want, but who's going to pay the rehab bill? Perhaps it's Dad's stability that lets some of us take reasonable risks that we would not otherwise take, just as it drives George to look for the fastest way, and therefore probably the illegal way, to catch up. In living the way he lives, Dad assumes part of our burden and enables our risks, good and bad, and for that we must always bear him gratitude.

With Uncle George safely in rehab, Brad and his father spoke to each other via their cell phones.

"Have you seen much more of Julia?" Dad didn't want to believe that she really was only a friend. Less than that, actually.

"Not so much lately."

"Well, we were glad to get a chance to meet her."

"She enjoyed it too."

"Maybe next time we come up, we could all go see a show or something. Of course . . . if we're going to do that we'd have to buy tickets in advance and let you know we're coming." And so he was able to tell Brad that he wasn't going to visit him by surprise again.

"That sounds good." And so Brad was able to tell his father, hey, come on up.

32. Meredith McCallister Strikes Back

THE STUDENT MUST SURPASS THE TEACHER, THAT IS THE natural order of things, but is the teacher supposed to sit there and be happy about it? What if the teacher's own career, which should have been a brilliant one celebrated by the Academy, was cut short by nothing more than bad luck? By some clueless, angry producer who thought it would be neat—that's what he said, "I thought it would be neat!"—to have Meredith McCallister eat the poisoned caviar. Willa couldn't let the bitterness go. The sudden and undeserved success of Nicole Garrison seemed to illustrate by contrast the unfairness of her own descent into obscurity. She had not even garnered enough fame, now that it was gone, to attract the attention of those "Where are they now?" shows. *After rising from the New York food and beverage industry to spend two whole years playing the villainous Meredith McCallister on Love and Loss, Willa Bernhard wanted to give something back to the craft, so she became an acting instructor . . .*

She could have accepted a moderate Nicole Garrison success. If Nicole had landed an entry-level agent—not *the* Ray Bernstein himself—and a small part in a limited-run off-

Broadway show or a low-budget independent film that would make the rounds of second-tier festivals, fine. But getting contract work on a soap opera, and worse, on *Willa's* soap opera, that was not okay. What on earth could Ray Bernstein see in this gangly Nicole, who was pretty enough but no beauty, no Gwyneth or Cameron or Julia? Bernstein had rejected Willa several times back in the day, before she finally signed with her own struggling agent, a man who now rarely returned her phone calls and who, last December, in a telling lapse, failed even to mail her the annual holiday card with a little squiggle on it that was supposed to be his signature.

Ever since Nicole had announced in class that she was set to join the cast of *Love and Loss,* Willa Bernhard had been in a grim mood, relieved only by periods of bitter conversation with herself, usually alone in her apartment but sometimes walking down the street. Yesterday a tourist mother had tightened her grip on her little girl's hand and tugged her to the side as Willa approached. Willa, assuming that behind her must be some brick-wielding homeless menace, whirled to avoid him. Seeing no one, she froze in epiphany. I am the menace. That woman is afraid of what I'll do to her kid. "Wait," she called after the woman, "I'm Meredith McCallister from *Love and Loss.*" Pulling her child by the hand, the woman hastened her escape.

The worst part about Nicole's success was that it strengthened Willa's unpleasant suspicion that her own time had passed and was now irretrievable except by scrapbook and anecdote. It was a feeling that had begun with the horrible turn of the millennium. As a much younger woman she had liked to imagine where she would be in her career in the year 2000, when she would be how many years old? Well, that depended on how good a liar she was. She was in truth now about to turn forty-three. She was a good looking forty-three, to be sure. The yoga, the weights, the stationary bike, the practiced air of self-confidence. But none of that stretching and crunching and sweating seemed to be helping her career. Straight out of Yale she had imagined there were two paths she could take. Path number one: the theater in New York, martinis with the intelligentsia, a few odd independent films, tragically uncommercial despite the accolades of the Big Apple elite. Path number two: big movies in Los Angeles, a superficial wonderful life of fun, hanging out by the pool in designer shades and partying with the beautiful people, and on the screen diving from fireballs and winding up in the arms of handsome leading men in exotic locations.

She had not anticipated path number three: a two-year soap career in New York, and then the broken phone, or maybe my agent has died—but, no, I just saw him in the society pages. She had checked the phone line a hundred times. And then, in an act of desperation, she had taken on a few students, "to give back to the profession." My ass. More like a desperate attempt to get the electricity turned back on and avoid eviction.

Making it as an actor was the toughest thing in the world. So far none of her students had landed anything more impressive than small speaking-parts here and there. Over the years as she continued to teach and her students continued to fail, the two-year soap career stopped seeming so unimpressive. Under the right circumstances, and within the right segment of the nonworking New York actor population, one could be positively divalike. That was something else she got out of teaching besides the rent: validation of the choice she'd made long ago to become an actor rather than, say, an advertising executive like her father.

And now this with Nicole. Since June, Nicole had been doing an alarming amount of extra work on *Love and Loss*. Willa could cope with that. But then, with Ray Bernstein's muscle behind her, the undeserving, only moderately talented non-Yale graduate had landed a starring role. Oh, the way she had waltzed into class to announce that she was about to sign a contract to join the cast. She had been very sweet about it, and full of herself, thanking Willa so profusely and telling the other students to "hang in there because it is possible!" Suddenly the expert. Perhaps in retrospect she would realize that her enthusiasm was a little hard to stomach. But they were all actors in that room, and everyone mustered the congratulatory hug, the *mmwah* kiss not quite on the cheek.

Nicole's breathlessness was unprofessional, Willa thought, and in poor taste; it indicated that she had not paid her dues in full and was not yet ready. If there were any justice in the cosmos Willa would have been the one announcing to the class that her character, whom the *Enquirer* had once included in a list of "Soap Villains We Love to Hate," at number seventeen, was about to come out of her poison-induced coma, and she, Willa, would no longer have time to teach. But it's been great, and good luck to you all!

This might seem cruel, she thought as she reached for the phone, but it is the right thing to do. She dialed the number of Jurgen Togel, one of the producers of *Love and Loss* with whom she still had a decent relationship, meaning she was fairly certain he would take her call.

"Jurgen, it's Willa!" Not wanting to test him, she quickly added, "Bernhard!"

"Oh, hi! Willa!" She wanted to believe his enthusiasm was real, to attribute it to the effect of her voice rather than to the simple fact that he was an exclamatory gay man who probably talked that way even to his plants. "How's it going!"

"Well, it's going very well," she said, her voice rich with recent credits too numerous to mention. "I'm working of course. Some really experimental pieces that are helping me push my limits as an actor. I'm also doing some teaching, not much, and not for the money of course. I feel the need to give something back to the profession. How're you?"

"Oh, God," he said, in a tone of dramatic weariness. "Chaos as usual. What do you expect? But the ratings are up nice and high."

"Actually, I'm calling about the show."

Defensive suddenly: "Willa . . . you know I can't do anything about the coma thing. You ate poisoned caviar. Our medical consultant says there's no way you can feasibly come out of a coma that's lasted this long without brain damage. Are you ready to play a brain damaged vixen?" He laughed. "Don't answer that."

"Oh, I'm not calling for me," she said. "Don't be silly. I'm beyond all that, and I haven't the time. The most I could possibly manage would be a guest appearance and then only if the scheduling worked out. Maybe I could come back in a dream sequence or something. But I'm actually calling about one of my students who is close to signing a contract with your show. Nicole Garrison?"

"Why, yes, a lovely girl. Ray Bernstein sent her to us. She's a fine actress. You taught her?"

"Everything she knows." Willa paused, as if reluctant to continue. "And I know everything about her. And look, Jurgen, signing that contract would be a big mistake for the show and for her. I wouldn't intervene except that it's for her own good, you understand. I love her to death. I worry that she might not be able to take the pressure of the show and the rigors of the day-to-day schedule. I mean, I don't want to talk out of turn here, my main concern is for her mental health. You could continue to give her small scenes every now and then, and I'm sure she'll be fine. In class she's usually great, and I'm sure she auditioned well because I gave her lots of tips. The problem is that she's got a little mental problem that requires medication. I'm sure when you saw her she was all doped up. It makes her charming and wonderful, but really she's just so fragile, and we owe it to her to let her recover. I beg of you, don't interfere with her treatment. I do not want to go down to the hospital at four a.m. again to hear from the doctors how much ground glass and what kind of drugs they pumped from her stomach."

In the silence that followed, she could tell she had gotten through to Jurgen. An unreliable actor on daytime TV could plunge the show into chaos. "Well, Willa, my God, I don't know what to say. I really appreciate the information. I mean, she is *such* a lovely girl."

"I know, that's why this is so important."

"And I wouldn't want to do anything that might cause a setback."

"I knew you wouldn't. That's because you're a prince, Jurgen."

"Well, should I ask her about it?"

"Actually, I think that would cause a relapse." Willa went on, sounding regretful and reluctant. It was best, she explained, that Nicole not learn of this phone call. "As fragile as she is, she might not understand that I have only her best interests at heart."

"Of course."

Willa made another pitch for the revival of Meredith McCallister. Since when did soap operas adhere to the restrictions of medical reality? Meredith might return not with brain damage but with *increased* mental capacity, perhaps even some degree of clairvoyance.

"And what about your physical condition." He was toying with her now. "You'd be out of shape after lying in bed for three years. You can't come back looking like you just showered at the gym."

"Oh, yes I can. I wouldn't have it any other way."

They both had a good laugh at that. Jurgen thanked her again for the intelligence about Nicole and promised he would look into the possibility of some resurrection of the brain-dead Meredith McCallister.

"Could you do me a favor?" he asked. "Just so I can pass along the news to my superiors, could you send me an e-mail documenting your concerns about Nicole?"

"Absolutely. And I'll make my pitch about getting back on the show if I ever have a break from my other work."

33. Steven Strikes Back

THROUGHOUT THESE WEEKS OF EVASION AND DECEPTION—
the Monday morning pep talks for the whole company followed by the Monday afternoon secret discussions among senior staff—Steven Bluestein's sense of outrage continued to grow. What was happening here struck him as a possibly criminal injustice and certainly an immoral one. His hatred of the man who thought the color of his last name was brown was now diluted by his growing resentment over the Sierra–Kharrazi relationship. She was AllMinder's Yoko. In her manicured hands were the reigns of the company. And Brad Smith turned out to have no backbone. The way he so willingly adopted the role of figurehead in his own department (a department of two!) was enough to qualify him as chief schmuck officer. Anyone with any self-respect would have resigned.

It had been much easier back when Jonathan Scarver alone seemed to personify everything that was wrong with AllMinder. This new apportionment of blame to several other parties had complicated Steven's thoughts about how he should attack the injustice that had led last week to sweeping casualties. Seventy percent of the company gone. Granted, many of those folks were growth-spurt bloat, but that wasn't *their* fault. They'd been wooed from good jobs and assured that the future was bright. Then they'd been dumped on their asses back into a job market that was no longer receptive. The stigma of having worked for a dot com would follow them to the next interview, and the next. You thought you were going to get rich, did you? You're the kind of person who wants to make the big score, huh? Well, here at company so-and-so we tend to take a longer, more patient, more *reasonable* view.

With so much blame to go around, the question was no longer how best to expose Jonathan, but how best to expose everyone, and the answer Steven kept coming to was a virus, one that he would create himself and then unleash in the AllMinder e-mail system.

If Steven could develop a virus that forwarded e-mail messages from your inbox to recipients chosen at random from your address book at a rate of, say, one per minute, the better not to crash the company's mail server, then eventually everyone would know everything. Jonathan's notes to Barbara Lubotsky and to Raj Gupta would wind up in general circulation and posted on FuckedCompany. Same with the Sierra–Farouk correspondence. Even Maria's frustrating infatuation with Mr. Green would come to light. There would be some pain—innocents too would suffer—but eventually history would come to regard Steven's anonymous act of cyberwar as the necessary corrective effort of a levelheaded anonymous hero.

In his capacity as systems administrator of AllMinder, Steven had intercepted and defeated numerous viruses, from the potentially devastating to the mildly inconvenient. He retained samples of each. Some combination of these viruses, modified slightly and made to facilitate the random message selection and random forwarding, would take care of Jonathan, Farouk, Sierra, Brad—everyone—once and for all.

Sierra continued to consolidate her new power.

"What do you think we should do about Jonathan?" Farouk asked.

She could tell that he had an answer in mind. The game was to come up with what he was already thinking, which in his book would make you a genius. "I think," Sierra said, "that at this point he's of little use to the company." Farouk's face acted as a thermometer, telling her whether she was getting warmer (the skin of his face would be lighter and clearer, as when he was happy and laughing at brunch in Miami) or colder (his face darker, sign of an incoming storm), and she made adjustments accordingly. "But," she said, "it might be worth keeping him around long enough to help effect some kind of sale. He's not a bad front man, and he can still explain the vision, even if he never delivered on it."

Kharrazi's face darkened. She was about to reverse herself when they were both surprised by a photographer's flash. Farouk dispatched one of his bodyguards with a wad of cash to buy the roll of film. He didn't want to become the subject of a tabloid newspaper story that his wife might use against him in court. They were eating at Asia de Cuba, one of Farouk's favorite restaurants. The staff knew him and they took care of him. He was loudly complimentary, a good tipper, and qualified as that recently ascendant form of celebrity: the really rich guy. Having successfully squashed the photography incident, he seemed to have forgotten about Jonathan.

"It might be an old man's vanity." He leaned toward her across the table. "But I want more kids."

Sierra said, "I'd love to have kids, but I'd have to be married to the father."

His face was the good color. "Well, soon I will no longer be married to my wife . . ."

"That's an okay answer for now. But Farouk, I'm a serious person. I'm not someone who can just take things as they come. I'm a planner."

"That's one of the things I like about you."

"It's against my better judgment that I'm involved with a married man. I never meant to fall in . . ." She stopped herself; for now, let him imagine the next word.

"I can't live without you," he said. "I will do what I have to do." He let a moment pass and then returned to the earlier subject. "And what do you think we should do about Brad Smith?"

Brad Smith who had hired her. Brad Smith who seemed to resent her for what she had done to the coke fiend Rinehart. Brad Smith who could probably never *not* think of her as a stripper. The guy whose very presence reminds her: I'm a stripper. What to do about him? She watched Farouk's face—ready to play *getting warmer, getting colder*—and gave her answer.

During the two weeks after the late September layoffs, Brad drank to excess only twice, and both times felt guilty about it in the morning, missing the early morning clarity of mind that had enabled him to produce a hundred or so pages of fiction about his time in New York this past remarkable year. The hangovers began to feel irresponsible. He had begun to tell himself: *I will not wind up like Uncle George.* He knew that in some significant way Dad was right: Brad and his uncle were birds of a feather. That's why the guy phones me. He phones because he *recognizes* me. Takes one to know one. Now that he was out of rehab and supposedly removed from his drug-running pals, George was already making the same promises that he always made when sober. He'd never do it again; he was sorry to have been such a pain in the ass; you guys can trust me now; I *swear* on a bottle of Stoli! Ha—just kidding about the Stoli! See, I can even joke about it, that's how *cured* I am.

Rinehart showed up at Brad's apartment. "I told you I was going to have a reverse intervention if you stopped drinking, and I was serious. Here I am. I feel like I used to know you, man. We could relate. But then sobriety got hold of you. And this, all this while I'm trying to deal with the whole Sierra thing."

Rinehart, sitting on the sofa, guffawed when Brad handed him a Diet Coke. "You've gotta be kidding!"

"I'm serious, man, you'll feel better in the morning."

Rinehart jumped up and began opening the kitchen cabinets. Brad could tell by his dramatic "Ah-ha!" that he'd found the Jack Daniels. "This'll fix it right up." Back on the couch, two sips into his drink, he said, "Let me ask you something, Brad. Do you think we're going to live a full life? Living here in this city, the number one terrorist target over the next twenty years, just when weapons of mass destruction are becoming more easily available? You know how we're going to go? It's not going to be liver damage. We'll be walking down the street one day, and it's going to be over. A flash of nuclear light, like someone taking a surprise picture, and you go from being Brad Smith, with all of his insecurities and his talents, to being a cloud of burning vapor. Or maybe it'll be something biological, which I for one would *not* prefer. I don't feel like spending a couple of days watching my tissues liquefy. Either way I'm not all that worried about what kind of shape I'll be in at sixty, because I really doubt I'll get there. When I was younger, I could envision myself as a party boy—late-thirties guy, rich, having fun in New York, and *voila*, here I am." He flourished his hand as if to conjure himself. "But I can't envision myself at sixty, all settled down. It doesn't compute. That must be a sign that I'm not going to get there. And I suspect you might not either."

"But in the meantime," Brad said, "I think I might want to be more clearheaded."

"I don't know what you do all day in dot com land, but in my world I'm clearheaded too much of the time. I treasure my moments of self-obliteration. I treasure them especially when you're along for the ride." Rinehart's eyes teared up. Sure that this was about Sierra, Brad was about to offer consolation when Rinehart said, "I lost three million bucks this year in the market."

"So what, you're down to *only* ten or eleven?"

"In that general ballpark."

There was no point in expressing sympathy. Sorry you have only twelve million bucks? There was something unseemly about even thinking it. Yet Rinehart was sincere, genuinely upset about the decline in his net worth.

Brad said, "Well, if it makes you feel any better, I'm down to negative four thousand dollars. That's what I owe on my credit card. My bonus is gone—couple of bad trades and a few months of living beyond my means. I live paycheck to paycheck. So don't expect me to give you a loan."

He would have liked to explain to Rinehart how uncomfortable his situation had become at AllMinder, but he could not have done so without mentioning Sierra. She and Farouk were having apparently endless meetings with creditors and strategists, and Brad was no longer invited. He sat at his desk all day reading news sites and FuckedCompany. He wandered back to IT and made small talk with Steven Bluestein—that's how bored he was. Bluestein was as shifty as ever, pulling up his screensaver as if he were up to something top secret. Delusions of grandeur, that guy. A little would-be spy.

The more Steven thought about the virus he had created, the more he realized, with an increasing sense of pride, its potential destructiveness. The rough version of the virus had been ready to go for days, and would have served Steven's purpose within AllMinder. The problem was that it would also have worked externally, would have spread across the country and the globe, wreaking havoc on people who'd done Steven no harm. That would have been too much destruction on his conscience, too much like raising a curtain on people's private thoughts coast to coast. Steven didn't want to hit the world, just AllMinder. This was a tactical nuke, not World War III. He also knew that the virus, even with the minute delay between forwardings, could, if let loose upon the world, result in such a massive overload that parts of the Internet might crash. He was sure he could survive any questions at AllMinder, but a nationwide crash would spur an FBI investigation, and Steven had no illusions about being able to slip through the fine teeth of that comb.

So he took a few days to enhance the virus, making it domain specific to AllMinder. He was fairly certain that he got it right. A QA technician would have advised him to test it, but QA technicians were always too cautious. Besides, there was no way to test it because there was no way he could totally reproduce a separate instance of the AllMinder network environment. He was going to have to trust his own programming skills and his own sense that the virus was ready to go.

Then, with the virus on a floppy disk, he took the R train from Queens, where he lived, to Times Square. He walked first to a small Internet cafe on Thirty-ninth Street, where you were allowed to upload attachments via floppy. He set up a free Web-based e-mail account under an alias, opened a new message, attached the infected file, and typed in Jonathan Scarver's address. He did not hit send immediately—best not do everything from one terminal—but rather saved the e-mail in his Drafts folder, then walked to Burger King on Forty-second Street between Eighth and Ninth Avenue. You buy a meal, you get twenty minutes of free Internet access, time enough for Steven.

As he ate his fries at the terminal and pecked at the plastic-sheathed keyboard, he considered his work. Jonathan would receive an e-mail, the subject of which would be "Here is the file I promised." The file itself appeared to be a simple Word document entitled "As Requested." Did he really want to do this? The effects would be devastating. Who was he, Steven Bluestein, to play God with his colleagues? Then he steeled himself. Who were Scarver and Kharrazi to play God? Who the fuck was Sierra to be secretly planning to fire her mentor, Brad Smith.

He hit Send, and nothing would ever be the same.

Part 3

34. The Shot Heard Round the World

IN SEATTLE THE NEXT DAY, GAVIN MILES, FOUNDING CEO of a regionally successful retail computer and software chain, received an e-mail from one of Farouk Kharrazi's lieutenants. Gavin had met with Kharrazi six months earlier to pitch a distribution deal and royalty strategy that he believed would motivate the sales force to sell more of Kharrazi Enterprise's products. Perhaps emboldened by Kharrazi's apparent openness to this argument, the way he was nodding and smiling, Gavin made the mistake of adding "and boost your sagging stock price." Kharrazi exploded, started talking about "picking his sword" and cutting off people's heads. "Your sales people need to be selling my stuff anyway!" he yelled. "Otherwise it's anticompetitive and I'll see you in court! I don't want any more talk of me giving you more royalties. Why? If my products aren't selling in your stores, it is a display problem, or your salespeople are ignorant and incontinent or worse, they are thieves!" *Incontinent?* As he crammed his papers back into his briefcase Gavin almost laughed. Farouk said, "You are blackmailing me for better store space. That is what you are trying to do!"

That was six months ago, and thankfully no weird lawsuit in the meantime. No knock on the door from a hit man either. Now here was an e-mail from the silent notetaker Kharrazi had brought with him to that contentious meeting. Gavin would have been happy never to hear from Kharrazi or his people again. Let the existing sales agreement expire next year and wash his hands of that crazy Arab, or whatever he was. He was tempted to delete the e-mail. On the other hand, the market had been soft lately, and Kharrazi's stock price had fallen so low that perhaps now he was not so high and mighty.

The subject of the e-mail: "Here is the file I promised."

Gavin opened it.

The enclosure was a Word document: "As requested."

Later, too late, after the damage was done, Gavin would kick himself for not recognizing the signs of a virus. The bland multipurposeness of the subject header. The assertion that the recipient had requested a file, though Gavin couldn't remember having done so. It was possible, he supposed, that, after the recriminations and the yelling at that meeting six months ago, he had attempted to salvage some sliver of normalcy by suggesting that someone send him some information. It might have been a way to pretend that everything had gone all right, and that Kharrazi had not stormed out of the room red faced, forgoing or forgetting the courtesy of a goodbye handshake.

And so he opened the attachment. It was unreadable, just a bunch of seemingly random characters, not all of them alphanumeric. He wrote back, "Glad to hear from you. Looking forward to taking our business relationship to the next step. Alas, file seems to be corrupted. Please resend." He got through the rest of his new e-mail—responding, flagging for follow-up, and deleting as he saw fit—and then went to a meeting to explain to a consulting firm that, no, they certainly had not fulfilled their contractual obligations to his firm and, yes, he was perfectly entitled to withhold the final quarter of the agreed upon payment until the matter was rectified. He was angry, righteous, but he did not threaten to cut off his counterpart's head. That was beyond the pale. That was reserved for people who thought *incontinent* meant incapable and unqualified.

Throughout the meeting he kept thinking about that garbled attachment. What was it supposed to have been? Perhaps a spreadsheet outlining terms favorable to Gavin and his company? If the terms were good enough, I wouldn't have to be here now trying to browbeat these assholes into holding up their end of this deal. I would never have to negotiate with these jackasses again. The right deal with Kharrazi Enterprises, even as beleaguered as the share price had been lately, and Gavin would be set for years. Why did that file have to be corrupt?

When he returned to his office to see if Kharrazi's guy had re-sent the file, he found that he had received nearly a hundred new e-mails in the two hours he'd been gone. Even for Gavin, who conducted his life mostly on e-mail, that was a lot. Oddly, most of the messages were forwards. What was it, National E-mail Forwarding day? Scanning his inbox, he saw his wife's name a few times. She had forwarded several messages with the subject line, "Why is it like this?"

He skipped hers for now and began opening messages from his business associates and employees. They were not addressed to him. In every case they seemed to be candid exchanges between the forwarder and some other correspondent. They had nothing to do with Gavin. Here was one from one of his floor managers. The guy was apparently writing to his mother-in-law to firm up plans for Sunday dinner. What?

Why was everyone apparently forwarding messages to Gavin Miles? And they were still coming in at a rapid rate.

His cell phone rang. The screen showed his wife's name: Bonnie.

"Hi, hon," he said.

"Well, I have to say that even for someone who is horrible at confrontation and would give his left nut to avoid it, this is a new low. I can't believe this is how you chose to tell me. And why today, I wonder. Why not yesterday or tomorrow or for that matter never?"

"I'm not sure what you're talking about, hon."

"Not only did you cheat on me, but this is how you tell me? By forwarding me her e-mails where she tells you how much fun it is? And *then*, minutes after you forward them, you pretend you don't know what I'm talking about?"

He was already in his Sent folder, assessing the damage.

"Your plans to meet at what *hotel?*" Bonnie continued. "I can't believe she bought that stupid line about how the cheap ones turn you on. A scrimper, even in your infidelities. Little does she know. Let her marry you, and then she'll find out that cheap *everything* turns you on. Cheap dinners, matinee movies, the worst hotels everywhere we go for nearly thirty goddamn years now. 'Only the cheapest for my wife!' you joke." Her voice shrilled. "You wrote that you like to kiss her tattoo? Jesus, Gavin, slobbering all over a butterfly on, let's see what you call it . . . oh, yes, her *sweet tiny ankle?* I could've gotten a tattoo for you. But of course you would've wanted a cheap one. You write about going down on her, she tastes like dessert? Did you come home and kiss me with that mouth?"

Yes, his Sent folder confirmed that somehow an e-mail string between himself and his former girlfriend had been forwarded to his wife. The errant forwarding was not just to his wife, he realized, but apparently to everyone in his contact list. For the past two hours—*ever since he'd opened that note from Kharrazi's guy*—he had sent more than a hundred e-mails apparently at random to various friends, family members, employees, and business associates. That his wife received this exchange about the weekend he'd spent with young Sally Marwood in San Francisco six months ago—yes, at an *economical* hotel—was purely accidental. It might as easily have gone to Farouk Kharrazi. Wait a minute—it *did* also go to Farouk.

In a state of hot shame he read again what he had written to Sally: "Don't worry about the age difference, you are wise beyond your years," and worse. It had been an ill-advised affair. At every single moment when he was not actually in her immediate presence, unable to resist touching her warm smooth flesh, he had felt horribly guilty. When he was by himself, he knew that the affair had to end and that, as much as he would like to unburden himself to Bonnie and beg her forgiveness, that would be a selfish thing to do, perhaps more selfish even than the affair. And so several times he went to Sally determined to break it off. But she would shut her office door and press herself against him, making him thick in the head, hard in the crotch, weak at the knees, and unable to refuse what she offered. There in the office. Like Bill Clinton, but all the way. Twenty-seven years old, her body. Twenty-five years younger than his. No way he could turn that down without hating himself just as much, but in a different way, as he did for taking her. In not taking her he would have denied himself, pretended to be someone he was not. Pretending he was content sexually with one woman for the rest of his life— bullshit.

But finally he had refused her offer. Sally had not cried. "You'll be back," she said, and he realized: *she considers me a weakling.* So far he had stayed away. The truth was he hated himself for fucking her in the first place. All of his rationalizations, all of that be-true-to-myself crap was just that: crap. He could not have two women. It wasn't in him. He had rationalized his infidelity, but in his gut he felt acutely the wrongness. How could he have betrayed the memory of raising their kids together? Well, never again. For him from now on it was just his wife. So there was no reason for her ever to know. He should have deleted Sally's notes, of course, but he couldn't bring himself to do that. He liked too much to go back and reread them, remind himself: I still have what it takes, even if I don't take advantage of it. Twenty-five years younger than me. And somehow his computer had forwarded Bonnie the correspondence.

"Why did you do it?" Bonnie asked.

"Look, something's wrong with my e-mail. I'm looking at my Sent folder now. It's forwarding things at random. This is some kind of misunderstanding." It occurred to him that perhaps this was Kharrazi's belated revenge, but no point in trying to explain that.

"Why, Gavin?"

"I have a couple of notes here from you," he said. "Forwards, no less. Let's see what we've got." The silence on the other end of the line became a little less smug. "Here's one you wrote to your old friend Jessica." Later, recalling that Bonnie had not tried to stop him, he would conclude that she had wanted him to read that note. Perhaps she was experimenting to learn whether she still had the power to hurt him. The note to Jessica was a catalogue of heartfelt complaints about him. Everything she felt was wrong with the marriage, she told Jessica. Everything that annoyed her about him, she told Jessica. Apparently he was a cold fish who cared only about his work and took little sexual interest in his wife. Perhaps, Jessica opined, he was impotent. Get some Viagra.

"What have we here?" he said now. "This is really surprising. I had no idea you felt this way about me, no idea how miserable I was making you, how much you despise me."

"I don't despise you," she said.

"I don't despise you either."

It was the most romantic thing they had said to each other in months. Whatever happened to "I love you"? He couldn't muster it.

He pulled the network connection out of the wall to prevent further damage and turned off his cell phone. Of course it was too late. His important business and personal relationships had all been damaged by bits of truth that in the days before e-mail he would have kept locked in his brain. Later, when they finally tracked down the guy who did this, some dot com squirt in New York, Gavin would favor the death penalty, despite the prankster's claim that he had not intended the virus to have any effect whatsoever outside his own company.

Twenty-nine years ago he and Bonnie had faced each other before a minister and a church full of friends and relatives and vowed to love each other forever, forsaking all others. He was pretty sure it was over now. He thought of his parents. That was going to be a difficult call to make, made no easier by the fact that—oh, no—they too had gotten the Sally Marwood e-mail. *You taste like dessert.* Jesus.

It wasn't just his wife he was worried about now. His computer had sent messages nonstop for more than two hours. His partners were among the recipients. His employees. The minister of the church he occasionally attended. Now he was trying to control his breathing, his heart rate, and his shaking hands. Not all of the notes were from Sally Marwood, of course, but plenty were from people he conducted business with every day, and a few were from lawyers detailing strategy in two ongoing lawsuits against vendors in default. One of those notes had actually gone to the vendor being sued. The implications! Big corporate customers who paid him tens of thousands of dollars throughout the years were now privy to the superior discounts he had been giving to some of their competitors.

Bonnie called back on the land line. "I've got Vince Ingle for my lawyer. So you can't have him."

"He accepted the case?"

"Yes."

"But he's *our* friend. Mine too."

"Well, he's *my* lawyer."

"Bonnie, don't do anything rash."

"You'll have to discuss it with Vince."

"Fine. Fine. But don't say anything about this to the kids until we get our story straight."

She laughed. "They haven't called you yet?"

His kids! He checked the Sent folder. Holy . . . yes, his children too, daughters both, one a graphic designer living in Denver with her boyfriend, the other in grad school at Berkeley, were now privy to their father's sexually explicit love notes to a woman whose age fell directly between theirs.

The carnage began spreading across the country within minutes after Jonathan opened that morning a note the FBI would soon discover had been sent from the Burger King on Forty-second Street between Eighth and Ninth Avenues, from a free Web-based e-mail account that had been set up minutes earlier. The straightforwardly dubbed "Forwarding Virus" would sweep across the nation and indeed around the world within hours, wreaking the kind of devastation no amount of money could repair. That some of the revealing Sierra–Farouk strings wound up in Rinehart's e-mail box was hardly a tragedy when considered alongside more serious breaches, such as the one between Gavin and Bonnie Miles. The voluminous forwarding properties of the virus caused such a spike in e-mail volume that parts of the Internet were crashing. Respected pundits on the talk shows debated whether we were witnessing the first large-scale act of cyberwar. Was this an electronic Pearl Harbor?

At an impromptu press conference, the director of the FBI himself said, "This is a very sophisticated, very malicious virus that could only have been written by someone who is at once highly skilled and highly motivated to act against our technological infrastructure. Rest assured, we will find that person. This so-called Forwarding Virus could lead not just to the kind of societal destabilization that we're already hearing reports of, and not just to the crash of the Internet and consequent loss of billions of e-commerce dollars from our economy at a time when the stock market is shaky and the upcoming election is among the closest we've seen in years, but it could also lead to a dispersal abroad of industry and state secrets."

"So the Bureau is treating this as a terrorist act or an act of espionage?" a reporter asked.

"It's too soon to speculate."

At home, wide-eyed in front of CNN, scared shitless, the traitor-terrorist himself: Steven Bluestein. Despite his anxiety, he couldn't suppress a smile. The director of the FBI had praised his virus and called him highly skilled!

The untested safeguard he had put in place to keep the virus from leaving the AllMinder domain had failed. To say the least. Intending only to expose various AllMinder-specific deceptions, he had managed in addition to jeopardize state secrets and make himself the as yet unnamed target of an inevitably successful federal manhunt.

Steven closed his eyes. I'm fucked. But highly skilled!

35. The End Is Near

IT CROSSED HIS MIND TO FLEE THE COUNTRY, BUT HE WAS not one who felt the appeal of a fresh start in a new place. He was a pack rat. He'd lived in the same apartment for ten years. There could be no thought of leaving it and all the accumulations that it stored, a sedimentary history of his life since college. Besides, his sudden unannounced departure would be so uncharacteristic that it would eventually draw the curiosity of the authorities. At first perhaps they would consider him a missing person, but then, "So, he's a computer programmer, huh?" Wouldn't take a genius to put two and two together.

The best course was to keep going to work and hoping for the best. He longed to return to the Burger King at Forty-second Street to make sure the security cameras really were trained only on the registers, as they had seemed to be when he cased the place as a possible launching point for his creation. It would have given him such peace of mind to walk in there again and confirm that the few minutes he had spent at the Internet terminal had not been recorded on camera. But no. If they'd figured out that it came from that Burger King —likely—then they'd already have the place staked out.

Besides, he realized, because he had to order a meal to use a terminal, he could take no comfort even if the security cameras were trained only on the registers. Best case, he was taped at the register a few minutes before the computer virus was mailed to Jonathan Scarver. The steps he had taken to protect his anonymity as the distributor of a localized, company-specific virus that probably wouldn't have garnered the attention of any law enforcement authorities now seemed hopelessly inadequate in the face of a federally supported nationwide investigation.

Everyone at work was talking about the virus. Everyone had been hit. He himself had intentionally opened the infected file yesterday, a tactical move to deflect suspicion. Couldn't have been me, I got it too, and I'm the guy who's supposed to turn this type of thing away at our electronic border. He had to shut down the mail server. So far, no one had developed an effective patch against his virus. The irony was that although Steven had successfully exposed Jonathan Scarver's catalogue of crimes and misdemeanors, Jonathan was—at first—protected by safety in numbers: everyone else was exposed too, and worried only about themselves. Jonathan? Who cares about him? I've got my own problems to deal with, my own damaged relationships to repair. But in a matter of hours another natural human reaction would kick in: let me find someone who comes off looking worse than I do.

Jonathan made everyone feel great: the Gupta kickbacks, the blatant misrepresentation of Kharrazi's intentions regarding layoffs and bonuses. Jonathan had withheld information, had lied, had made decisions with his own bank account in mind rather than the best interests of the enterprise. Steven could see him in the glass conference room, yelling on the phone, probably to his wife. The affair with the supposedly impartial VP of HR, Barbara Lubotsky, however inconsequential it might have seemed from a purely business point of view, was, Steven surmised, hardly inconsequential to Olivia Scarver.

In the IT room, the Gupta Technology Indians were chattering in Hindi, obviously distressed. "It's not that we're worried about this particular job for the job's sake," one of them told Steven in heavily accented English. "The problem is with our visas"—pronounced *weesuz*. Apparently, Steven learned, if you're in the United States on an H1B visa, you have to be working or else you get shipped home. Steven was dismayed. His Gupta Technology buddies were not the ones gouging AllMinder. *They* were being paid a small fraction of what Raj Gupta and Jonathan Scarver were taking for themselves.

"Isn't there anything you can do?" he asked.

"Short of getting another job, no, and the market is a lot tighter now." The guy rubbed his temples. "My family depends on a certain amount of money coming in from me every week. My mother needs it to make ends meet due to my father's high medical expenses."

Steven had never felt so low. This depression, he told himself, was punishment enough. There was no reason to suffer any further, to subject himself to a legal ordeal which, after all this mental anguish, would be meaningless anyway, except that it would embarrass his family and end his career. He resolved to do whatever he could to keep from getting caught.

Which was nothing. He sat back and pretended to read, staring at the pages of his science fiction book, turning a page every now and then for show. Oh, why had he allowed himself to snoop in the first place? He should have stuck to science fiction. And great, here was garrulous Brad Smith, walking around chatting about the virus.

"They're saying the virus seems to have originated in the tri-state area," he reported, sipping his coffee. "Maybe even right here in New York City. Which would be interesting. It seems like they usually begin in some other country, some bunch of kids."

Steven asked the question of the week. "Did you get hit?"

"I'm in PR. I know better than to put anything incriminating in writing. Ever. I don't put anything in writing that I wouldn't be comfortable seeing printed in the *New York Times*. All my incriminating activities are conducted by cell phone, usually after midnight and several drinks. So, yeah, several of my e-mails were forwarded, but nothing too damaging."

"If you didn't get damaged," Steven tried to smile, "people might start thinking you're the one who did it."

"Anyone who thinks that greatly overestimates my programming skills. The best kept secret around here is that I'm pretty much computer illiterate."

"How are you going to spin the whole Jonathan kickback stuff?"

"Kickback? No, that wasn't a kickback. That was an 'inadvertently undisclosed arrangement that was intended to maximize his leverage over the vendor, to the benefit of the company.' We're glad he did it."

"That's not bad at all," Steven had to admit. Even as he asked his next question, Steven knew that someday Brad would be called before a courtroom to repeat it, but he couldn't stop himself: "What kind of PR advice would you have for the person who created the virus?"

"Now *that* would be an interesting assignment." Brad stirred his coffee while he thought. "It would depend on the circumstances. I'd probably say the whole thing was an accident that got way out of hand. He didn't intend to turn the world on its head. He didn't intend to violate state secrets and jeopardize national security. He just wrote a little program that actually was supposed to *help*, yes, that's it, *help* people better manage their e-mails by automatically forwarding them from one account to the other, each account being owned by the same person. But the virus developed its own intelligence and mutated—"

"Stop, that'll never work. Trust me, whoever wrote this thing knew what they were doing."

"Well, I don't know, then. I guess I'd try to argue that the virus has done as much good as harm. We just haven't heard the good stories yet. What about all the couples that this thing might bring together? Maybe some girl gets a message indirectly from some guy who's too scared to tell her how he feels, and maybe she feels exactly the same way about him, and she's been scared too. In a message written to some third party, some friend, he says how much he loves the girl in question, but he can never tell her this because he fears the interest is not reciprocated. And then she gets the e-mail. Turns out she feels the same way about him. They get together, and the rest is history. Maybe it all evens out."

"I like that." Steven thought of all the lovers his virus had brought together, the babies that would come of it, the feuds his virus would help to end, the peace he had wrought. I am the *last* guy who deserves to be punished.

"And maybe there's no harm in a little honesty. Maybe we're all better off if we can keep ourselves from lying, cheating, and stealing." He paused for a moment. "But since we're human I guess the only way to do that is to put a bullet in our heads."

"No thanks."

Brad said, "I sometimes wish I were a programmer.

Something's wrong, you just go in there and change a line of code, and *voila*, it's fixed. I know that's an oversimplification, but I sometimes feel like you guys live in a less complicated world than the rest of us do, because you can fix yours if it's broken." He shook his head at himself. "I realize that might sound condescending. I don't mean it that way. I'm sure your job comes with its own difficulties."

The nation's number one most wanted criminal, a man hunted by the FBI and publicly disparaged by none other than the agency's director himself, said, "You have no idea."

The next morning, secret fugitive Steven Bluestein slouched to work in his usual fashion, with his backpack slung over one shoulder, his science fiction novel open as he walked. It was one of those lucky mornings when apparently you will have the elevator to yourself, for the door is closing . . . closing . . . and then suddenly a wonderful sight: Maria Massimo rushing breathlessly toward you, needing your help: "Hold the elevator!"

At the last possible second he bravely inserted his arm between the two closing doors. They squeezed his wrist for a second and bounced back.

Stepping on, she said, "Thank you." She was dressed to go out after work in a low-cut pink blouse with a faux fur collar, a leopard-skin skirt, and platform shoes that aligned her breasts perfectly with Steven's wide eyes. She picked a piece of lint out of that collar and let it drop. Steven watched it float down to her painted toes.

Considering the likelihood that he was soon to be arrested, Steven guessed that this was it, his last chance to assert himself to Maria. If no one else stopped the elevator on its rise to AllMinder—one of the overnight delivery couriers, say, going from floor to floor—he had about twenty seconds alone with her. He got his courage up and said, "The virus forwarded me some of your e-mails. You seem pretty impressed with this Mr. Green character." He laughed to indicate that he didn't disapprove, didn't hold her sluttishness against her, but the way it came out . . . he sounded, he realized, like a spying pervert.

"You *read* some of my e-mail?"

"Well, at that point in time, I didn't know about the virus yet, so I thought you were forwarding them to me intentionally."

"Oh, right." She rolled her eyes.

He retreated. "Look, Maria, Mr. Green is none of my business, I apologize. I shouldn't have brought it up. I'm sure he's like some big perfect Wall Street guy and you're in love with him and you want to marry him. For me"—he smiled, raising his science fiction book—"a literary guy, a quiet guy, I know there's no hope."

She looked as if she pitied him. She handed him her purse. "Go ahead, since you're so interested in my private life. Open it up. You'll find a clue about Mr. Green in there."

Steven eagerly accepted the purse, feeling that he had finally broken the ice with Maria. He dug into it with a hand that his excitement rendered no more precise than a dog's paw. And then he saw it. His eyes widened. This explained everything. He was no match for a perfect Wall Street guy, but this he could compete with. Was she showing it to him because she was interested in him? Was she open to the possibility of letting him use it on her? He had seen plenty of pornos, he knew what to do. He could recommend with assurance a little hotel called the Mayfair, which seemed to be popular for off-site AllMinder meetings. Having regained the use of his opposable thumb, he lifted from the clutter of the purse a ten-inch vibrator.

It was fluorescent green. It was Mr. Green.

Steven's breath had gone shallow and his knees were rubbery. A corresponding weakness in his brain made him activate the device by twisting its base: *buzzzzzzzz*. He heard himself guffawing in geekish delight. He raised his eyebrows at Maria. She sneered at him, arms folded. Mr. Green was still buzzing.

And that was the scene upon which the elevator doors suddenly opened on the newly renovated AllMinder floor, where stood waiting the only person in the company who began and ended each day holding in her two manicured hands Farouk Kharrazi's very balls: Sierra Hamilton, shocked, narrowing her eyes, finally saying, "You two, I don't think this is appropriate workplace behavior."

"You *two?*" Maria said. "He's the one who read my e-mail."

"She gave me Mr. Green," Steven said. "She let me look through her purse."

"I'd like to see you both in the conference room." She checked her watch and winced. It was tough being such a busy executive. "Oooh. Maybe we can do it after Farouk and I meet with Brad."

Brad was tired this morning, but not, as would have been the reason mere weeks ago, because all of his physical systems and resources were engaged in recuperating from margarita abuse. This time it was because he had stayed up until one o'clock last night writing. He slept fitfully, half-dreaming about the scene he had just written and the one that was coming next, and he awoke spontaneously at five a.m. to resume his work. He poured a cup of coffee from the pot that had been on all night. At eight his alarm sounded from his bedroom, startling him. He had forgotten to turn it off. Reaching for his coffee, he was pleased to find it cold. Not for the first time during his writing sessions, he had forgotten to drink it. Always a good sign. At nine-thirty he decided to shower and go on to work. Maybe there he could get some rest. Back in the early days of AllMinder he would have been at his desk for an hour by now, but since the layoffs what was the point? No one was doing any work anyway. There wasn't even the tenuous incentive of the stay bonus to motivate people now that the Forwarding Virus had revealed Jonathan's assumption that the bonus was a "nonexistent carrot." A good day at work was getting through the hours without seeing Farouk and Sierra laughing together in one of the glass-walled conference rooms, without receiving from her some weird grunt-work assignment, and without having to thank her for her insincere expressions of concern about Uncle George. Why had he ever confided in her?

The anxious boredom at work had reached a new high a few days ago when Farouk had a couple of coldhearted custodians take away the basketball goal and the pinball machine. "Just following orders," they had said. Everyone who read FuckedCompany knew there was no future for AllMinder. With Sierra's help, Farouk was going to extract as large a fraction of his investment as he could, and then he would let the place fold. Ordinarily Jonathan would have tried to counter the demoralizing effect of the essentially true gossip, but the Forwarding Virus had given him notice about two forthcoming personal problems that rendered minor the question of the company's survival: Farouk was considering criminal charges related to the Gupta kickbacks, and Olivia was considering divorce. To Jonathan's credit he was concentrating solely on the latter problem. In his one phone conversation with Brad he had seemed genuinely contrite, a flagellant, willing to do anything to keep his family together. "I don't think you'll be seeing me for a while."

"Do what you have to do," Brad told him.

"AllMinder's over, huh?"

"If we weren't floating that loan, if Farouk wasn't distracted by Sierra, I'm sure we'd already be shut down. It'll happen soon enough. He'll figure out a way."

"It was the right vision. We had the right vision for AllMinder, didn't we?" Jonathan asked.

"Sure. Yeah. Sure we did."

Bored at his desk, Brad made a habit of visiting FuckedCompany.com and reading the latest posts about AllMinder. Some of Jonathan's e-mails were posted there now, and even some of Sierra's and Farouk's, along with more of the same kind of bilious, vituperative commentary that had accompanied the initial posts. Someone revealed Sierra's former profession. Brad immediately suspected Rinehart, and thought of him downtown at GSR Investments, exacting some small portion of revenge against the only woman, since he'd become a millionaire, to give him a taste of rejection.

"Brad, can Farouk and I see you in the conference room for a few minutes."

"Oh, hi, Sierra." He didn't bother lowering his feet from his desk. "Bad stuff about this virus thing, huh? Rinehart's been getting e-mails from all over the place"—including some between you and Farouk, he did not have to say.

Bristling, she pointed toward the conference room. "Immediately, please. Farouk is very busy today."

Farouk sat at the conference table before a patchwork of AllMinder documents. Brad recognized one of his own press releases. "We've got a big presentation coming up to the rest of the board," Farouk said. "And I bet a guy like you is really good at PowerPoint."

Brad sensed an assignment coming. Having done no actual work in weeks, he wasn't sure he could make the adjustment. "To tell you the truth I've been relying on Sierra for all my PowerPoints. She's gotten really good."

"I'll be happy to give you feedback," she said.

Farouk beamed at her. "I'm sure she's excellent at PowerPoint, but I have more important things for her to do. I need you to create a PowerPoint presentation for the board meeting. We'll show where the money has gone and we'll list examples of various types of mismanagement. Sierra knows what I want, so she'll get you started, and you'll submit your work to her for critique."

"That's not really PR work. I'm really no PowerPoint expert."

Kharrazi said, "But it's the only work we have for you. Sierra is taking over the PR work, at my request."

"I see."

"Make it look nice," Kharrazi said. "We have a lot of explaining to do to the board."

Sierra said, "I'm thinking something using mainly bluish tones."

36. Retrenchment

FOR SOME UNKNOWN REASON THE *LOVE AND LOSS* CONTRACT had fallen through, and this *after* she had mentioned it (in retrospect *boasted* about it) to anyone and everyone. Sharpening the sting was Willa Bernhard's imminent triumph, her return to *Love and Loss* to resume the role of Meredith McCallister, "twice a week in dream sequences," she had announced to the class, "while the writers work on bringing me out of a coma in a way that will explain why, after all this time in bed, I still look like a million bucks. It's one of the hazards of staying in such good shape. It's sometimes an art slash reality disconnect." That Nicole was not truly happy for her acting coach made her feel petty and bitter, and gave her another excuse to chastise herself. The bottom line, Willa continued, was that she was going to have to cancel two of her classes, and this, unfortunately, was one of them. She would do what she could to "squeeze you all" into her remaining class, though, truth to tell, she would have to cancel that one too, as soon as the *Love and Loss* writers revived her from her coma. "Of course, Nicole, you won't be needing that, will you? Since you'll also be starring on *Love and Loss*. I am so proud of you."

"Actually," Nicole said, and already it was too late to shut up. Her classmates turned toward her. She read in their eyes the poorly concealed hope that *Love and Loss* had fallen through. "It looks like I'm not going to be on the show after all. I don't know why. They called my agent and retracted the offer."

Dramatic expressions of shock, sympathy, and anger: *That's terrible, why, I thought it was all set! Didn't you say you'd signed a contract?*

"I was close to signing a contract. They said, 'You're going to sign a contract.'"

"That's a verbal!" said Gina Sullins, suddenly Nicole's advocate. "You could sue!"

Nicole shook her head. "Sure, I could sue. But my agent, Ray Bernstein"—that was still a coup worth mentioning—"says that I want to make my name in the business, not in the courts." Baffled, Ray had called her to report that the offer had been withdrawn. He asked Nicole if there were anything sordid or unprofessional in her past that might have come to light to the producers of the show. She assured him absolutely not. "Well, then," said Ray, "I just don't get it. Something must've happened."

Willa said, "I think he's right. I'm so sorry, Nicole. This must be very disappointing, but I hope you'll learn something from it." She addressed the whole class now, clasping her hands like a funeral director. "Our career trajectories all happen in their own good time. If it didn't happen this time, for some reason it wasn't meant to happen. Your career will continue to develop, and, who knows, you'll probably wind up on another soap before too long. That they even thought for a minute that you might be remotely desirable for the role is encouraging, and you shouldn't forget that. This kind of thing goes on, you know.

Maybe they had a change in the story line and the character you were going to play is no longer needed. You shouldn't worry even if Ray Bernstein loses interest in you."

"That's right," one of her classmates echoed. "Just because he doesn't want to represent you anymore doesn't mean that someone else won't pick you up."

Willa said, "Someone who's not as big and not so used to success will see you more as a project, and that might be good for you."

After class she called Ray in tears. "Are you going to drop me?"

"What?" He seemed offended. "Listen, honey, you aren't getting off that easy. You've got the talent, and you've got the backbone, and in yours truly you've only got the best agent in New York and LA. It's only a matter of time. Nicole, I've put you and a guest on a list for a certain party I want you to attend. The Museum of Film and Television is throwing a party to kick off its European Directors Series."

"What am I supposed to do, pass out my headshot and résumé?"

"Don't you dare. Just go and enjoy yourself." He recited a list of famous names. "They're all going to be there, and I want you to hang out with them. You need to get used to hanging around famous people without being giddy."

"Well, it's not like I have to get up early and go to work on *Love and Loss.*"

He ignored the bitterness in her voice. "And whatever you do, Nicole, don't open the Forwarding Virus. It could wreck your life."

The comment reminded her that in her recent depression she had neglected not only her workouts and voice lessons but also her e-mail.

Borrowing a roommate's laptop computer, she checked it now as she sipped coffee fom a mug.

Having been a victim of one of the many e-mail-borne computer viruses that had circled the globe before the Forwarding Virus unlocked so many secrets, Nicole knew not to open unexpected attachments, even those that appeared to be from acquaintances with whom she often corresponded. She did not immediately open the e-mail bearing the attachment that she received from Willa Bernhard. She planned to ask her about it first. *Did you send me anything?* Later, reading an article in the *New York Times,* she would match up the subject line of the e-mail and the name of its attachment and realize that Willa's e-mail would indeed have infected her.

Evidently Willa herself had not been so prudent, for also in Nicole's inbox were several messages forwarded from her. There were notes from other acquaintances too—even several from Dale—but these did not hold her interest like the ones from Willa. The proper etiquette, all the pundits were saying now, was to delete the e-mails. Do not read them. But she couldn't bring herself to delete Willa's.

For Nicole, Willa had been a few years earlier a mythic, all-powerful figure, an acting coach who really thinks I've got potential! It had taken time, but gradually the apprentice's natural and necessary disillusionment with the mentor had set in. Nicole had even taken to skipping a class or two every month, forgoing the hard folding chairs and the musty Garment District space that Willa, all red hair and bracelets, called a studio, as if to name it thus made it so. Nicole had been with Willa long enough to have heard for a third and in some cases even a fourth time the supposedly ad-lib wisdom, the off-the-cuff remarks that had seemed so fresh and spontaneous the first time around but were probably even then repeats. After so many years, the teacher's grooves ran inescapably deep. Round and round, same old song.

And now these e-mails from Willa, turning the computer monitor into a window on the life of someone who had once held so much sway over Nicole that a simple compliment could float her for a weekend, just as faint praise or dismissiveness could make her think her attorney cousin was right: time to give up the vain dream and get a real job.

In Willa's notes the first surprise was to see that her coach harbored such desperation. "I'm teaching five classes a week. The same stuff. Mom, I didn't become an actor for this. I didn't go to Yale for this. I do not intend to live out my life teaching these two-bit hacks from the food and beverage industry how to act. My students have no talent, but they each have fifty bucks, which is my main requirement." Willa wrote to a girlfriend that becoming an actor had apparently been a big mistake. "You know what I should've done was marry Frank. Hindsight is twenty-twenty. He's gone on to become a multimillionaire. Hell, he had a million bucks back when he proposed to me. Fifteen years ago. I saw him on CNBC the other day talking about the downturn. He's like some sort of authority now."

In the complaint of the notes, in their depressing regretful tone, Nicole feared that she was reading her own future. We do not expect those who have worked harder than we have and advanced farther—as Willa had advanced farther than Nicole—to be capable of such unhappiness. Was this guy Frank like Nicole's Ed Larsen? Would Nicole someday regret walking out on Ed's proposal? She hadn't heard a thing from him since that night she'd left his diamond ring on the table. Some day she would see Ed on CNBC. If when that happens I'm inspired to write a note like the one Willa has written about Frank, God, please send down a lightning bolt. In spite of Willa's description of her students, Nicole felt a great wave of pity for her acting coach. She wanted to go to her, to hug her, to let her know that what she had done with her life had really made a difference to so many people, for example Nicole.

And then she got to another of Willa's forwarded notes. The subject line read: "N.G. and *Love and Loss*." She opened the note Willa had sent originally to Jurgen Togel.

As Nicole read this false account of her own mental instability, her drug dependency, and her general forgetfulness and unreliability, the likelihood even that she was the one responsible for the theft of a classmate's wallet, she began to feel sick with betrayal. For a moment the room seemed to spin. In an attempt to steady herself, she gripped the edge of the table in front of her with enough desperation and violence to slosh a few drops of coffee onto her roommate's keyboard. She blotted at it with the edge of her sleeves and tapped the keys with her fingers. They seemed to work fine, thank God. The last thing she needed was the expense of having to repair a laptop or buy a new one. Discover your coach has betrayed you and then douse your friend's computer circuitry in coffee: that'll be two grand, please.

Nicole resisted the urge to gather her roommates around the laptop to show them Willa's note and narrate the tale. It wouldn't have felt good. It would have been too much like saying, "Hey, listen, someone shoved my face into a pile of shit, what do you think of that?" Willa had committed an atrocious act of professional sabotage so unconscionable that the only way for a third party to deal with it was to suspect there must be some truth to her accusations. If she shoved your face into a pile of shit, you must've done something to deserve it.

This was the worst betrayal Nicole had ever suffered. This

made the waitress-chasing Dale look like a saint. She'd gotten so much momentum out of that Dale–Gina business card incident, which had propelled her to the East Village, and the Ed Larsen proposal, which had heightened her career aggressiveness, but what could she do about this Willa e-mail but sit down and cry?

Her first instinct was to hit Reply and write back to Willa. Her second instinct was to hit Reply and then add, in the CC line, not just Jurgen Togel from *Love and Loss*, not just her agent Ray Bernstein, but everyone in the acting class and maybe the *New York Times* and the *New York Post* and the *Daily News*. Hey, listen, someone shoved my face into a pile of shit! Especially her fellow actors in Willa's class. They had a right to know that Willa suffered from the coach's equivalent to Munchausen syndrome, the kind that causes afflicted parents to keep their children sick. She actually composed an e-mail that began, "I want everyone on this list to see what Willa Bernhard has done to me," and then went on to address the issues of trust, professionalism, and likely long-term damage to Nicole's earning power. But then she thought better of it. Never write an e-mail in anger.

She did call Ray.

"Wow," he said.

"Should I sue her?"

He repeated the advice he had already given her about lawsuits: "You want to be famous for a sensational performance, not a sensational trial. If producers think you're going to go to court over every little slight—I know this isn't a *little* one—they'll be gun-shy around you. You can't do anything. You have to walk away from it. Look, I'm submitting you for Aidan Fagan's new pic." He gave her the address. She copied it down sullenly. For the first time since moving to New York, the prospect of yet another audition gave her no hope for the future but merely a clear perspective on the length of her unsuccessful past. Looking back, she saw audition after audition, endless and fruitless.

Of course she skipped the next Willa session. Later, during her shift at the Film Center Cafe, she heard from one of her classmates that others had also received the e-mail Willa had written to Jurgen Togel, and one of them had confronted her with a printout. "Is this the kind of support we can expect from you?" Willa had denied everything. The Forwarding Virus must have done that to her, she said, must have actually inserted those damaging sentences into her e-mail to Jurgen. She made no sense whatsoever. She began to leave messages on Nicole's cell phone. "Nicole," Willa said, "I think there's been some misunderstanding related to this horrible virus. I'd really like to talk with you about this." Nicole didn't bother calling her back.

Aidan Fagan lived up to his reputation for being eccentric by not showing up for Nicole's audition. She went through with it anyway of course, reading lines opposite a name brand actor who was to play the male love interest. Their audience? A couple of backslapping producers whose forced jocularity struck Nicole as a form of suppressed anger. Perhaps it was her eagerness to get out of there and get to the gym that imbued her performance with whatever it was that prompted them to give her not just a callback—they were moving too quickly for that, they declared—but a callback for a screen test.

"But I didn't even meet the director," she told Ray.

"A callback is a callback. No, I take that back. This is more than just a callback. This is a screen test. You're going to be dressed by Wardrobe in period costume. They're going to put makeup on you, the whole bit. You've got to memorize the scene, so it's off-book."

"I was in and out of there in like five minutes. There's no way this is going to work. These people must not know what they're doing, if they think anyone's going to want to watch me walk around London in some Victorian dress. Besides, *no one* does a screen test without first having a regular old callback. That's what all the acting books say."

"That's probably what Willa says too."

"I'm just trying to be sensible."

"I hope your negative attitude didn't come through, young lady."

"Young, huh? That's nice of you to say."

Over the next few days, as Nicole memorized her scene for the screen test, she continued to brood on Willa's betrayal. This person whom she'd paid to advance her career had done exactly the opposite and now *she*, Willa, was going to be on *Love and Loss* again. It was unbearable. She recalled with regret all those times she had ignored Dale's suggestion to please find a new acting coach. Whatever his faults, he was good at being suspicious. This was one of those times when she was nostalgic for his more impressive qualities, never forgetting the bad, the womanizing, the binge drinking, the sloppiness around the apartment, never wanting him back but understanding better why she had been with him in the first place. She was so low in the days after she received that forwarded e-mail that she began imagining—not exactly really *considering*—a reconciliation with Dale. She even began to give more weight to the words of her discouraging cousin. Maybe it was time to give up. Maybe she should go crawling back to Ed Larsen to see if his proposal was still good. Defeat wasn't an orphan after all. Defeat was a girl raised by her own parents and a huge extended family out in Colorado Springs. If she had accepted Ed's proposal she would be living comfortably by now, eating out whenever she wanted, shopping in all the right places. But no, no, no—this way of thinking was not hers. She was not interested in being anyone's wife if that meant being his possession.

Her mood was briefly encouraged by the screen test, which took all day. It had been too long since she had felt the heat of a cinematographer's lights. Once again Aidan Fagan was inexplicably absent. Two weeks went by, and no callback.

"They obviously hated me," she said to Ray.

"That's not necessarily true," he said without conviction.

"They said they wanted to move fast. They must have already picked someone."

"Look, you need a break," he told her. "Don't even *think* about trying to find a new acting coach yet, and don't worry about the screen test. Just concentrate on the auditions I'm going to send you out for. Go to the party at the Museum of Film and Television tonight."

She did go to the party. There she saw plenty of famous people, recognized several directors, producers, and actors, but ended up stuck in conversation for ninety minutes with a man who had mumbled his name in an Irish accent and seemed intent on keeping her to himself for the rest of the night. Except for the accent, in which she could at least take a professional interest, he was most unappealing. Short, fat, bald, with a habit of plucking at the dark hairs that grew on the shells of his ears, he was also a heavy drinker and seemed irritated that she was not keeping up with him as he raced over and over to the bottom of his glass, almost as if drunk was the only way he could stand her boring company. She longed to make her way to the sides of the famous directors, to tell them how much she loved their work, to mention casually that she was an actor and her agent was Ray Bernstein, just in case you want to get in touch with me. But she was stuck; she was too gentle to break away. Too gentle for this business, she sometimes thought. Finally the man announced that he had to "drain the snake," and Nicole, no longer up for the kind of conversation that networking in this environment would require of her, left the party altogether, sure that she was at the lowest point of her career.

37. Laid Off

SIERRA AND FAROUK TOLD HIM THAT HE'D DONE A GOOD job. "The PowerPoint presentation especially was top notch," she said. "I really like how well you take direction." This had nothing to do with performance, they assured him, but strictly with the needs of the company. "If not for that bastard embezzler prejudiced-against-Persians adulterer who was supposed to be running the place," Kharrazi said, "maybe our prospects would be different and you'd still have a job. But the bottom line is we no longer need a full-time PR guy. What for? So that coverage of our disappearance is favorable? We'll be gone! It's like worrying what people say about you after you're dead. The fact is, Sierra has picked up on the PR side of things so well that she could probably do it with her hands and feet tied behind her back."

That must be fun, Brad thought, unable to resist a glance at Sierra. She crossed her legs and smoothed her skirt over her knee. "I told him, and I'm telling you, I really appreciate you for giving me my chance. I'll always be grateful. But it's not gone unnoticed that you're hardly busy all day. Not your fault. You are in fact doing all the PR work there is to do . . . there's just not enough to justify keeping you around. It's like Farouk says, 'This is not a welfare organization.'"

Brad was already nodding, ready to wrap this up. He had the sense that the meeting was not for his benefit but for theirs, so they could be amazed at how much they agreed with each other, what a connection they had.

"And I share Sierra's gratitude," Kharrazi said. "I want to ask you. Do you think Jonathan Scarver is an idiot?"

Well, no, he was a product of the time, a creation in part of Farouk's own IPO dreams. Brad was furious with Jonathan for having established such an obviously improper relationship with Gupta Technology. You could call it an "inadvertently undisclosed arrangement" all you wanted, but the weakness of the spin revealed its desperation. To any rational observer, and especially to an irrational one like Farouk Kharrazi, it seemed as if Jonathan had pushed Gupta on the company to help an in-law and to line his own pockets. It seemed as if during the first round of layoffs Jonathan had made decisions that were contrary to the best interests of the company in order to pro-tect this arrangement. Anyone could have seen back then that the thing to do was to let go of Gupta Technology. With the site up and running there was no reason to keep a phalanx of overpaid StoryServer developers on the payroll. One or two for minor development and bug fixes would have sufficed. Scaling down the Gupta operation would have allowed AllMinder to keep more of its regular employees on board.

But in response to Kharrazi's question all Brad could say was, "Jonathan has made some mistakes. But so did a lot of people."

Sierra winced and fixed her eyes on the pad of paper before her. Kharrazi's face darkened.

"I feel raped!" Kharrazi exploded. "I feel as if someone has come into my house and taken my Picasso off the wall. I am going to do what I can to put Jonathan in jail. I have two severance offers for you. One, you sign the standard termination letter promising not to sue, and we give you four weeks' pay. Or two, you sign a letter saying that not only will you not sue, but you are willing to testify against Jonathan Scarver in a court of law. Sign that letter, and I give you"—he paused, reading Brad, what'll it take to buy his testimony?—"sixteen weeks of pay, even at your overinflated salary, which I did not approve. It's not that I don't think you've done a good job. I'm sure that you are not"—he looked at Sierra and smiled—"*incompetent.*"

She winked at him.

An extra twelve weeks' pay, on top of the standard four, if he would help put behind bars a man who, for all his human weaknesses, for all his business misjudgments, was still a decent person, at times a friend. Besides, he was probably going to lose his family over the Barbara Lubotsky sessions, and that seemed punishment enough for his crimes.

Brad said, "I'll sign the four weeks."

Kharrazi slammed the table. "Fool!"

"I'm not interested in helping you try to blame your investment loss on Jonathan. What if he had been more careful with the money? Would we have an extra month or two now? That's peanuts. We'd still be out of business because of market conditions. Fact is you misjudged the future, and now you've got a case of the scapegoats." He reached for the four-week letter. "Besides," he mumbled, "who the hell are you to criticize someone for adultery."

"What!" Kharrazi snatched the unsigned agreement back and stood up.

"He didn't mean that," Sierra said. "Farouk, he's just very emotional."

"I did too mean it." Brad looked Farouk in the eye. "Who the hell are you to criticize someone for adultery. What are you and Sierra doing in your hotel suite? Playing checkers?"

"Farouk is working on the divorce," Sierra said. She stood behind Farouk now, her hands on his shoulders. "It's complicated in his case."

"I'm glad you think the money I've lost is peanuts," Farouk said. Her touch seemed to keep him from yelling. Under her influence he sounded almost reasonable. "You know why you think that? Because it's not your money. It's my money. It becomes a whole lot harder when you realize that the money someone's been wasting is your own."

"Oh, I'm sorry, I thought you were upset because I implied you are a hypocrite."

Kharrazi remained frustratingly calm. He placed a hand over one of Sierra's on his shoulder. "I don't care what you think about that. You can never know what two people are feeling, whether they're married or not."

"Right. The same for Jonathan then."

Another explosive tirade. Kharrazi shrugged Sierra's calming hands from his shoulders and started yelling. Already fired, not even sure he was going to get *any* severance pay, Brad had nothing left to lose. He could afford to sit back and watch the fireworks. He could afford to interrupt. "Look, Farouk, I'm not really interested in your investment philosophy right now. You know why? I've got to go find a new job. I don't have a billion dollars in the bank. And do you know what? I've been thinking about this. I think I'm happier than you are."

"That's because you're not as smart!"

"I disagree. I think I'm smarter. I'm certainly more well-balanced as a human being. I bet I have a better time than you do. I bet the only difference in our lifestyles is that you can take a better vacation. I bet you spend more hours at work. It clearly stresses you out. Look at you, you're like a heart attack waiting to happen." He turned to Sierra. "Better watch his Viagra intake." Back to Kharrazi. "You should get out more. Sit on a beach somewhere. Relax. Contemplate your life. If you live it too quickly and it's all a blur, what have you got? The U–Haul stops at the graveyard." He sat back, stunned to realize he'd just quoted Mom and Dad.

"Money is not about having a good time," Kharrazi said. "It's about responsibility."

"I guess I have a different view."

Sierra took the four-week letter from Kharrazi and handed it to Brad. Kharrazi had crumpled the lower half in his angry grip. Brad had to smooth it out on the table with his palm before he could sign it.

His world had contracted considerably in the past eight months. Back in March, the day the bonuses were paid, he had assumed that he would never again be in the red financially. Now, if he didn't find another job right away, he would have to ask his father for help with the rent. At thirty-four years of age, ask his father, whom he'd recently lectured about religion, for help with the rent! Ridiculous! And he would deserve the stiff arm, the loud *No, Mr. Know-it-all*. But his father would oblige, the money would come, and without a lecture. Dad knew that sometimes silence carried the stronger message by allowing the recipient to imagine for himself the unspoken words.

In short, Brad had every reason to be pessimistic and angry with himself as he walked down Park Avenue South toward the Gramercy Park apartment that he could no longer afford, carrying in a cardboard box his personal possessions from work; indeed, angry at the world for changing the rules on him as if just to keep him from winning.

And yet as he passed through Union Square he could not suppress his elation, for this was still such a beautiful city, and here between the grime on the subway tracks and the view from the top of the World Trade Center, here among the spires and the crackpots and the crazy fucking speculative real estate and stock market bubbles, the goldrush mentality, the dooms-day mentality, here he was home. This was a beautiful place, and Rinehart and Julia, whom he had called with the news of his financial disaster, were meeting him at 5:30 at Cibar to buy him a few glasses of consolation.

Sierra and Farouk laid off two more AllMinder employees that day: CTO Rick Stevens and Executive Assistant Maria Massimo; Rick because he had allowed the Forwarding Virus to get into the building somehow, *and* he had allowed Jonathan to hire the Gupta Technology consultants at above-market rates; Maria because Sierra had caught her harassing Steven Bluestein with a vibrator on the elevator *and* because Farouk had never authorized a personal assistant for anyone, least of all Jonathan, who was no longer with the company anyway.

It made no difference when Rick protested that he had in fact *opposed* the use of the Gupta folks. "Who was CTO?" Kharrazi asked. "You or Jonathan?"

"I was, but he promoted Gupta heavily, and in the world we were living in at that time we didn't really have a lot of choice. Even if I had stuck to my guns, it's not like there was this vast pool of idle StoryServer developers in the early spring of 2000 waiting for my call. And as for the virus, the FBI says that we were apparently among the first to be hit. There's even a chance that we were *the* first to be hit. They're trying to determine that now. So it's not like we had any warning, and the virus was more sophisticated than the antivirus software that was out there at the time! I had my best guy on it, Steven Bluestein. Look, if it got past him, it could get past anyone."

"Don't blame it on your underlings."

"I'm not. I'm saying Steven Bluestein is a fine sys admin, among the best you'll ever know, and he had all the appropriate security measures in place. Somehow the virus got by. There was nothing we could do about it."

Didn't matter. He was out of there.

Maria's turn. Her attitude toward Steven was the opposite of Rick's. She tried to blame the whole episode on him. He'd upset her by making reference to private comments in her e-mail correspondence. "And guess what? I checked my Sent folder, and the Fowarding Virus never sent my notes about Mr. Green to Steven. I think he was reading my e-mail."

"There's no need to make spurious accusations," Sierra said. "Maybe the notes went to someone else who was also infected, and from there to Steven."

"If you want to believe that. Look, I need the job. Maybe I overreacted by allowing him to discover Mr. Green, if it like traumatized him or something—"

"Mr. Green?" Kharrazi asked.

"That's her nickname for the device," Sierra explained.

Farouk Kharrazi actually blushed, but he wasn't susceptible to Maria's pleading. She was fired. Dressed for a night on the town clubbing, dancing, she planned to meet her girlfriends later, and to keep from having to make her way back to Jersey she would go home with some as yet unknown lucky guy. The plan was still on. There'd be plenty of time tomorrow to worry about getting fired.

But never go quietly. Always give them a shock, something

to think about. She fished her vibrator out of her purse and tossed it to Farouk. By reflex he caught it.

"You two have fun with that," she said.

And then they called into the glass conference room Steven Bluestein himself, who, along with the other few survivors of this second round of layoffs, had been sitting at his desk hoping *not* to be called to the gallows. Now he assumed that he too would be executed, which was fine since he also expected to be arrested at any minute. He'd seen Brad Smith and Rick Stevens start packing their desks. He'd heard Maria on the phone saying, "Fuck it, you know? I can get another job."

He walked slowly to the conference room. It's been nice, he thought, sitting here reading science fiction and other people's e-mail. I'll miss it when I'm in jail.

"You are the future of the company," Kharrazi told him. "As the systems administrator, you are the one who is going to keep this place up and running so that Kharrazi Enterprises doesn't have to write off the loans we've made to AllMinder. You've done a great job. I don't blame you for the virus."

"You don't?" For a second Steven thought Kharrazi knew he had written it.

"No. I understand that the virus was a new variation, designed by some malicious person specifically to circumvent high-grade security measures like the ones that you put in place. The FBI tells us that we may have been the first to be hit." He raised his eyebrows. "So there's no way you could have stopped it. I don't know if you're aware or not, but we've already fired your worthless boss. I'm promoting you to"—his pause revealed that he hadn't yet considered a title—"director of . . . the management of . . . technology."

Steven smiled. "Are you sure?" Now is exactly when the FBI agents would probably burst through the door. Using a program that was supposed to delete files permanently, he had already wiped his hard drive of all evidence pertaining to the virus, but he was not confident that this would stump the FBI experts in computer forensics. Even if the FBI lab could produce no evidence, who's to say they couldn't plant some? That the people who wanted to jail him would be the same ones "analyzing" his hard drive struck him as a serious conflict of interest. They might just analyze something right onto it that wasn't there before, mightn't they?

Steven finally muttered, "Thanks."

"Aren't you happy?" Sierra asked.

"Well, it sounds like a lot of responsibility. Director of the management of technology, wow."

Sierra said, "We can work on the title, right Farouk?"

"Call him CTO for all I care."

"Okay. I'll take that," said CTO Steven Bluestein.

How to tell the guy, look, I'm about to be arrested. Steven let the opportunity pass. There was after all a slight chance that he would get away with the Forwarding Virus stunt. All it took was some malfunction of the Burger King security cameras. Perhaps the tape had not been changed in a while, and the resulting images would be blurry enough to conceal his identity.

But he was not optimistic. He walked to and from work looking over his shoulder. At home, before opening the door he checked to see if a matchstick that he had wedged in the crack was still in place, indicating that there had been no FBI intrusion. Inside he kept the blinds drawn. He did a lot of nonincriminating Web surfing, hanging out at CNN.com, never clicking on the virus story. Or *should* he? Yes, considering his profession, the FBI would find it odd if he showed no interest in the story. He clicked on it just to prove that he was a normal CTO.

Underlying all of these efforts was Steven's frustration that he could not take credit for the virus, which was, after all, quite an accomplishment. It had ended marriages, true, but it had started marriages; it had gotten people fired, yes, but also hired, and himself promoted. That there were anonymous posters in hacker-related chat rooms taking credit for his virus was maddening. As much as Steven wanted to avoid prison, he also wanted at least a few people, close friends only, trustworthy only, to know about what he had done.

He phoned a former colleague with whom he'd also had a few computer science classes in college. "Can I trust you?"

"Of course, man."

The guy was impressed. "That was you? The Forwarding Virus? That thing defeated all of our security measures, that was tough, man."

"That was a mistake. It was supposed to stay within AllMinder."

"Ha! I bet you about shit your pants when you realized it had gotten out!"

"Look, I could be in some serious trouble, you can imagine. But I had to tell someone. I had to clear up my conscience a little bit, but there's also pride of authorship, you know? I never meant to cause any harm except to my own company. But now they've gotten rid of the CTO and promoted me—"

"To CTO?"

Steven let there be an affirmative silence.

"That's great, man!" his friend said. "I always knew you'd make it."

Steven recounted the history of AllMinder, his justifications for snooping through people's e-mail, and he told what he learned from reading Jonathan's. "I mean here's this guy, our leader, right? Our guy. He's feeding us bullshit." And he described in detail how he had created the virus, and his morning trip to the Burger King with Internet access on Forty-second Street, where he unleashed it on the world.

"I can trust you, right?" he asked again.

"Absolutely. It was a nice piece of work, Steven."

But if you tell one person because the information is so interesting that you cannot contain it, and you crave the feeling of importance that you get from revealing what you know, why do you expect your listener to be immune to the same desire to be the newsbearer? It's not as if the FBI needs any help. By now they have closed in on the Forty-second Street Burger King. By now they have the security tapes, which are not blurry. They have decent images of everyone who ordered a meal in the minutes prior to the creation of the Web-based e-mail account and the launch of the virus.

A few days later, looking through those odd mug shots, each one containing a cash register and a hungry person counting change from his hand to the counter, Jonathan Scarver—recipient number one—would feel a sense of worth that he had not felt since early spring, certainly not since Kharrazi let him go and his wife kicked him out. Now he had something to tell the bartender at the Applebee's near his one-bedroom apartment on the outskirts of Westchester county. He had something to tell his wife too, still hoping to win her back. "These FBI agents stopped by with all these photos, and I recognized this weird little science-fiction-reading creep from our IT group."

38. Closure

IN A MOMENT OF WEAKNESS SHE AGREED TO MEET DALE. Just for coffee, but still it was against her general philosophy of breakups, which required a sudden, total, and permanent removal of one person from the other. The Band-Aid approach. Tear it off all at once. You're going to feel just a little sting. Her sudden, unannounced, undebatable move to the East Village back in January had been consistent with this approach, and throughout the eleven months since then she had been faithful to it, even during the particularly good and bad times, when it was so tempting to pick up the phone and call Dale, not because he was perfect for her, not because she wanted him back, but because he knew so much of her history, her wants and hopes, that he would understand how great it was that she had signed with an agent—and none other than Ray Bernstein!—and because he would have shared her sense of anger and betrayal over the Willa Bernhard incident, and her general frustration over the fact that her thirtieth birthday insisted on being two weeks away despite the fact that she was still not a working actor, to say nothing of being a star, co-star, or even a bit player. Birthdays should be awarded based on achievement, not doled out uniformly on an annual basis. It reminded her of the way kids who can't read are automatically passed along to the next grade just because it happens to be next year. Somebody please hold me back.

From his sometime girlfriend Gina, Dale had heard about the Willa incident. Outraged on her behalf, he had sent her a note suggesting this meeting.

She read that note on a Friday morning, shortly after learning from her parents that her grandfather had died. You can rebel against your family and run away, but then they keep dying on you, and you have to go back, the New Yorker dressed all in black, wearing your shades at the funeral, shaking hands with all the people who used to muss your hair and now think you're a little off your rocker, wanting to be an actress, and how old are you anyway? There'll be younger women there who've been married for five years and already have their children. No, this time, she wasn't going back. How could she? Her credit cards were maxed out, she had only eight hundred dollars in the bank, and seven hundred of that was for rent. She would have to ask her roommates to float her portion of the power bill. She might even have to resort to the petty argument that, hey, she's not home all that much, so she must not be the one running the air conditioner nonstop. Feeling this way—detached from her family and financially inadequate—she saw Dale's note. Maybe Dale would be in her life, years from now, as a friend. Her roommates were interesting and for the most part considerate, but time, and not much of it, would cause the foursome to drift apart, and she would be with another set of roommates. She would continue to live a life of discontinuity, of fits and starts, of passionate friendships killed by distances of mere blocks and absences of mere weeks and months. She couldn't even afford to fly back to Colorado

Springs for the funeral of her mother's father. So, goddamn right it was good to see Dale's name in her inbox, and hey, it wasn't a forward!

In her imagination the year 2000 for Dale had been nothing but great business, designing all those Web sites, and great fun, getting to know his new girlfriend, Gina, meeting her family if the relationship had veered toward seriousness. What did his own family think of the sudden break with Nicole? She often wondered if they missed her. She'd spent a week with them at the beach, and one Christmas, and now what did they say when, flipping through the photo albums, they came across her picture? She regretted especially that she no longer saw his younger sister, thirteen and just heading into that awkward stage, and treating Nicole like a big sister. She hoped they lectured Dale: "You really let a good one go that time." She hoped that Gina suffered by the inevitable comparison.

She watched him walk into the Coffee Pot and look around for her. She waved. His face broke into a smile of condescending sympathy that reminded her it hadn't all been great; it's not always cool to be hanging out with someone who knows your weaknesses and during arguments can count them off on his fingers. Things cannot have gone well without me, his smile seemed to say, and I know about the way you got screwed over by your acting coach.

Nicole gave him a smile that said, "I'm tough, things are great," and they hugged. He tried to peck her lips. She countered with a quick one to his cheek, setting the tone for what she knew would be a purely platonic encounter.

"Here." He handed her a photo album. "I was looking through these the other day, and I realized how much fun we had. It surprised me when you didn't take any of them. I think you should have a few at least."

"The Band-Aid approach," she said.

"Yeah, well."

As she flipped through the album she was surprised by how glad she was to have this compilation of photos, a few pictures from every trip. Dale meant well. He always meant well, or nearly always.

They sat in mismatched armchairs that needed reupholstering, facing each other across a small round table with a faux marble top. They sipped coffee and talked. Dale bought a giant chocolate chip cookie, and they broke off pieces throughout the conversation. "I'm really glad to see you again, Nicole. I want you to know, I never cheated on you, not all the way."

"No, you just desperately wanted to, and that was almost as bad, in a way."

He shrugged. "What's the gift if there's no sacrifice in being faithful?"

"I don't want there to be any sacrifice. Somewhere out there there's a guy, I know this, and I'm totally perfect for him, and totally *enough* for him. He won't want anyone else. Just me."

Dale shook his head. "Stay away from that guy. He wants to keep your severed head in the freezer."

They reached for the cookie at the same time. Dale grabbed her finger, and there was a second or two when the move might have developed into a full-blown hand-hold. But no, Nicole tugged it away. "Listen, tell me how you've been, Nicole. I tried to respect your decision to move on, but I'd be lying if I said I haven't thought a lot about you and wondered how you were doing."

"It was hard at first." She told him about the sense of discontinuity. She didn't want to die unloved, a fear that she had not known she harbored until she articulated it now. She told him about her grandfather. He advised her not to skip the funeral. "You need some money?" She turned him down, lying, "No, it's not the money." The truth had to do with her and her family's mutual inability to understand each other. "I'm the one who wandered off to New York with crazy ambitions and no qualms about shacking up with some guy, some 'graphic artist,'" she said, imbuing the job title with her father's condescension. "I'm totally different, I'm like a freak to them."

Dale said he felt the same way, but she doubted it. "Did you pick up a lot of girls this year?" she asked.

"I was thinking about you too obviously, I guess. They could see it in my eyes. I seemed to have better luck attracting other women when I was with you."

"Yes, because then you weren't thinking about me."

"I wouldn't say that."

"You had me all lined up at home. I was your safety net. You knew you were getting laid. It must have given you an air of confidence that made you attractive."

They moved on to the Forwarding Virus (Dale had suffered embarrassment but nothing more) and to the Willa Bernhard issue, common ground on which to reunite against an old enemy whom only Dale had recognized as such back in January. To his credit he resisted saying, "I told you so."

"But at least you've got the agent now," he said. "I'd take an agent over an acting coach any day. Not to mention that it's Ray Bernstein. It's not like you're ever going to give up acting, so you *will* recover from this."

She retracted from the moment briefly and tried to imagine herself *not* acting. How did other people fill their days? No, even after the Willa betrayal and the *Love and Loss* disappointment, she could not possibly stop being an actor. As a person might from birth until death be black or white or brown or yellow, her color was actor; she was of a separate race.

Dale said, "You're not thinking of quitting acting, are you?"

"God, no."

"You had me worried for a second. I'd hate to see you turn your back on it after investing so much work into it." He knew better than to say *so many years* or *your whole twenties*.

Now why couldn't Ed Larsen have had that attitude? Because Ed was looking for a wife in the same methodical way he might choose a stock. A woman needed to have certain characteristics, be willing to make certain shifts in life strategy in order to win his approval. A wife who wanted to run to auditions all the time, a wife who might actually, God forbid, land a part on a soap and suddenly not want to have kids, that wasn't on his agenda. Dale was more supportive, more easygoing.

He reached out and put a hand on her knee. "I have to say that although I think I needed some space and although I have on occasion made the most of it—there were some good times—" He stopped himself, and she could almost see him retrieve the words. "I think that was something I needed to get out of my system, and it's gone now. And I've come to the conclusion that overall our separation was a step backward for me as a person." Sensing some grand overture, she tried to interrupt him, but he held a hand up to forestall her. "Nicole, this is hard for me to say. I'm not exactly the most humble person in the world, I do have some pride. Bear with me. I was wondering actually if you'd consider starting over with me—slowly at first, and then we could see how it goes."

She raised her eyebrows. "Gina?"

He shook his head. "It's going nowhere. I see her only once a week, if that. The sex, when it happens, which is hardly ever, is boring. The relationship has pretty much run its course."

Realizing what he'd said, he raised his eyebrows and covered his mouth. "I did not mean to put it exactly like that."

"You need to grow up, Dale. I don't care about your wild nights. I don't want to hear about you and Gina having sex, because somehow it still hurts me for some stupid reason. But I could never take you back. You know who you remind me of? Bobby Parnell, this kid I knew in the eighth grade. A friend of mine let him put his hand up her skirt, and he went around all day at school letting the other boys sniff his fingers. I've got to say that our separation was hard on me too at first, and not just financially. Also because I was scared to be alone again. At my age. Growing up in Colorado Springs, hanging out with my parents' church friends, I never knew any woman who by thirty wasn't married and settled. I guess that affects me deep down, even though I know intellectually that it's bullshit. I'm pissed at myself about that now. I've turned down a serious wedding proposal, by the way. I left a two-carat diamond ring on a restaurant table and walked out to a chorus of gasps and sighs because I couldn't make a compromise. I couldn't give up my life. I've learned a lot about myself, so for me the breakup overall has been a great step forward, and that makes me strangely sad, if that makes any sense."

Dale had withdrawn into his high-backed lounge chair. He adopted a semi-intellectual pose, almost as if he were discussing a hypothetical proposition made by some other man to some other woman, rather than one made by himself and rejected by Nicole. "Sort of, but remember what it was like when we first met? The mental connection we felt. And the physical. How we couldn't wait to see each other and couldn't keep our hands off each other and people used to shout, 'Get a room'? Maybe we could get some of that back."

Despite her residual anger and pain, she had to smile at the memories Dale had just evoked. May she please feel that way again someday, with someone else. In her current mindset, this new power and maturity, she could not imagine ever again succumbing to the giddiness that she once found so pleasurable, the silliness of saving a man's messages on her answering machine and jeopardizing her New York City cynic's credentials by making out with him passionately in public. In the checkout line. On a bench at Union Square. Waiting to cross the street. His hand kneading her ass right there in front of everyone walking by—kids, grandmas, puzzled dogs, frat boys: "Get a room!"

"That was all nice, Dale, but it was spontaneous and uncontrollable. It's not something you can cultivate. We didn't come to some sort of careful agreement that now we're in love and can't not touch each other. It just happened to us. What we had most in common was some sort of gap. We each thought the other could fill it. We imputed to each other qualities that we wanted to be there and maybe after all weren't, Dale. A grade-school mistake. We can't have it back."

Even as she said this Nicole felt a pang of regret for how true it was, how inevitably the relentless passage of time wrecks us. She really had once been in love with this man. For two years she had gone to sleep every night with her head on his chest. Now, beyond the normal awkwardness of two former lovers trying to have a civil conversation without stepping on any of the land mines left over from the former conflict, there was also the sadness of remembering a passion that she might never feel again with anyone, in part because it hadn't been real in the first place. This emperor had no clothes. Did she really misread the whole situation back then; was she that stupid? She hoped so. Because if she read the situation correctly, she held a world of love in her fists and had only to keep her grip, but could not do it.

The conversation drifted into cordial distance. Thwarted in his overtures toward reconciliation, Dale was feeling anew the blow of her departure, her perhaps unforgivable determination to leave him, the way she lugged those goddamn suitcases down the stairs. He remembered now the sympathetic comments of a neighbor who, seeing Nicole heft her bags into the back of the cab, had correctly read the situation. He remembered feeling at once the great insurmountable hopelessness and, the other side of the coin, his new freedom.

Nicole's cell phone rang. She was grateful to be distracted from Dale's silence, his obvious contemplation of things past. Her screen display: Ray Bernstein. She showed it to Dale as if to prove to him, hey, my high-powered agent calls me regularly.

Ray sounded upbeat. No, he sounded ecstatic. "How are you doing my beauty, my star? Listen, when I signed you I knew you were going places. Your beauty is too sophisticated for you to be the next Bond girl, that's not you. You are a thinking man's beauty. You are an elite. If a man is not intelligent enough, he's going to overlook you and go straight for some bottle blond, and they make movies for people like that dumb guy. Fortunately, they make movies for the rest of us too—"

"Ray, Ray, Ray, what are you saying?"

"The screen test."

Long enough ago that it took her a moment to remember. She had stopped asking Ray if he had heard anything about it.

"The screen test," he repeated, "for Aidan Fagan."

"That? I figured he already cast it." She raised her eyebrows at Dale. That he was sitting here watching her about to get a good piece of news only proved that her parents were right: there is a God. Solely to give Dale the backstory, she said, "The screen test I did for Aidan Fagan was weeks ago, and he wasn't even there. I didn't even meet him." At the mention of the famous director Dale perked up and leaned forward in a pose that reminded her briefly what it was like to strategize with him about her career.

"Believe it or not, apparently Fagan himself didn't look at the screen tests until yesterday."

"I can believe it, since he didn't even bother to show up."

"Well, he recognized you from the Museum of Film and Television party."

"What? I didn't meet him."

"Apparently you talked to him for an hour and a half." As Ray described him, Nicole realized that Fagan had been the annoying Irish guy who had plucked at the hairs on his ears while keeping her away—she had thought—from all the directors.

"He wants me for the lead?" Nicole said. She felt Dale's hand on her back, a gesture not of comfort but of congratulation. She managed to keep herself from screaming, and from fainting, but she did squeeze parallel tears from her eyes.

"Principal photography begins next month. Principal photography begins next month *in London*. Not that you'll have much time for sightseeing, but maybe you can tack on a week at the end of the shoot." In a tone of understatement he added, "I think you'll be able to afford it." When he told her how much money she would make, her credit card debts suddenly became as inconsequential as the price of the coffee she was drinking.

There was a contract to sign and a script to pick up. There were travel arrangements to make. Ray told her to stop by his office if she had time (she laughed at that), and they would go through it all.

"Nicole, I want you to realize that if things had worked out with *Love and Loss*, you would have been contractually bound to the show during the same period when Fagan is shooting.

You would have missed this great opportunity. So it turns out Willa whatsername did you a favor."

When she got off the phone, she looked at Dale, tears in her eyes. So many times when they were living together she had hoped to get a call like this in front of him so he would see that his emotional support and financial help through the lean times had been justified. Now it was bittersweet. She tried to feel vindicated, she tried to lord it over him, but couldn't; the call had left her too weak and humble. She knew she could do the role; she knew she was going to give a performance that critics would praise. Suddenly she had a career.

At that moment of supreme happiness she felt as giddy as during the get-a-room stage, and for a moment she wished it could have worked out differently with Dale. If only . . . if only they were completely different people maybe they would walk out of this coffee shop hand in hand and be together forever.

"Dale," she said. "I didn't just get the part, I got the lead," and after years of being tough about her career she finally, now that she could afford to, burst into tears. She was grateful that Dale was there, not so she could rub it in but so she could feel his big dumb arms around her. He'd been there from the beginning. He deserved to share this moment. She would share with him nothing else.

39. FBI

STEVEN BLUESTEIN AWOKE TO THE SOUND OF KNOCKING. It was six a.m. He already knew who it was before he put his bare feet on the cool wooden floor, before he looked through the peephole and asked, "Who is it?" And before they answered.

Two days ago CNN reported that the FBI had settled on the Forty-second Street Burger King and was studying the security tapes. They took still shots from those tapes, blew them up to eight-by-tens, mass produced them, and distributed them to high-tech firms throughout the city. Sierra was among the recipients. Not having time to look through the mug shots herself, and guessing that Steven would have a better chance of knowing the geeks, she handed the pile to him. "Would you please give the FBI a hand and look through these?" Back at his desk he flipped through the photos, and there he was, not quite plain as day but very definitely himself, Steven Bluestein with his long black hair at the register. The time printed on the photo showed that it was taken fifteen minutes before Steven hit Send.

He e-mailed Sierra: "I don't recognize anyone." Then he

went home for the day, knowing that across the city his colleagues were looking through that same stack of photographs. FBI agents were probably showing them to Jonathan Scarver, recipient number one. It was over. There would be the thrilling shock and a feeling of self-importance as these high-tech deputies, members of this scattered posse of technologists, dialed the FBI's Forwarding Virus Hotline. In the end he would learn that among the first to come through with the information was the former college buddy to whom he had pridefully confessed his authorship of the virus. He would explain to Steven that once the fast-food mug shots started proliferating throughout the city he felt he had no choice but to come forward lest he be considered an accessory to the crime.

Knock Knock Knock.

These two guys were here to end life as he had known it since high school, when his father bought him his first computer and Steven realized that it was his soulmate, the unguided raw intelligence contained within that box. The succession of computers he had owned since then—the upgrades: more megahertz, more RAM, larger monitor, flatter screen, better joystick, first modem, faster modems, the beeps and chirps of his first connection to a BBS, and eventually high-speed cable access to that live and evolving record of human consciousness, the Internet—all of this took him more deeply into that same inexhaustible spirit to which his first Commodore 64 had given him what would turn out to be a mere hint of access. It was a peephole. The Internet was the endless beyond. And even now, *even now*, after trillions of dollars had been thrown at the Internet, it was still years away from fulfilling its promise. It was like a tool fallen out of the sky. It's great, it's fantastic and exciting! What exactly does it do? In answering that question, hundreds of reasonably intelligent but overexcited people with top-tier MBAs had produced business plan after business plan, skipping the part about profit, and ordinarily shrewd venture capitalists, blinded by the promise of this great thing that had fallen from space, bankrolled them anyway. You became CEO of a hundred-person company by little more than self-proclamation. Before the Forwarding Virus problem, Steven Bluestein had been looking forward to being a shaper of the evolution of the Internet. That's how he viewed his career so far, and that's what he saw himself doing in the future. In chat rooms and IT groups he would help to improve this alternate, better world, where no one knows you're a dog. Perhaps the Forwarding Virus, which some considered an attack on the Internet, *was* a part of his contribution: a way to expose vulnerabilities so they might be corrected. Nothing is ever fixed until it is first broken. This wasn't an attack on the Internet. This was a love tap, a little smack on the behind that was very definitely going to turn out to hurt the spanker more than the spankee. They didn't just send you to jail for this. Sometimes the judge would forbid you from ever again having Internet access. Cruel and unusual punishment. What he'd done had helped! For the Internet there would be more extensive precautions and higher security. For Steven Bluestein?

Again the knock.

Standing there in only his boxers, barely thirty seconds awake but not at all groggy, he asked through the doorway, "Who is it?"

"FBI."

40. Not Yet

ONE MORNING IN EARLY DECEMBER, ON HIS WAY HOME from the gym, Brad picked up the *Times*. On the front page was a picture of Steven Bluestein and an account of his arrest. *Ho-lee shit!* He leaned against the building and read the article straight through. *Ho-lee shit!* Back home he called his dad. "You'll never believe this, but . . ." And before the week was out he would have his own visit from the FBI. "Did Steven Bluestein ever mention anything about a virus?" "No, not that I can recall." "Did he seem odd to you? Anything unusual?" "Oh, sure. I mean, he's a systems guy. They're all a little crazy." "Did you ever go out drinking with Steven Bluestein?" "No." "Heartland Brewery ring a bell?" "Oh, that's right, wait a minute, I ran into him at Barnes & Noble, and . . ." His brush with notoriety inevitably comes up during his job interviews. "You worked at AllMinder? You must've known Steven Bluestein." People see AllMinder on his résumé and want to bring him in to chat.

He has only two more weeks in which to meet Nicole before she flies back to Colorado Springs to spend a triumphant Christmas holiday with her family, and then off to London to shoot the Aidan Fagan picture. Of course, he does not know this.

And for her part, she is not looking for anyone. She's in town for only two more weeks, not enough time for any new relationship to gain traction. Besides, neither one believes that there exists on the planet anyone who is perfect for anyone else. They're New Yorkers: they don't believe in perfection; they believe only in the pursuit of it. Perfection doesn't exist in anything: food, apartments, and certainly not love. That two people might be perfect for each other strikes them as a quaint pre-Letterman notion, perhaps vaguely 1940s, though even back then, c'mon. No way.

On this particular night in December, Brad, still unemployed but with two job offers on the table, thanks in part to his association with infamous hacker Steven Bluestein, walks east from Union Square in a full-length wool coat, enjoying the cold and the sense of promise that comes with the realization that you are highly employable, that putting food on the table is not an issue for you; it's putting a Porsche in the garage someday. One of the jobs he is considering—the one that he will take— will require him to travel to London once a quarter. Sign me up.

He recently managed to complete his grand jury testimony in a mere half hour, having convinced the prosecutors of the truth, that he had known nothing of Steven's little side project that briefly had brought down parts of the Internet and inspired the wrath of the Federal Bureau of Investigation.

"But he did ask you an interesting question after the virus hit, didn't he, Mr. Smith?"

"Yes."

"And what was that question?"

"He asked me what kind of PR advice I would have for the person who created the virus." Brad went on to recount what the prosecutor called his "good intentions defense," which maintained that Steven's sentence should reflect that he had intended to do no harm, but to serve the greater good.

But that is several days behind him, and now he is going to meet Rinehart at Cibar. In his shirt pocket he carries the disk containing his novel-in-progress. He has become so attached to it that he cannot imagine leaving the only copies in his apartment. What if someone broke in? What if the place burned down?

"Ketel One martini, straight up with a twist," Brad says.

"Thank God," Rinehart says. "I was worried you were getting carried away with the whole abstinence thing."

"I've cut down a lot, but I realize it's who I am. I'm a drinker."

Someday he will quit. He knows this the way he knows that someday he will die. He sees it out there, but he would like to put it off as long as possible. The acute clarity of mind he has enjoyed these past few weeks while writing his novel comes at a price, the sacrifice of drunkenness and its virtues: the dulling of pain, the contraction of your world view to right here, right now, these girls at the bar whom you just met and are now chatting up, all three of them beautiful, and even more so with each successive drink. He feels good right now. The conversation flows as if he has written it himself. One of the girls is the assistant to a famous photographer, and she is full of stories about celebrity photo shoots. Who was a jerk, who was nice, George W. Bush's attempted banter. If we began the year harboring no interest in numerical technicalities, we are ending it obsessed with them—a matter of personal and electoral votes down in Florida, and who will be the next president. The group makes a pact: we will not discuss this ongoing election dispute; and may we someday forget all that CNN has taught us about "chads."

The novel in Brad's shirt pocket is four hundred pages long, and it is nearly finished, but maybe he can put the photographer's assistant in there, add her like a spice, for she is so very New York. He doesn't know what the hell one does with a finished novel, but will ask around. Rinehart's ex-girlfriend's brother's ex-girlfriend is a literary agent. On the strength of that personal connection, maybe she'll have a look at it.

Absent Sierra is like a ghost standing behind Rinehart, the explanation for everything he does, the way he's trying so hard for that photographer's assistant. Desperate to find a graceful way to let her know he's wealthy, he manages to mention that his Porsche is in the shop. They all decide to leave together and go to Underbar.

If only they had stayed.

Three minutes later Nicole and her East Village room-mates and a few of her Film Center Cafe co-workers walk into Cibar and occupy the very barstools that Brad and company just vacated.

If only Brad and Rinehart had stayed it would have changed everything. Brad and Nicole would have started talk-ing immediately. The conversation would have been easy. "Is that a computer disk in your pocket?" "My novel." And then. "Oh, you're going to London too? I'll be there shooting a movie." "Well, we should get together." The Forwarding Virus would come up. "You *know* Steven Bluestein? He exposed my acting coach as my career saboteur." On some subsequent out-ing, perhaps in London in a few weeks, Nicole would tell the story of Dale Caulfield and Gina, that whole business card thing, and Brad would realize this is the same story he heard from Julia Dorsey, maybe a year ago, that night at El Teddy's, Julia having heard it from a temp who was in the acting class. Or something like that. Back in New York they would run into Dale Caulfield, and Brad would realize, *I've met this guy some-where*. At a party, yes.

Being perfect for each other, they would have immediately begun to enjoy a passionate life together of intellectual, worldly, and sexual fulfillment that neither thought possible and that their friends would have suspected was an act, a front for some sort of unspeakable turmoil that no doubt existed beneath the surface. To believe otherwise, to believe that they are actually *that* happy, that's just too fucking corny.

But Brad, Rinehart, and the three girls they met at Cibar are gone before Nicole and her friends walk in.

Now it will be ten years before Brad and Nicole meet, time enough for both to marry unwisely and divorce painfully, Brad without children, Nicole with two; time enough for both careers to take off, for Brad to have seen her movies and later her television sitcom, and for Nicole to have read in paperback the novel that he carried on a disk in his pocket the night they should have met at Cibar. How had her acting class incident gotten in there? And perhaps it will be Rinehart after all who introduces them. Mr. Big Shot now, coke free since 2002, running for political office, paying for his own campaign, showing off his accomplished friends. Hears Nicole Garrison is in town and invites her to the party. Has been hanging out with Brad all these years. They shake hands. This can't be happening. I am one marriage beyond infatuation and way past love at first sight. Over the next few weeks it will occur to both to wonder why they could not have met ten years earlier, maybe at some place like Cibar. And in subsequent years the only opportunity that Brad sometimes thinks he might have missed, the only woman he senses might have been this perfect, is the one on that escalator at Barnes & Noble in Union Square, whom he saw only from behind and who was gone by the time he tore himself away from that leech Steven Bluestein and made it to the first floor checkout lines. He will feel mildly guilty of betraying Nicole with the memory of another woman whom he will never know has become his wife.

Brad and Nicole will meet. The city will see to it.